Audition for a Legend

The Hell Hole Saga:

Book II

S.L. Kotar and J.E. Gessler

Ahead of the Press Publishing
St. Louis, Missouri

Library of Congress Cataloguing-in-Publication Data

Audition for a Legend
The Hell Hole Saga: Book II
 / S.L. Kotar and J.E. Gessler / authors
/E.J. Rossi / illustrator

ISBN   Paperback   978-1-950392-08-7
ISBN   KINDLE   978-1-950392-09-4

This story is a work of fiction. The names, characters, places and incidents are products of the authors' imagination. Any resemblance to actual events, locals, or persons, living or dead is entirely coincidental.

Manufactured in the United States of America
Ahead of The Press Publishing
St. Louis, Missouri

Table of Contents

SUMMARY OF HELL HOLE SAGA BOOKS
First Draw

Book I

Hellhole, Kansas, was no ordinary town. Like other places, it was comprised of desultory businesses, saloons, livery stable, bank, and clapboard homes, clinging to life by their figurative fingernails. What set this hider town apart from other post-Civil War outcroppings of civilization was that it also housed a United States Marshal's office. Hellhole was known to the authorities in Topeka as the place where lawmen went to die.

Claw Kiley had served in the Union Army during the Civil War, being discharged, as he had entered, a private. That fact hardly qualified him for a Federal position, yet he knew something about deputing, having served under the legendary Marshal Jack Duvall before the War. Duvall was widely regarded as the best man ever to wear the badge, yet he had been gunned down on the street of some unnamed town by a man seeking a reputation. Kiley had been the youth who outdrew the man who killed Jack Duvall. That alone made his resume worth considering, and as his life expectancy was deemed to be short, the government agents offered him the job on the expectation he could do little harm in the time he served in the position.

Bright-eyed and with faith in the almost mystical power of the badge he wore, Marshal Kiley drew three rapid conclusions about his new town: the residents of Hellhole still seethed over the outcome of the War Between the States; a girl working at the Lowdown Saloon would become very important to him; and outlaws held no respect for the Law. His first order of business was to teach the citizens to put the late conflict behind them and develop a respect, if not a friendship for the Federal man. His second, get to know Miss Cougar Bradburn; the third, to survive against those who took what they wanted by the power of guns and sheer audacity. How he succeeded would determine not only his own fate, but how the law of the land was to be carved out of hell.

DEDICATION

"Audition for a Legend"

This book is lovingly dedicated to our long-time friend, Nancy J. Stewart, who held a vision for helping humanity and saw it through against all odds. Established traditions in hospitals are hard to fight, but you saw the light and made 3-North the standard of excellence for geriatric care long before the concept ever became popular. You always believed in us, Nancy, and we hope, in some small way, our grateful acknowledgement repays you for your care and concern.

SLK and JEG

CHAPTER 1

"It's hot enough to fry eggs in sand."

She could hear him say it. Right down to the peculiar emphasis he put on the word, "fry." It conjured up images of grease-darkened frying pans, sand blowing so hard it pried the eyelids open, eggs costing two dollars a dozen and not having a dime to her name.

Those were the good memories.

In truth, there was only one bad memory associated with that statement.

The man who originated it.

The man she had heard repeat it, time after time. One thousand times. Until she was so tired of hearing him utter such nonsense, she told him if he said it once more, she would leave him.

Which was a lie.

It was he who ended up leaving her.

For a grave on boot hill.

Lowercase "b," small "h."

Not a famous cemetery, not in a notorious cow town.

In a no-name graveyard, in a town that would not outlive the railroad tracks bypassing its borders.

If it had been for another woman, she would have forgiven him. If he had tottered away under the influence of too much red-eye whisky, she would have understood. If lightning had struck him, she might have accorded such as the Will of God.

If he had developed fever and withered away under its burning tortures, she would have nursed him to the last, without question. If he had been trampled on in a stampede, thrown from the back of a wild mustang, been crushed in a rock slide, she could have borne her grief with dignity.

If he had died of old age, she could have accepted his passing with grace.

Of all the ways to die on the frontier, only the last was improbable.

Which caused her to laugh. The first mirth she had expressed in years.

Improbable?

Impossible.

Her man had been a lawman. He had worn the Badge.

Uppercase "B."

For "justice," he said.

The irony was, he meant it.

Justice.

Justice of acquittal for men accused of crimes they did not commit. Justice of the rope for men who used guns without giving a damn who they shot, or why.

Justice for homesteaders driven off their land; justice for Wells Fargo, recovering cash boxes filled with other people's gold.

Justice behind bars for swindlers, card sharks, brawlers and water witches.

The only one not accorded "justice" under his system of law and order, was his wife.

She was expected to understand.

Fairness was for others.

That was part of the deal he made for both of them when he pinned that "tin badge" on his chest.

"For better for worse."

She could hear him say that, too. He had only said it once. It was enough to sear the sentiment into her breast.

Closer to her heart than his head lying on her bosom.

He stood tall that wedding day, a brave man sweating under the burden of the oath he was about to take. Comfort. Honor. To love and to cherish. He had nodded gravely at each word, pledging his troth with a stiff nod and a firm, resounding "I will."

He swore to love, to have and to hold, to keep himself only onto her, "as long as ye both shall live."

He was not generally a swearing man, but he took that oath, kissed her on the lips and paid the itinerant preacher ten dollars in gold for his trouble.

He said afterwards, it was the most expensive swearing he had ever done in his life.

She asked him once, what oath he had taken when he first put on the badge. He knew what she meant and did not answer her.

Their marriage had many silent days, many cold nights.

If his death had a purpose; if it had made a difference; if anyone had cared, the widow might have been left with a memory warm enough to sustain her one single night.

It did not seem too much to ask. One night. Eight hours.

She did not get five minutes.

Nor five seconds.

Where was the justice in that?

To be sure, there were the graveside testimonials, the two-paragraph obituary in the weekly, out-of-town newspaper, condolences from his superiors in Topeka. The governor had sent a hand-written letter, penned by an anonymous aide.

Nowhere was the word "justice" mentioned.

Which, it its own ironic way, was a form of justice.

Without meaning, without empathy.

No one could understand her loss. She was expected to grasp the meaning without being told. She was a woman of the world.

A world exactly ten feet deep and four feet wide.

There had been no money for a headstone. Someone from town carved his name on a wooden cross.

The gesture held no meaning for her.

He was dead. That was the only fact she understood.

By God, there was no justice in that.

Just a cold, hard fact.

Stone cold and as hard as her heart.

As endurable as flint.

It was hot enough to fry eggs in sand, yet she did not sweat.

He had said once, sweating was for cowards.

He expected her to follow his lead. She was the wife of a United States marshal.

In her life, she had come to understand much.

Her understanding was nothing, compared to the hatred she bore.

It was more alive than her empty womb.

"Yes. Of course," she said.

"I hope you understand," the banker said.

"I understand."

"Without an income...."

"I understand."

"I'm sorry."

Which meant he was not sorry at all. She was a bad investment. She did not sell whisky to the Indians, branch water to the converted, spurious land deeds to the pioneers, worthless railroad stock to shop clerks, shirts to the dry goods store or services to dirty cowboys.

She did not have a ranch to sell, for they have never purchased a square inch of any dream they ever owned.

He left no life insurance.

Premiums cost money. They had talked about the necessity of such a policy, yet somehow, never got around to buying one.

"For your security," he promised.

"You are my best security," she had replied.

It was a game they played.

She did not have jewelry to pawn. Diamonds were for "city folk," and gold was for jingling around in a pocket the day after his check came in from the state capital.

Once a month, like clockwork.

Someone had forgotten to wind the timepiece.

They opened a bank account once. She forgot the name of the town. He had said it was to show faith he could defend that worthy institution from robbers. He had been a sheriff, back then. When the bank was robbed, he had been unable to recover the money. For two weeks, fourteen endless days, fourteen empty nights, she waited for his return, not knowing whether he was dead or alive.

One by one the deputies straggled home. To their wives, their loving children, their warm beds and their safe, secure jobs. Only he did not return.

When he did come back, bone weary, shoulders drooping, spirits sagging, the town officials called for an election.

He stood on his record of honesty, dependability, experience.

They moved out of town the next day.

Never let it be said she did not understand justice.

The word "justice" did not appear in the marriage compact. It was a concept too ethereal for two people pledging mortal fidelity.

Their worldly possessions included one horse, one six-shooter with belt, two rifles, a box-and- a-half of shells and the clothes on their back.

He was buried in his clothes.

She wore hers to his funeral.

The badge belonged to the State.

A lien was put on the horse. It was sold at auction to pay her back room rent. The rifles went next, for a sum total of six dollars and thirty-six cents.

She thought she would keep the pistol for sentimental reasons. It had been his constant companion, in sickness and in health.

It went for a week's worth of meals and a stage ticket.

Out of town.

The man who purchased the gun said he did so for sentimental reasons. The marshal had killed a lot of men with it. One day, he said, he might donate it to a museum.

He would be famous by association.

She wished him well and thanked him for the money.

It was the least she could do.

It was also the most.

The lady dressed in widow's weeds set her carpetbag down on the floor of the stage coach. Without help from either of the two male passengers already seated, she hoisted herself in. She sat by a window and averted her eyes.

There was nothing out there for her to see. Her vision was directed inward.

Neither of the passengers were local men. One was a peddler. He looked like a peddler, smelled like a peddler, sounded like a peddler.

The other was a sharper. He had not gotten out of the stage at the depot. Someone had apparently neglected to tell him the marshal was dead.

"Sure is hot, ain't it?" the peddler asked. He was used to making small talk and familiar with being ignored. That suited him well, for the gambler and the widow already knew it was hot and saw no need to comment.

"Goin' far?" he inquired of the gentleman sitting opposite. The man shrugged, then took out a small nail file. He rubbed it against the tips of his fingers. The peddler appeared intrigued. "Never seed a man do that befer. Seed him file off a nail, or trim one wid a knife, but I never seed him file his fingers befer."

"Will wonders never cease."

It was not the gambler who spoke, but the widow. Her comment was meant to be taken sarcastically, but in the companion-starved confines of the coach, the peddler saw his chance and took it. He prefaced his address to the lady by tipping his hat.

"Seen you befer, ain't I, ma'am?"

The woman realized her mistake and made a noncommittal motion. Knowing beforehand that if she simply ignored the man or turned her gaze outside the window to state at the monotonous, uninspired scenery, the peddler would continue his prattle until her already frayed nerves were shot, she reached into the small handbag she carried.

Taking out a letter directed in her name to "General Delivery," she gazed bleakly at the bold, sloping hand, then opened it. She had read the contents before, but perused it now as though the news was strange, foreign to her eyes.

The return address was the "United States Marshal's Office, Hellhole, Kansas." She had never been to Hellhole, never even passed through. She knew it for a hide town, new and raw and rough. She did not have to know Hellhole to guess the best hotel in town was called the Hellhole House and the best restaurant was named Regent.

She did not need a tour to describe the Marshal's office, brick by brick. She could have sketched the hand-painted sign, listed the names of four out of five outlaws whose faces were tacked to the bulletin board.

She knew the desk chair had a squeak, the coffee pot was dented and that the wood used to burn it was piled in a stack just behind the rear door.

And that it came dear.

Everything came "dear" to a man making "sixty a month and found."

Another one of *his* expressions.

And just as accurate as the temperature being hot enough to fry eggs in sand.

Whatever her man "found," he returned. He had never stolen a penny in his life and would not have been able to live with himself if he had. Men were like that. They could afford the luxury of a conscience.

Women were different. They were the realists. They knew that a penny found is one cent farther away from the poor house.

They fully understood that a dead man's purse would not keep the corpse warm at night.

They knew what it was like to sell what, to a man, was his "dearest" possession.

The widow knew the Marshal's Office had one desk, one table, one checkers board and two jail cells. On Saturday nights, those two cells could hold six men.

When the herds or the hiders came to town, they could hold ten.

She knew where the peg on the wall was placed and exactly how the marshal hung his hat on it. Underneath, he occasionally slung his gunbelt.

A six-shooter, worth exactly a week's worth of meals and a stage ticket.

She could elaborate on where the gun rack was and how many rifles it held. She could even name the rifle manufactures and make a fair guess which drummer had sold them to the Law.

The Law.

Capital "L."

The marshal, small "m," was the Law.

She was a lawman's widow and knew how it Was.

Emphasis on "W."

As in "widow."

Small "w."

Marshals and widows Were small players in the Larger game of Life.

She knew there was a half-pound of coffee in a can by the pot-bellied stove, two boxes of cartridges in the upper desk drawer and three deputy's badges.

None of that required any guesswork.

Even if she had been wrong about the maker's name on the rifles, or where the hat peg was, she was absolutely sure of one thing.

The office contained only one bed.

That, as they say, was written in stone.

The same type of stone which is planted, but never grows, on Boot Hill.

"Don't you have any kin you can apply to?" another banker had asked. Different time, same type of man. They were all the same, those bankers. She could have written their Code of Honor. "Someone who can help you out?"

She had shaken her head slowly. It was a familiar ritual.

"No one."

"No family back east?"

She always wondered why people used that expression: Back east. Men in the west had an uncommon faith that widows and orphans all had family "back east."

Back east must be a wondrous place.

She had never been there.

She had never been to heaven, either. And has as much faith in one as the other.

"Children? A married daughter who can take you in?"

They also placed a great store on marriage. The implication being, of course, that an unmarried daughter would be unable to accommodate her.

Or support her in the manner to which she was accustomed.

"A son?"

The Law Widow shook her head and looked down at the letter in her hands. The stage jostled her, jarring her bones but failing to divert her watery blue eyes from the signature at the bottom of the letter.

"No," she said. "I had a son. But he's dead."

Adding, without further explanation for her change in tense, "He is a United States Marshal in Hellhole, Kansas."

"I'm sorry," the banker said.

"So am I," Ada Duvall replied.

CHAPTER 2

It was the greatest evening of her life.

As Cougar Bradburn surveyed the empty whisky bottles, the spilled beer glasses, the piles of damp sawdust on the floor, she knew she ought to frown. There would be a great deal of cleaning up to do in the morning.

What was she thinking? It was already morning. Six o'clock in the morning to be exact.

She was not the least bit tired.

Stifling a yawn, the new owner of the Lowdown Saloon drummed her fingers on the bar, then looked up into the mirror behind the counter. From that perspective, she could see behind her without turning.

A glimpse of the past.

Three or four men were slumped over tables, fast asleep. Their snoring made a familiar, if not soothing, accompaniment to the crickets.

The swinging batwing doors were moving slightly, indicating a man had recently come in or gone out. She heard no one leave. Therefore, a man must have entered. She had seen no one.

Craning her neck to view the furthest reaches of the Lowdown's dark corners, her piercing blue eyes scanned the room. No one. Returning her vision to the bar, she locked behind it, more from force of habit than expectation. She had sent the bartender home an hour ago.

As expected, no one lurked behind the long, dark-stained mahogany bar.

Then he had gone upstairs, this interloper. Pursing her lips, Cougar glanced upward. No one lurked by the closed doors of the girl's rooms. Neither had any of those doors been opened. Floorboard creaks, door squeaks, mattress sighs. She knew the sounds by heart.

She ought to. Until three hours ago, she had lived behind those doors.

"Buy the lady a beer?"

Cougar started to shake her head before her numbing mind identified the voice.

"I've had enough beer tonight to last me..."

She did not finish the sentence. The words "a lifetime" were left dangling.

Unspoken.

Unuttered.

"Claw!" He grinned sheepishly, blushed, then looked down. "How...? Was that you who came in just now?" He nodded softly. "I saw the doors swing but I didn't see anyone come in. Where were you?"

"Right behind you."

She shook her head.

"No. I was looking in the mirror. I would have seen you. Fiz, maybe, could have hidden behind me," she teased. "But not you."

"I was there."

The marshal did not seem nearly as amazed as she.

Perhaps she had missed him because she was tired. More tired than she realized. If he said he was there, then he was. There was no two ways about it.

"I'm afraid the lady has had enough to drink. How 'bout you?"

Claw shook his head, removing his cowboy hat as he did so. With a boyish-like shake of his head, he took in a deep sigh and leaned against the bar, taking care his body should not touch hers.

Having been a saloon girl all her working life, Miss Bradburn noted his seemingly casual effort. While she might have preferred otherwise, their relationship had changed. It would be foolish to deny it. Twelve hours ago, Cougar Bradburn was a saloon girl with no more prospects for advancement than a cowboy's lewd proposal of marriage.

It had been bravado on Bix Bradley's part. He had been winning big. A man knew when his luck would hold, so when the audacious woman in his employ asked if she could take part in the game, he had acceded. Why not? While he did not need to win money from Cougar to own her body, the game provided added impetus to his desires.

No one standing around the table gave the woman a chance. No one even considered the possibility Bix Bradley's luck would turn. He had played for the house often enough. He was known for his shrewd ability, an uncanny talent for sizing up the competition and for the occasional manipulations of fortune.

Bix Bradley was a man.

Cougar Bradburn was a woman.

In the natural order of things, she did not stand a chance.

A man might as well expect a red Injun to walk in and beat the pants off Bix, than for a woman to strip him of all he held dear.

Yet, she had. It had taken hours, but slowly, painstakingly, Cougar had whittled down Bradley's pile of coins until he was forced to put up cr shut up.

What he "put up" was his ownership of the Lowdown Saloon. What she staked against him was just as precious, but had less marketable value.

Five dollars a jump, to be exact.

After gratuities to the management.

She had won big and she had won it all, becoming the new mistress of the premiere drinking parlor in Hellhole, Kansas.

Put that way, it sounded less auspicious than it was.

Cougar Bradburn won a business, a home and a chance at dignity.

Of the three, the last was the most important.

A man - or a woman - might calculate the worth of a business, set an amount per acre on a home, but no one could put a price tag on honor.

She had gone from nobody to somebody by the kind twist of fate.

An the dexterous work of her own two hands.

"Hey."

Cougar looked up sharply, startled by the voice. She had forgotten Claw was standing beside her.

"I think I fell asleep on my feet," she confessed. "What about you? You must be as dead as I am." A poor choice of words. "You must be as tired as I am," she rephrased. He nodded, his red-rimmed eyes spilling over with reflected pride. Whether she knew it or not, it had been the best night in his life, too.

"Going to bed?" she asked. It was not an invitation. She was relieved to see him shake his head.

"No. I thought I'd see Bix Bradley off on the morning stage. Nine o'clock. After that, maybe I'll put my head down for a bit."

"Does that mean you will, or you won't."

It was not spoken as a question.

He shrugged.

"Depends."

"You ought to try."

"Yeah."

"I'll remind you this evening about your offer to buy me a drink."

"Will I see you?"

The question, softly articulated, held behind it all the unspoken distance which had arisen between them. When he was a newcomer, a lawman on his first independent assignment as a marshal, and she a saloon girl, there was a modicum of equality between them. It was an equality which would shift over time, as he became more entrenched, more respected in his position, while she sunk further and aged more in her inferior position.

All that had radically altered. While Claw Kiley's position remained relatively unchanged, Cougar Bradburn had vaulted from the bedroom and the bar, to the owner and the employer.

As much as things remained the same, they changed.

That was the Rule of Life. Those who could not adapt perished.

There were no rules, however, on whether or not such transitions were easy or hard.

Or whether or not the parties involved wished to participate.

Life never asked.

"You'll see me."

She tried a smile, hoping it did not reveal her nervousness.

"Then I'll be sure and stop by." He turned, back to her and took three steps before stopping and slowly revolving to face her. "I'm real glad things worked out the way they did."

"You are?"

"You betcha."

This time, Miss Bradburn did not have to force a smile. It came to her lips unbidden.

She thought, after he was gone, that she should have walked him to the door. That had not been her privilege as a working girl, but as the new owner, she could do what she wanted. A woman who walked a man to the door was a woman with the right to invite him back.

To invite him anywhere she wished.

But she had not thought about it until too late.

"There will be other times, other nights," she mused to herself. And perhaps it had not been an oversight, after all. She would have other nights for him, but only one for herself.

One first night as owner of the Lowdown Saloon.

Gathering her wits about her by the simple gesture of drawing in the flowing folds of her dress, Cougar walked toward the stairs. She did not have to count the distance; she knew it by heart from every corner of the saloon.

Now, when she did her calculating, the sums would add up to a new equation.

It was a heady feeling.

Almost like being married, as though she were setting out on a new course in life. The companion beside her was not a flesh and blood man, however, but an inanimate building of wood and glass.

"No one would ever call this place 'inanimate' on a Saturday night," she spoke aloud, trying to make sense of it all.

"Inanimate" was one of "Fiz," short for physician, Ward's words. He had used it once to impress his listeners. She remembered the occasion well. She and Fiz and a hider were sitting at a table toward the back of the saloon. They were well into their third bottle of red-eye whisky when Fiz slapped his hand down on the green-felted table and declared, "In a week, this town will be inanimate!"

He was referring, he later explained, to the imminent departure of the hide skinners who had brought in their hides and pelts. In seven days, their one-living commodities would be sold, money exchanged, men paid off, the leather and fur bundled and shipped out.

Neither the hider nor Cougar understood the meaning of the ten-dollar word. There had been a pregnant pause, then the skinner had imitated Fiz's action by slapping his hand down on the table and declaring, "By Gawd, I don't need a week to be 'in-and-outta' nuthin'!"

"In-and-outta" being as close as he could come to defining "inanimate."

Which had prompted an invitation upstairs by both men.

She and Fiz had gone up together, she remembered, and "were in-and-outta" bed for a week.

Thus more-or-less confirming Fiz's prediction.

While adding four ten-dollar gold coins and one ten-dollar word to her personal fortune.

Up the steps, one at a time. She had ascended them often, seldom alone. To do so now was a thrill equal to a blushing bride's trip across the threshold.

Down the hall, one foot in front of the other. To her right was the railing, then the wide-open space of the second story. She had seen six men fall from that railing in her tenure at the Lowdown, one of whom had been pushed, the other five fallen from drunken stupors.

None had survived, which, as Fiz Ward, in his great wisdom and one-dollar words had put it, "Was a damned good thing."

Which had nothing to do with the extent of the injuries they sustained from the fall.

To her left were the three rooms the girls stayed in. To have said, "the three rooms the girls slept in," would have been a misnomer, for very little sleep was accomplished behind those closed doors.

One did not get paid for sleeping.

Bix Bradley had reminded her of that fact a time or two.

Or three.

Not much sleeping was done in the room at the end of the hall, either.

Another fact he had reminded her of.

More than once.

Cougar paused, lips pursed. For one long moment of gall and bitterness, she hoped the bastard would refuse to board the stage. That would give Claw Kiley all the excuse he needed to shoot him.

Between the eyes.

That would be a kindness. If she were packing the pistol, she would aim lower.

At a less fatal but far more deadly area.

Below the belt but above the knees.

"No."

She startled herself by the sound of her own voice.

No.

No, what?

No, she would not shoot Bix Bradley? The hell she would not.

No, she would not shoot the bastard in the crouch? She sure as hell would.

No, she would not let Claw Kiley do her killing for her.

That was what she meant. If a man needed killing; if he had offended her, hurt her, stole, cheated, lied to her, she was perfectly capable of shooting him herself. It would not be the first time. She had never sought help from the law, redress from any lawman. She would not start now.

Not even if that lawman's name was Claw Kiley.

She would never lean on him. That was not her way. She had been independent from the day she was weaned off milk. Cougar Bradburn had never looked to anyone - man or woman - for succor. She had asked for advice on occasion, borrowed a few dollars from dire need, but never, ever had she surrendered her independence.

She was not about to start now.

Not even for a lawman whose name was Claw Kiley.

Not even if she loved him, which she was not sure she did.

Love was a four-letter word, after all. Of all the four-letter words she knew, this was the one with which she was least familiar. Love was for ladies and gentlemen, school marms and governor's daughters.

Not for the likes of her.

Not for a saloon girl.

Not even for a saloon owner.

Between the one hand and the other was money.

For a man, money equated to dignity. The dirtiest skinner, with twenty dollars in his pocket, was a king to a penniless saloon girl. The meanest-mouthed cavalry officer who married the girl with a dowry became a cattle baron. The girl became nothing more his wife. The most savage Injun fighter was a hero to the scribes from Back East. The best dressed female in Hellhole was a spinster, no more than a target for anyone in britches.

For a woman, money equaled the right to go to bed alone.

For the moment, it was enough.

Holding her head high and stiffening her back, the new owner marched past the three closed doors. As though to mock her assessment of how little sleep was done, she heard gentle snores from all three rooms.

She would have to think about the six girls Bix Bradley kept on the payroll.

There were either five too many or one too few.

"Just let me get some sleep."

She had never talked to herself before. Perhaps being raised on so low a plain, she had not felt worthy of answering herself.

The door at the end of the hall was unlocked. She was almost sorry. Without the key, she would have had to seek a different bed for the night or kick the door in.

She knew someone whose credentials included that talent.

Unlike him, however, she did not have the State of Kansas to pay for the damages.

Opening the door, Cougar stood on the threshold and looked inside.

Bix Bradley had not needed a lock. She would have one installed.

It was a night of sentimentality.

If it had been one o'clock, two o'clock, even three o'clock, she would have had the strength to rip the linen off the bed and change it. She did not want to lie on a mattress smelling of Bix Bradley's cologne and a woman's cheap perfume.

Which reminded her. Now that she was the owner the Lowdown, she would need a new wardrobe.

Including a new perfume.

But it was well past three and she was tired. Bone tired. As weary as she had ever been in her life.

The excitement of the night had drained her. All she wanted to do was crawl into bed and close her eyes.

"No."

There was that word, again.

Not "crawl."

All she wanted to do was get into bed and close her eyes.

Unlike a frog grown from a polliwog, she no longer had to move about on all fours.

Which was not quite the same analogy as referring to herself as a fledgling, grown wings and flown away, but it was close.

As near as she ever expected to get.

No complaints.

Complaints were for sore losers.

She had been sore in her life and she had occasionally been a loser, but not tonight. Tonight, she was the Big Winner.

A smile came to Cougar Bradburn's face. Starting at one corner, it spread across her lips, like a ripple transforming into a wave.

There were not many waves in Kansas.

As many as there were honestly-played poker hands.

The thought did not diminish her smile.

Not one "wit."

She crossed to the window, then, from force of habit, stepped to the side before opening it, so she could not be seen from the street below. Now that she owned the saloon, there was no need for caution. This was her room, now, and if she wanted to open the window, she damn sure would.

But old habits died hard.

And, she reminded herself, one seldom died from an overdose of caution.

Suddenly, Cougar was no longer tired. Sleep faded away from her as though she had just awoken, rather than been up all night.

He was out there. Bix Bradley. His back was to the upstairs window of the Lowdown, so he did not see her.

From her heightened perspective, he appeared larger than life; formidable. Danger clung around him like a cloud.

She saw him motion to a man across the street. Her eyes followed his wave. The man was known to her. Ray Hailey. He crossed the street. The two men shook hands, then bend heads in whispered conversation.

The hair on the back of her neck rose.

Bradley and Hailey. They were up to no good.

Hailey was a lawyer of sorts. The same way Phillip "Fiz" Ward was a doctor. He had been educated in his trade, hung out a shingle and charged accordingly.

That was where the similarity ended.

Mr. Hailey was unscrupulous, greedy and hell-bent-for-leather when a client stiffed him on an invoice.

Fiz Ward was honorable, generous and complained a lot.

If Bradley was asking Hailey to represent him over the loss of the saloon, then her elation, her new-found sense of security had been a cheat. Hailey would file an injunction, force her to move back into one of the three "girl's rooms." He would see to it Bix had the opportunity to rape the safe of all its contents.

Her mouth grew dry, her breathing rapid.

Not from fear: from shame. She had allowed herself to believe there was some good in the world; that Fate had provided her with an unexpected opportunity to succeed where so many others failed.

How could she have been so stupid? So blind? So naive?

She was not born yesterday; far from it. As saloon girls went, she was already old.

They started at eleven or twelve years old.

As soon as they "became a woman."

Or sooner. No one especially cared about the technicalities.

She was a decade past eleven. She had been around the bend.

And back.

Now she was on her way again. Back where she came from.

The thought made the idea of long life a farce.

It obliterated any concept of love.

Love. That was a joke. A bad joke. She would have to get Fiz liquored up one Saturday evening and get him to tell some medical jokes about "love."

Her favorite was the one about the Cyprian's Curse.

It had something to do with the transmission of venereal disease.

Ray Hailey squared his shoulders, hitched up his trousers, scuffed his polished boot in the dust and looked up. Directly into her eyes.

He knew without being told, he was being stared at.

Important men and men who thought they were important always knew when another's eyes were on them.

"Move along!"

Her head jerked involuntarily, seeking the shape of the speaker. There he was. Coming out of the Marshal's Office. Cougar wondered if Claw had been watching, too.

There was nothing he could do. She knew that. The law was the law. He was in Hellhole to uphold the Godamighty Law. He would not, could not, go against Ray Hailey. It was not a matter to be settled by a gunfight on Main Street or a brawl in the Wolf's Pelt Saloon.

Where injunctions were concerned, the paper was mightier than the pistol. Legal documents would be drawn up and brought to James Jackson, the circuit judge, for his signature. He would not want to sign them, probably - but he would. With the West as wild and wide open as a cattle stampede, men like Jim Jackson and Claw Kiley were pledged to play their part in taming the wilderness.

Bringing law and order to prairie towns was their prime concern. Judge Jackson would sign the papers and Marshal Kiley would enforce them.

She wished she had never been born.

"Move on, I said."

She could have heard his order had she been standing on the dark side of the moon. He did not speak the words loudly, but his tone of command was unmistakable.

She forgot he had been a soldier.

Apparently, Union privates did a lot of officer's work.

The South would have been well-advised to follow that example.

It was a morning of water over the bridge.

Ray Hailey said something in return. She did not catch the words. Then Bix Bradley waved his hand. It might have been mistaken for a threatening gesture.

Come to a court of law, she would have sworn to it.

Claw hit him squarely in the jaw. The former owner of the Lowdown Saloon went flying. He landed on his ass, ten feet away from his newly hired attorney.

"Try that again and I'll place a slug between your eyes," the law man warned.

Bradley flipped, flopped, got to his feet. His nose was bleeding.

The lawyer raised a hand to his hat, prefatory to removing it. Miss Bradburn was sure he was going for the derringer concealed beneath it. She remembered hearing him brag about it, once.

Doctor Ward would stand as a second witness.

Apparently, Claw had heard the story, too, for he was taking no chances. With a fist as hard as iron, he smashed it into Hailey's tender stomach. The man retched, gagged, turned purple and fell onto the street in a dead faint.

All of this without saying one articulate word.

"The stage stops over there," Claw directed Bradley. "I wouldn't want you to miss it."

"You can't do this. It's against the law."

Her heart caught.

There was that word again.

"Is that a fact?"

It was the first time she ever heard Claw Kiley utter those words. The first time she ever detected sarcasm in his voice. She would hear him repeat that statement one hundred times, in exactly the same tone of voice. Never would it lose the significance of this moment.

"Yes. It is a fact."

Claw appeared to consider while he un-holstered his gun. His mind was made up by the time it took him to point it at Bradley's chest.

Dead center.

It was not a quick draw, exactly. By her estimation, the simple act required two seconds.

"Let's go buy your ticket, Bix."

Bix turned on his heels and marched.

The stage was half an hour late. When it departed at nine thirty-seven, Bix Bradley, former owner of the Lowdown Saloon, was on it.

Ray Hailey, attorney at law, and been removed from the street.

"Shoveled up," was how she expressed it later.

It was only after the four-up was well on its way out of town that the law man looked up at the window.

He smiled and nodded.

Someone unfamiliar with the gesture might have put a crude meaning to its significance.

He would have been wrong.

The marshal was not reminding the saloon owner she owed him a favor.

He was telling her to get some rest.

He was telling her he understood.

The fact he was also reminding Cougar he knew exactly where her new bedroom window was, had absolutely nothing to do with the fact Miss Bradburn turned away with a grin on her face.

It was a new respect for the law which lit her shining blue eyes.

CHAPTER 3

When Cougar awoke, the light coming in from the sun told her it was afternoon. A closer examination suggested the time to be somewhere after two o'clock. A chill of fear rippled from the back of her neck to the tips of her toes. She was due downstairs by noon. There would be hell-to-pay for her tardiness.

It was only when she reached for the robe to throw around her shoulders, lightly dusted with red freckles, that a new awareness stole over her.

The devil had already gotten his due, in the form of a stage ride out of Hellhole. Bix Bradley was gone, never to return.

In twenty-four hours her world had turned upside down.

Flipped over like a flapjack on a hot grill.

Which reminded her she was hungry.

Starving. Ravenous.

There was no privy upstairs. The girls routinely used chamber pots to relieve themselves if they were too tired, or two occupied, to make it outside. The men simply pissed in the corners or out the windows.

It was a lesson learned early in life.

Never stand under an open window of a saloon.

And watch where you walked.

Wrapping the robe tightly around her, then tying the belt with a deft, "do not disturb" knot, the new owner of the Lowdown Saloon opened the door to her bedroom and shuffled barefoot out into the hall.

It never occurred to her that her hair was in disarray, her robe threadbare and "second hand," her make-up worn into uneven splotches on her face, or that her feet were bare. She might as well have questioned why men grew hair on their faces or why their breath was inevitably sour in the morning, than waste time considering how she looked upon rising.

A girl was paid in advance. How she appeared upon rising, therefore, had no bearing upon anything important.

It was only when she reached the foot of the stairs and had begun to make her way toward the back that she caught a glimpse of someone out of the corner of her eye. Turning quickly, she saw it was the bartender.

"Good morning," she said.

"Good afternoon," he countered.

Which lost him his job.

She was new at being an employer, but not at dreaming. There had never been a saloon girl born who had not fantasied about what she would do if she ever won, stole or married into the ownership of a tavern.

The first thing she would do would be to open a bottle of the most expensive champagne on the shelf. The second was to dismiss all those who did not know a superior person when he looked at one.

Cougar had forgotten about the first dream in her excitement, an oversight she intended to rectify. She had not forgotten about her second dream.

"Pack up your things and get out," she said with an unemotional coldness she had rehearsed for two-thousand, nine-hundred and seventy-six years.

"I got a week's wages comin' to me."

He did not seem surprised at his dismissal.

"Take it up with Mr. Bradley."

Ordinarily, Cougar would have sympathized with the bartender. As a general rule, they were likable, lower class men who knew better than to hassle the girls. Not above slipping a few coins into their own pockets, they regularly sampled the beer, tested the strength of the red-eye and took a bribe on occasion to supply an alibi for a disreputable-looking man.

She did not know whether Bix owed the bartender a week's wages or not. Inheriting the saloon, she readily assumed responsibility for its debts and obligations. However, she was not a fool. It did not take a banker or a railroad man to understand that when a property changed hands, the new owner was accorded at least as much respect as the old.

In this case, the new owner demanded more respect than the old one had received. The bartender had failed to live up to that expectation. So much the worse for him.

"I'll complain to the Marshal," he said.

Her blue eyes narrowed into slits and the corners of her mouth tugged in annoyance.

Was the man threatening her because he knew of her relationship with Claw? Or was he simply taking a shot in the dark? Or more unlikely, standing up for what he perceived to be his rights by applying to the law?

It was an irritating question, doomed to go unanswered.

"All right," she decided aloud. She had emptied the till last night, hiding it behind the bar for fear of having the safe broken into by someone who already knew the combination. She gave the bartender a direction by tilting her head to the left. He responded immediately by stepping out from behind the bar.

Cougar assumed his former position, reached into the empty whisky crate and removed a handful of currency. She did not have to be staring at his face to read the expression.

Damn fool.

A more careful scrutiny would have supplied him a slap across the face.

"Here."

She counted out five dollars, which was his due, then added another dollar to the pot.

It was her first full day as a saloon owner. She did not want to mar it by having a former employee leave with a bad taste in his mouth.

"Thanks," he said, vindicating her generosity.

"Where will you go?"

She did not especially care, but asked from professional curiosity.

He shrugged.

"Six dollars an' what I got saved up won't buy me a stage ticket to San Francisco." He tried a smile. "Guess I'll ask around Hellhole. Maybe Blade will take me on at the Wolf's Pelt."

They both knew better than that. Blade tended bar by himself. He was too tight with a dollar to hire anyone who did not bring the potential for additional revenue under her skirt.

It was not the improbability of his getting a job which made Cougar regret her decision to fire him. It was his statement, or, more accurately, the destination he would never reach which moved her.

San Francisco.

She, too, had thought about San Francisco; looked to it as a far-off locale of wonder and new hope.

It was disconcerting to hear her own dreams verbalized by another.

A man, no less.

"You might try San Louie," she tried, pronouncing "St. Louis" with a slight French dialect she had unknowingly picked up in New Orleans.

He shook his head.

"Came from there."

"Really?"

"Yeah."

"Why'd you leave?"

"Why'd *you* leave where *you* came from?"

Which was as much as to say, "Mind your own business. I got my secrets, you got yours."

She regretted asking him.

"Good luck."

"Thanks."

It never occurred to him to ask why she fired him, or to plead for his job back.

It never occurred to her to ask him to stay.

Some things were better off left unsaid.

Without waiting to see whether he left, Cougar took her temporary strongbox of money into the back room. There, she stashed it under a table behind several wooden crates, broken whisky bottles and a mound of dust. The table, crates and broken glass were not formidable obstacles in themselves, but the dust balls could have held off an attack of charging buffalo.

With that thought in mind, she went about her morning ablutions. The outhouse was something else she would have to consider. It needed a complete decorating job. This redesign did not include curtains or amenities such as bum fodder. It required a new hole - deeper, this time, and as far away from its former home as possible.

The current necessary needed liming and a burial.

It would be convenient to have a privy indoors, as well. While Kansas winters were not particularly severe, performing one's business in ten degree weather discouraged men from ordering a third or a fourth beer.

Whoever thought she would be worried about outhouses?

Withstanding a barrage of horse flies which had fled the livery in search of live game, Cougar retraced her steps back inside. The bartender was gone.

She instinctively glanced over at the wall, where the high-priced liquor and wine were stored. None were missing.

By paying the man one dollar more than he had coming and exchanging a few words with him, she had saved herself twenty, maybe thirty dollars.

To say nothing about a severe chastisement at her own gullibility and forgetfulness. This was her business, now. It was up to her to keep an eye on the stock.

"Excuse me, Miss Bradburn."

Cougar turned toward the speaker and saw Gail, one of her girls, standing by the foot of the stairs.

Miss Bradburn.

It was a wondrous thing, to contemplate the value of respect.

What was in a name? The leap from owned to owner.

There never would be a sweeter sound than "Miss Bradburn." There might be more endearing ones, but never one which conveyed with it the spirit of independence.

"Yes?"

As with the bartender, it did not occur to her to correct the woman, to invite her to resume their former familiarity. A man might be called by his first name and be considered "fair." A woman called by her first name was "fair game."

"Excuse me, but are we to be kept on, Miss Bradburn? Me and the other girls?"

By Cougar's promotion, Gail had been elected spokesman. It was as well for both parties to understand the new power structure.

News of the bartender's departure spread fast.

Cougar would have appreciated more time to consider the question, but she did not blame the girls. They were scared.

She had been scared a time or two in her life.

"Yes. We'll run things pretty much as they were for now. It's going to take a little time for me to get adjusted."

"Thank you, ma'am."

Gail made a small courtesy and scampered back up the stairs with the good news. Her gratitude made Miss Bradburn smile. It was an odd sensation, having the power to grant life and death.

It made her feel like a marshal.

Which was something she would not have had the audacity to think a day ago.

Owning a saloon gave a woman the balls to savor authority. And the money to back it up.

Which was something no marshal ever had.

She needed breakfast. What was more, she could afford to go out to eat it. The thought was irresistible. No matter that it was just past two o'clock. She could go to the Regent and order anything she wanted.

One thing was for certain. She had made her last pot of coffee. From now on, a freshly brewed pot would be delivered daily, at ten A.M. She would wait and consider what to do about cooking later. Bix Bradley had taken all his meals out, but that was not only expensive, it invited conversation. A man could sit alone at a table and no one talked about him.

A woman sitting alone was either an old spinster, too ugly for any man to bother with, or a prostitute no reputable gentleman wanted to be seen with in a public place.

Saloons were the exception. They came ready-made with excuses.

"Gosh, dear, they get paid to sit on my lap!"

"I'm sorry, honey, she just sort of bumped into me at the bar and the next thing I knew, we were sitting at a table together. Nothing happened. Honest."

Honest Injun.

As honest as a cigar store figurehead and just as truthful. The poor wife had no choice but to believe her husband. On one hand, being a "reputable woman," she had never crossed the threshold of a saloon in her life. On the other hand, even if she knew her man was lying, there was nothing she could do about it.

What were her options? Lock him out of the bedroom? In all her life, Cougar had never known one decent family to have a lock on any inside door. Refuse to cook for him? That would starve herself. He could always go out; he held the money. If she were lucky, she had egg money or the few pennies earned knitting socks for Mr. Anderson at the dry goods store.

Spend that money on herself and all hell would break out. Come Saturday and she did not have one dollar to give him for his night out, he would take a strap to her back. That money was for the household expenses he did not care to finance. It was not to be spent foolishly on personal items for the wife.

Tell her neighbors? They were in the same situation as she.

And just as helpless.

The Written Law - man's law - was always on the side of the husband.

The Unwritten Law was even more merciless.

Cougar could not go to the Regent or any other restaurant three times a day. It was simply out of the question. That left her with the option of cooking herself, something she knew as much about as knitting socks, or having someone prepare her meals.

She would ask one of the girls, she decided suddenly. They would appreciate the chance to earn a little extra money. There was a pot-bellied stove in the back. That would suffice. Once the back rooms were cleaned up, one could be converted into a pantry.

Problem solved. It was amazing what money did to problem solving.

She went upstairs and changed, donning her most conservative dress, then covering that with a shawl. It was almost too warm to wear a covering over her shoulders, but a gentlewoman was never overdressed. Adding the requisite hat to her outfit, Cougar checked her appearance in the glass and nodded in satisfaction.

Overdressing had never been a concern of hers, but for other reasons.

Walking with a lively step, Miss Bradburn emerged from the Lowdown with her head held back and her eyes shining with new luster. Three men were standing at the edge of her building, speaking quietly among themselves. When they saw her approach, all three tipped their hats to her.

"Good afternoon, Miss Cougar," one said. She had never seen him before in her life.

"Good afternoon," she replied. Saying "good afternoon" without the suggestive tone of voice asking him come back to see her in the evening was a new experience.

Another first.

She was learning fast and the education was exhilarating. The closest way she could describe it to herself was as though she had been transformed during the night into a man.

A man was born with respect. Another Law.

Amazing how her life had revolved around the Law and she never questioned it.

At the Regent, Cougar walked in, looked around, then selected a table toward the front. Her head was spinning. It was the first time she had ever been there alone, the first time she had ever selected her own table.

The first time she ever realized all the first times she had missed in life.

"Good afternoon, Miss Bradburn."

The waiter was a small boy, one of Jonathan Walker's sons. He was no older than fourteen although he looked twice that. She had never seen him in the Lowdown but knew his father well.

"What's cooking in the back, John?" she asked.

"Wednesday's beef stew is warming up," he offered.

"How about you ask - No," she corrected herself. "How about you tell the cook to make me two eggs, sunny-side up and serve them with bread and bacon. And put a fresh pot of coffee on for me. I'm so thirsty, I could drink it all."

"Yes, ma'am." He was back in two shakes of a longhorn's head "Cook says the coffee's fresh. But it ain't," he whispered.

"Tell Cookie that Miss Bradburn wants a fresh pot of coffee or she knows who to complain to."

"Yes, ma'am."

A cup of steaming hot, newly brewed coffee was served with her meal.

A day ago, that threat would have gone unheeded. Saloon girls did not blackmail cooks. If they did, they were more likely to get a shiner for their trouble than a fresh cup of coffee.

New life. New rules.

New respect.

No, that was incorrect. New life. New rules.

Respect.

Cougar ate her breakfast in glorious solitude, left a standing order for coffee, bread and butter to be delivered daily to the Lowdown, paid two weeks in advance and left John Walker twenty-five cents tip.

"Keep it for yourself," she advised him. "No one's the wiser but you and me."

He swallowed his gratitude.

She had eaten that for breakfast a time or two herself.

Not unmindful of her new status, Cougar walked back to her home, savoring the sunshine, the smell of the breeze which held a hint of wildflowers, sidestepping the wads of half-chewed tobacco. Hellhole was the same Hellhole but it no longer looked or felt like the Hellhole she knew.

There was a sense of ownership, of belonging. She was no longer a transient but a resident. If she could have taken an hour to go from the eatery to the alehouse, the trip would have ended too soon.

Pausing at the swinging doors, she turned and stared out at Main Street with a great desire to walk back down onto the hard-packed dirt and walk some more. This, she realized with a start, must be how Claw felt when he make his rounds. He, too, was no longer a man passing through, but a resident. What happened to this town affected him. Each building constructed added to his prestige; every new couple moving in came under his charge.

She was not a marshal but she was a property owner. Now, the buildings, the people, the hopes, dreams, the living and dying added or detracted something from her. It was not a duty but a dimension of a life he and she were now an inextricable part of.

Who would have guessed?

CHAPTER 4

He watched her from the window of his office. He saw her come out of the Lowdown, noting that the three men at the corner of the building tipped their hats to her. He waited while she ate. He was standing by the half-open door as she made her way back to the saloon.

It did not occur to him to approach her.

Not before business hours. A new sense of propriety had entered his life. They were not starting over.

They were starting anew.

He would wait until six o'clock. He was sure she would be downstairs by that time. He did not want to have to ask for her.

He could not have explained his reasoning, but she could have.

It was something they would have to work through.

Pride was a two-way street.

If she had known, she would not have come down until seven.

The hand-printed sign went up at precisely five-thirty. "UNDER NEW OWNERSHIP. First drink is on the house. By Order of Miss Cougar Bradburn."

It was placed in the window; the one to the immediate left of the swinging doors. He could read it from across the street. It stirred his blood.

The marshal prepared himself some supper, then forgot about it as he returned, shadow-like to the door. He was keeping an eye on his town. It was easy to rationalize.

He finally ate his food cold and never tasted it.

At five-forty post meridian, Doctor Ward drove his buggy east on Main Street, going toward the stable. The pace he kept would have put him in good competition with a snail. He was not known for his fleetness of foot.

Fiz was putting disease and death on guard: I will come at my own time and on my own terms. You have no terrors for me. We will do combat against one another. You have scores of symptoms, legions of lesions, "piles" of pusses, and poisons. You will win often.

I will never wave the white flag, show the white feather, while there is hope. I will pray to God, place my trust in the skill of my hands, the wisdom of my brain and the courage of my heart. I vow to stock my cabinets with healing herbs, and to ease pain wherever I find it.

Suffering may help the soul but it does nothing to promote healing.

I will neither stand in judgment, nor will I turn away any in distress.

This vow was not the Hippocratic Oath but one Fiz Ward had composed for himself, in place of that other. He never wrote it down, added to it when necessary, never shared it.

He saw the sign and reined in his horse. In the length of time he took to contemplate the words, he could have composed a sonata.

By five fifty-five, Fiz presented himself, freshly shaven and wearing a clean shirt, at the bar of the Lowdown.

"Where's my free drink?" he demanded in a loud voice. Turning to the new bartender, he squinted, rubbed his mustache with his right hand and leaned forward. "I want to speak to the owner."

"Is there something wrong?" the bartender inquired. There was no more than mild inquisitiveness in the question.

"Yer dern tootin' there is. I want my free drink."

"You may place your order with me, sir," came the tired response. "What'll it be? Whisky? A beer?"

"I don't want any of that flat beer Bix Bradley used to serve. And I don't want any watered down red-eye. What else have you?"

"For a man getting a free drink, yer mighty demanding." The bartender was droll.

"The sign says, 'First drink is on the house.' It does not say, 'First flat beer is on the house.' Or, 'First watered down whisky is on the house.'"

He leaned over the bar, staring at the high-priced bottles. By the way his eyes shifted from one to the other, one might surmised he had the labels memorized.

"I'll have a drink from that one," he continued, pointing with the index finger of his right hand. The exact same finger, incidentally, with which he had, so recently, rubbed against the grain of his mustache.

The bottle he indicated was French champagne.

"It ain't chilled."

"We'll send for some ice."

"From where? Saint Louis?" There was obvious skepticism in the bartender's voice.

"The Regent."

The bartender almost cracked a smile.

"I've never known the Regent to serve ice, unless it were the dead of winter and the coffee in the pot froze up."

The bartender had a regional dialect, half buffalo hunter, half Injun scout. It sounded phony.

The doctor did not seem to notice.

"That sign," he reiterated, turning with a nod of his head toward the window. "It says I'm entitled to a free drink and if I don't get what I want, I'll summon the law."

The bartender blinked three times.

Unknown to any, save, perhaps the medicine man, three was a Holy number.

All things came in cycles of three.

The Father, Son and the Holy Ghost.

Jesus, Mary and Joseph. Shouted three times in succession, it was said to be an effective curse.

The number of curtain calls, multiplied by ten, the Swedish Nightingale received after her solo concert performance singing "Home Sweet Home" and Italian arias at the Academy of Music in New York City.

Deaths. Deaths came in threes. It was as certain as all hell breaking loose during a full moon.

Perhaps the matter was academic.

"What seems to be the trouble here?"

The bartender looked up. The doctor turned around. The marshal towered over one and nodded respectfully to the other.

The doctor had a great deal of authority, but was out of his element. The bartender had less authority but owned the joint.

Money, like sentiments spewing forth from a drunk's mouth, talked.

"No trouble. Now that you're here." It was Miss Bradburn who spoke. Putting aside her temporary job as bartender, she nodded toward the quality liquor. "Fiz claims my sign gives him the right to demand a bottle of champagne. I wanted to celebrate tonight with a glass of something special. And you promised to buy me a drink. If you'll just pay up, Marshal, we can all retire to a table at the back."

Claw instinctively looked toward the rear of the saloon. The Lowdown was filling up fast.

"There aren't any tables."

It was a moot point.

"I can drink mine here."

"Thanks, Fiz," Claw muttered.

"Any time."

Cougar took the bottle off the shelf and ran it lovingly through her hands.

"It's been a long time since I had any of this. And the circumstances weren't exactly what I'd call memorable. You're buying, Giant. Would you care to open it?"

The fact of the matter was, Claw Kiley had never tasted champagne in his life. Nor had he ever opened anything more complicated than a can of peaches. He did know wine came with corks but he did not have the slightest idea how one removed such an object from the neck of a bottle, unless it were to crack it against the edge of a table.

"If I'm buying, then I'm not going to do the work." He glanced at Fiz in good imitation of how the professional man viewed disease.

"Don't stare at me," Fiz complained. "I just came in for a free drink. I don't need a job."

"There are some that say otherwise," Cougar quipped. He had set himself up for that and did not deserve to get away without the proper punishment.

"Thank you." Fiz scowled and looked down at the bar. As the self-appointed public health officer, his action held more than an implied threat. "Don't you ever clean this?"

"About as often as I clean myself."

No gentleman could possible make a comeback to that statement. Fiz let it ride.

If wishes were horses, the Marshal would be on one now.

That left Cougar to make the decision.

The answer walked through the door.

"Mr. MacPhearson, would you come over here, please?"

Startled to hear himself so addressed, the said Mr. Frankie MacPhearson hurried to the bar. He removed his hat and smoothed down his greasy, unwashed hair. His eyes glistened with permanent tears.

"I'm mighty proud to congratulate you on your new ownership of this establishment," he said with solemnity. "Fate is seldom so kind to so worthy a personage."

The words were crisp, even eloquently spoken. Fiz mumbled a "For heaven's sake" under his breath but it was more form than surprise.

"Mr. MacPhearson, will you do me the honor of opening this bottle of champagne? And then, we would be most pleased to have you join us in a glass."

Frankie was being admitted into the most elite circle Hellhole, Kansas had to offer. He had stood in many circles before, but none he would trade for this company or this place.

He was an extraordinary man.

"It would be my pleasure." His back straightened and his eyes dried, leaving only the indelible tracks of a broken heart which stained his face from eyes to chin. "I shall require a towel. A clean one."

If Doctor Ward ever cared to relinquish his title as public health officer, a new candidate had unknowingly stepped forward.

"I will get you one."

Cougar slipped away from the bar and disappeared into the back room. She returned almost immediately with a clean white linen cloth and a tray with six matched wine glasses.

Six being a holy number, doubled.

Frankie unwrapped the foil from the neck of the bottle, then placed his dirty, gnarled hand on the cork. With painstaking care, he rotated the glass container, working the stopper out until there was no more than a sliver of it remaining.

"The wine is warm," he observed to Cougar. "Please stand back in case the contents bubble over."

She moved back. Claw, who had no experience in effervescent liquids, remained where he was. Fiz picked up one of the glasses and inspected the inside for dust.

The cork came out with a POP. The operation had been performed with so delicate a hand, no wine spilled. Cougar clapped in spontaneous approval.

"You are wonderful, Frankie!"

Frankie MacPhearson was a man whom life had taught how to cry. Tears came easily to his eyes but not usually for the reason they spilled over the rims at this moment.

"If you will be seated at a table, it will be my pleasure to serve you," he informed his host.

Miraculously, a table at the rear suddenly emptied. Cougar led the small party to it. Fiz, hurrying after her, had the honor of drawing her chair back. While she seated herself, Claw stepped on Fiz's foot.

It was a tribute to his breeding that he did not scream.

A greater compliment was paid to Claw's strength when Fiz did not bluster with uncouth observations on the lawman's ancestry.

Frankie followed with the tray. The white linen was folded over his arm. After delicately setting the crystal down, he dispensed four glasses from a set of six, then poured Miss Bradburn the first drops of the delicately colored liquid. While it was not proper Philadelphia etiquette to offer the lady first approval, this was not "Back East."

Cougar sipped the wine and smiled.

"Perfect."

Frankie made a slight bow, wiped the bottle with the towel, then filled the doctor's glass. Youth was served last.

The effort was appreciated by all but one of the select gathering.

The marshal had never gone to charm school and attributed the action to the supposition Frankie owed the doctor money.

"Will you join us?" Cougar invited. It was, after all, her party.

Frankie swelled with pride at the invitation, then graciously declined.

"I think not."

There was too much behind his eyes for his refused to be gratified.

"Sit down," Claw ordered. Anything less would have sent the slender, emaciated man fleeing for his sanity, if not his life.

Frankie sat and Cougar poured his drink. When all four glasses were filled, they paused for a moment of silent acknowledgement to the Fates, before Fiz made the toast.

"To the new owner of the Lowdown Saloon. Long may she reign."

They each sipped, then Mr. MacPhearson turned to Miss Bradburn.

"To the most gracious lady in the world."

His voice caught between the words "lady" and "in," implying a rapid, silent consideration. His pause did not go undetected and was, therefore, the more deeply appreciated.

"Thank you."

Which left Claw. He took another sip of wine, this one larger than the first. Immediately bubbles went up his nose. His ocean-blue eyes opened in surprise and he swallowed quickly, hoping to lessen the imminent damage. His effort underwhelmed the gods, who saw fit to have him sneeze.

"What is this stuff?" he gasped in blind forgetfulness of the moment.

"Champagne."

Any one of the three could have supplied the answer. He could not be sure who spoke, for his ears were plugged with embarrassment.

Fiz tapped him on the arm with clinical righteousness.

"We're waiting for you to make a toast."

Claw determined never to pay another doctor bill as long as he lived.

"Cougar," he began, then paused to clear his throat. "I'm real happy for you."

It was not what he wanted to say and certainly did not come out the way he intended, but mercifully, it served its purpose. The gang drained their glasses, and Frankie refilled all but his.

He though to escape but the new owner of the drinking parlor had other ideas.

"Frankie, the bartender resigned this morning and there are twenty thirsty men at the bar. Will you draw them all a beer while I sit here?"

"At no charge?" he asked, clearly frightened by the prospect of handling her money.

"At no charge," she agreed.

His lips twitched as he contemplated the enormity of the task she had set for him, then he wordlessly slipped away. For one more day in his life, he would be a respectable citizen.

It is the moments stolen from reality which make life worth living.

His chair was not cold before Fiz spoke.

"Haven't you ever had champagne before?"

Claw shot him an appreciative look.

"Contrary to popular belief, the Union Army did not supply 'sparkling wine' to its soldiers."

Fiz grunted and looked away.

"That's not what I heard."

"I think I'll have to see about putting in a cold house," Cougar said, speaking over the last. "That way, I'll be able to keep the beer cold and have some ice in case any other big spenders come in."

Which reminded Claw he was paying for the celebration.

"I'll have some more."

It was Cougar who poured in Frankie's absence.

"Drink up," she offered.

"He ought to. He's paying for it."

Claw leaned back in his chair, drawing his Stetson back on his head with a motion not unlike how he would quick draw his gun.

"You know, Doctor Ward, it wouldn't surprise me any if one day you woke up in jail and someone had thrown away the key."

"Now, why would someone do that? You're here to enforce the law, aren't you? I'll look to you for redress."

Claw had no idea what "redress" meant but he was quick enough to realize it had nothing to do with the way the word sounded. It gave him the liberty, however, to wink at Cougar.

"I guess we all know a little bit about 'redress.'"

Cougar drew the same conclusion Claw did and laughed heartily at his joke.

Humor was where you found it.

It was a lot like life.

Fiz blushed. Another notch for Claw's gun. And this time, his victim did not require the services of a doctor.

Unless one considered the old adage, "Physician heal thyself."

"Drink up, boys. No sense letting the wine go flat."

The boys helped themselves.

When the champagne was finished, Cougar confiscated it with a small smile.

"I'm going to have my winning poker hand framed and put up on the wall," she explained. "As a remembrance. I think I will put a candle in this bottle and set it up on the table in the back. In case I ever have a fancy dinner."

"Sounds like a good idea to me," Claw approved. As the owner of the bottle, by dint of having paid for it, he was officially presenting it back to the lady.

"Yes. Well, I had better be going."

Fiz rose slowly to his feet and looked around the room with the eye of a man who only occasionally controls his own destiny.

"Why don't you stay?" Cougar invited. "There's no need for you to rush off."

"Oh, yes there is." He nodded toward the bar. "If I outstay my welcome, I know what I'll be doing until closing time."

"You think I'd ask you to tend bar?"

"There are some that say bartenders and doctors have a lot in common."

"Yeah. They both charge an arm and a leg."

It was Claw's best shot of the evening.

Fiz grunted and nodded to Cougar.

"Good night. Thank you for the drink." He hesitated, licked his lips, then resumed his habitual stooped posture and shuffled away, weaving carefully through the crowded room.

"He's an odd duck," the marshal remarked.

"Like all of us."

"I suppose so. How late are you planning on staying open?"

"Why? Are you going to come back and close me down if I don't shut the doors by ten?"

He looked startled.

"No. That wasn't what I had in mind. I just figured there will be a lot of blind drunk men tossed out into the street about the same time. Thought I'd be around to see they get home."

"Drunk on one beer?"

"The way Frankie's pouring drinks, I'd say your limit isn't being too strictly enforced."

"It's only for one night. Tomorrow I'll charge them double to make up for what I lost tonight."

Claw did not know whether or not she was teasing.

"Time for me to pay up."

He reached into his vest pocket but she stopped him by putting a hand on his.

"Not for the champagne, Claw. That was my treat."

"But I promised to buy you a drink."

"So you did. And I'll hold you to it."

The words were not meant as innocently as they sounded. There was a peculiar emphasis on the second sentence.

"Tomorrow, then?"

"Sure. Or later tonight? Maybe after closing, when it's a little less hectic in here?"

He grinned.

"Now, why do you think I really asked what time you were closing?"

"To usher the drunks home."

She dead panned the line, which did not mean she was lying.

"I'll see you later."

"You bet."

Claw walked across the floor, pausing long enough to separate two men who were in a heated argument over the worth of Andrew Jackson.

Cougar watched him go, then made her way to the bar, leaving behind on the round, green-felted table, one tray and six matched wine glasses. Four from the set had been used; two were untouched.

The situation, as it stood, had the potential for bad luck. There was only one remedy. The spirit of Marshal Jack Duvall nudged his wife's elbow. Thinking he was a breath of wind, she ignored him. It was only through persistence and a tug on her heart strings that Ada Duvall looked away from her empty window.

"Jack?" she said. "Jack?"

There was no answer. Nor had she really expected one.

From somewhere far below, on a street in a town she was not a resident of, Ada heard a man call out. His voice was deep, jovial.

"I'll drink to that!" he said.

She thought she recognized the voice, but that could not be true, for she knew no one in No Name.

"I'll drink to that," Ada repeated for no particular reason. She turned from the window and stared out. The speaker was nowhere in sight.

His spirit had returned to the Lowdown Saloon. Two drops of what could have been champagne dripped down the side of each previously unused glass.

A disaster had been averted.

Once a lawman, always a lawman.

A saying which could not fairly be coupled with "Till death do us part."

"I'll take over," Cougar offered as she joined Frankie. "But if you're interested in a job, I can use a bartender. I'm looking for a man I can trust."

He looked confused.

"There's the marshal," he tried in a plaintive voice. "I trust him."

"So do I, Frankie." Cougar smiled at him, then planted a kiss on his forehead. "Here. Take this with you. As a present from the new owner."

She gave him a full bottle of whisky. He hesitated, then accepted the gift.

"I won't have a drop of it tonight," he promised. "I've had my limit."

He was offering her the only gift he had. She pursed her lips and looked away.

"Oh, Frankie, go on."

Clutching the bottle with two hands, he hurried away.

When she looked back, the smile had returned to her face.

"Belly up to the bar, boys. Drinks are on the house."

A house, which had become a home, in a city which housed the dearest family she would ever have.

CHAPTER 5

Ten o'clock came and went and Cougar Bradburn did not notice the time. It was a night of celebration and she was kept busy tending bar. It was not until she caught one of the girls, hiding in the back room, rubbing her feet, that she realized how late it was getting.

"Call it a night," she ordered. The girl looked up with an appreciative nod. Seeing the expression on Cougar's face, she tried a grin.

"Big doings. They won't forget this in Hellhole for a long time."

"Not before the first thaw and the hiders come in, anyway."

A man's memory never went past his last free drink.

"Good night."

"Night."

It was too early for the new owner of the Lowdown to decide whether or not it would be a good night.

Returning to the front room, Cougar slapped her hand on the bar for attention.

"That's it, boys. Tomorrow is another day. Drink up and head on home before a posse of wives comes to collect you!"

There was a rumbling of discontent but no one complained too loudly. Miss Bradburn was right. She also had that tone of voice which promised, "pay up," if they overstayed their welcome.

Tossing "thank yous" and "g'nights" over their shoulders, the menfolk of Hellhole shuffled off to their homes, their families and their day jobs as respectable citizens.

"You, too, girls," Cougar called to her staff. They heaved a collective sigh of relief and made their way to the stairs. Cougar counted them as they went up, one step at a time, dragging their weary feet as though they had swollen to twice their normal weight. She knew the feeling.

She also made a casual observation. No men trailed after them up. Those who might have had an inclination were either dead drunk under one of the tables or had opted for another night. As the new owner, that meant a loss of revenue, for she was entitled to her "cut" of the nighttime activities. As the new, tired owner, she was relieved. It would be a quiet night.

Bed creaks were not conducive to sleep.

By quarter after eleven, Miss Bradburn was alone in the downstairs of the saloon. Systematically, she went from lamp to lamp, extinguishing the lights until only one burned by the entrance. She had not meant it as a signal, but as she stood by the double doors, staring out into the darkness, her awareness grew acute.

Where was he? Was he herding men home as he had promised earlier? How long would it take him to perform that civic duty? Half an hour? An hour?

The waiting had begun.

She had fancied that waiting at the empty door of her own establishment would lessen the expectation, take an edge off her nervousness. She was mistaken.

Of all the drunken men she had known, the violent men, the thieves, robbers, confidence men, trail bosses and hide cutters with sharp knives, time remained her worst enemy. Time reminded a woman she was lonely. A drunken man could be tossed out. A thief could be thrown behind bars; a gambler could be taken to the stage depot and unceremoniously dispatched out of town.

Only time remained. Or more correctly, time continued to move in its slow, insidious pace. Time kept the same rhythm as a heartbeat, yet time never aged.

"God, I'm tired."

She spoke aloud. There was no one to hear. She wanted to break her train of thought. Words were sometimes a hedge against loneliness.

Sometimes not.

It was a game all lonely people played with Fate. If you put fate on notice you were not waiting for someone or something in particular to happen, It might be deceived.

"I'll clean up in the morning," she said. "And I'm going to have to hire a bartender. I can't do all this by myself."

She rubbed her elbow for emphasis. It was sore from pouring drinks. Too sore for her to bother picking up all the chairs, placing them on tables and sweeping the place out. There was no hurry. It could wait until morning.

Her eye caught an overturned spittoon. Her lips twitched into an unpleasant grimace. To the victor belongs the spoils.

"Tomorrow."

Tomorrow was another day. But there was only one tonight.

Cougar let her shoulders sag as she revolved slowly in a semi-circle, running her red-rimmed eyes over the room. She had imbibed too freely with the celebrants. Her head was swimming. Call it a night.

Not a "good night." Just a night.

This was what she had wanted, what she had dreamed, struggled, fought for. What she had never dared hope would happen. She was the owner of her own establishment. The boss lady. It had cost her nothing more than her entire life's misery to obtain. And cheap at the price.

"A *am* tired!" she decided. She had just about as much strength left as would be required to drag herself up the stairs and slip into bed. She would not even bother changing, she decided. What was the point? Wrinkles came out of clothes.

"You know, that Tom Green has a mighty mean mouth on him." The words came from behind her. She did not turn around when she spoke.

"He's the son of a preacher from back east."

"I guess that explains where he learned them, then. I got cussed to damnation in more ways that I ever heard before."

A wry smile replaced Cougar's grimace.

What did men know of damnation?

"Wondered where you were, Marshal."

She felt a tentative hand on her shoulder and leaded back into it.

"I heard you talking. Thought there was someone in here with you."

"That matter to you?"

She had not meant to ask that question.

"Depends on who it was."

His voice was soft, tender. Young. She could not imagine how a man could be a United States marshal and still be wet behind the ears.

There was an implication behind his words and it hardened her heart. When Cougar faced Claw, her smile was painted on. Like a saloon madam's face.

"It takes a lot of money to run a place like this."

He smiled and raised his eyebrows in sincere astonishment.

"Never thought about it."

"It's something I've given a lot of thought to."

A lot of thought can be thought in a matter of seconds.

"I guess you'd have to."

There was a faint trace of light-colored stubble on his cheeks and his shirt was stained with sweat. One of the buttons was either missing or had come undone. She wondered how many shirts he owned and if he could sew on a button.

Two, she decided. And yes.

She was used to answering her own questions.

"You came back."

"I was here at ten but the party was still going on. Didn't see any sense breaking things up. You look tired."

"Thank you."

She gave no indication whether she was thanking him for allowing the saloon to remain open, or for the observation which went wide of being a compliment.

"Want me to help you clean up?"

"Claw, I think we need to understand one another."

His eyes opened wider. She had forgotten how blue they were.

"Reckon that'd be a good thing."

"I invited you back here tonight because I thought I'd take you upstairs. It's my place now and I can do what I like."

A tinge of red crept into his cheeks. He nodded. When she did not say anything else, he felt obligated to prolong the conversation.

"Yeah."

"Some men I take up by choice. Others because it's a business. Do you understand?"

The silence was longer this time.

"Yes, ma'am."

He did not understand.

"You face a man in the street. You don't want to kill him but you do. Because it's part of the job. The bank gets robbed and you're gone for two weeks trailing outlaws. Someone wakes you up in the middle of the night because a husband is beating his wife and you go break it up."

He nodded slowly.

"That's my job," he acknowledged. He had lost her tracks and was following on faith.

Belief was not to be confused with instinct.

"I have responsibilities, too. Different from what they were but no less demanding. This place needs a lot of upkeep. I have girls who work for me and need to get paid. I have to buy beer and whisky."

"I know one expense you won't have." He tried a smile. She did not return it. Nor did she encourage him to pursue the thought. "You won't have to bribe the law."

He was trying to be understanding, gentle. In his innocence, he blundered badly, digging the knife deeper than she intended.

"I have to make money."

"I expect you do."

"Do you have any idea how the owner of a drinking parlor makes money?"

He shifted his weight from one leg to the other.

"By selling drinks."

"And?"

He lifted his eyes. Not far enough to indicate heaven.

"Yes," she agreed. "It's a very lucrative part of the business."

His shoulders hitched as though he were going to draw his gun against an invisible enemy.

Not imaginary. Invisible. The difference was tangible.

"How many customers did Bix Bradley sleep with?"

He had on his Marshal's voice.

She did not appreciate it.

"There's the door, Claw. I'm not going to answer that question and I'm not going to argue with you. For the first time in my life, I have a chance to make good. Real good. But in order to keep this place afloat, I'm going to need capital. Lots of it."

His eyes hardened.

"What did Bix Bradley do when he needed money?"

She was almost glad he asked.

"He went to the bank and borrowed it. Do you think I would get the same consideration from Mr. Herbert? Think about it."

He thought about it. And said nothing.

"Good morning, Miss Bradburn," Cougar continued. She lowered her voice slightly, to indicate it was the bank manager speaking. Her voice was stern, chipped. Cold. Formal. Managing to convey both disapproval and distaste without losing Mr. Herbert's veneer as a gentleman.

"I was told by my clerk you wished to speak to me. Open an account? No? Borrow money? I see. Won't you come this way."

The "please" was conspicuously missing.

"Have-a-seat-Miss-Brad-burn."

The surname, thus pronounced, had the distinct association with "fire." Or "arson."

"Thank you," Cougar responded in her normal voice.

The drama unfolded before Claw's eyes. She had already seen the play.

"You wish to borrow one thousand dollars against your interest in the Lowdown Saloon?"

"Not interest, Mr. Herbert. I own it. Outright."

"You have a bill of sale? Something which would indicate the property was legally transferred to you? Without coercion?"

"No."

"You have some document proving the worth of your collateral to be over one thousand dollars?"

"I have an inventory of the stock; furniture, whisky, kegs of beer. I have receipts for the past six months, proving an adequate income from which I would be able to pay back the loan in installments."

"You have insurance on the property? Operating a saloon is a high-risk business."

"No."

She did not have to add no one would insure the Lowdown.

"You have life insurance?"

"No."

She did not have to add no one would insure her life.

"What experience do you have in the management of a business?"

"I grew up in the business."

"I specifically said 'management,' Miss-Brad-burn."

"None."

"You have a man keeping accounts for you? Someone who might have a respectable background?"

"In a pig's eye."

"There is no call for profanity, Miss Brad-burn. How much have you in your account at this moment?"

"Two hundred dollars; all the money the former owner left in the safe."

"If you had one thousand, or twelve hundred dollars in the bank - in a secured account that you agreed not to touch for the life of the loan - then perhaps I could see my way clear to loaning you... say five hundred dollars."

"If I had one thousand dollars in my account, I wouldn't be here now, Mr. Her-bert."

"I see. I appreciate your desire to improve the property, but I am afraid the bank's stockholders would take a dim view of my granting any loan without proper collateral. Or to any person who does not have established ties with the business community of Hellhole."

Cougar made a curt chopping motion with her hand, effectively terminating the interview and her one-sided conversation.

"Does that make it a little clearer, Claw?"

She had the peculiar impression he had shrunk in stature during her loan refusal.

"If I had a thousand dollars, I would give it to you," he whispered. His throat was dry, accounting for the huskiness in his voice.

"But you don't. And the odds of you ever having that kind of money are pretty slim. And even if you did, I wouldn't take it from you. Not as a loan; not as a gift. This is my business, Claw. Not yours."

"What about Fiz?"

He was trying, but his efforts brought more heartache than comfort.

"I do not have that sort of relationship with Fiz." He looked hurt. She softened her tone. "Besides, I doubt if even he has that kind of money."

"He came from back east."

Everyone who came from "back east" had money. It was an Unwritten Rule. Like so many unwritten rules, it had no foundation in truth.

She tried a smile. It was getting late and she had already placed her cards on the table.

"He's a Southerner. I heard he invested heavily in Confederate bonds."

Call it an ace up her sleeve.

Claw nodded thoughtfully.

"Oh."

"I played straight with you, Claw. I don't want a relationship based on lies. I don't want to feel your eyes on me every night at quitting time. I didn't say it would be forever."

She did not say, but expressed through her eyes, I don't want you to make me feel dirty.

His mouth twitched at the corner in the beginnings of a weak smile. Some hope was better than no hope.

Jim Bennett had said that.

"Did I offer to help you clean up?" he inquired.

"Yup."

"What did you say?"

"I said, 'How about coming upstairs and starting there?'"

He brightened considerably. Cougar wondered if that was how he had looked when someone gave him his first horse.

Standing before her with a grin in his eyes, he could have been ten years old. But he was not. He was a grown man in an adult relationship.

She wondered how she would feel standing on Boot Hill looking at his grave marker.

It was not the time for such thoughts.

All things considered, it never would be.

"What do you say we go on up?"

He offered her his arm. Cougar Bradburn, saloon girl, would have felt both girlish and professional accepting it. Miss Bradburn, saloon owner, felt a flush of pride.

She hoped to God he was worth it.

Arm-in-arm they climbed the stairs, pausing only casually at the door of one of the girl's room to listen to the silence.

"It's just the girls and you and I," she informed him for no particular reason.

Claw nodded. He understood where she did not. Being alone without paying customers made it more home-like. Without realizing, she had taken the edge off the hurt both of them experienced from Herbert's not-so-pretend refusal.

She opened the door and stepped inside. He lingered at the threshold while she lit a lamp. Only when the feeble rays cast back the dark shadows of memory did he join her.

With her back to him, Cougar did not hear him move behind her. It was the warmth of his body, the innocence of his being which finally alerted her. When she turned, it was into his arms.

Clutching her with all the protection he knew how to give, Claw found her lips. They kissed, a long, passionate yet strangely asexual touching of two lonely souls. It was only when they broke for air and gazed into each other's eyes that their heat rose into a more pressing, urgent need.

His hands wrapped around her arms, drawing her closer. He was strong and youth cursed through his veins. They kissed again, as he pushed the material of her dress down her shoulders, baring them. The night air was cool to her flesh, raising her temperature.

She shivered but not from chill.

"What am I going to do with you, Giant?" she teased. She felt his shoulders shake as he chuckled.

"Lock me up, I guess."

"I thought that was your job."

He released her, crossed to the door and turned the key in the lock. When he faced her again, she was already undressing. He whistled and her pulse took off, soaring to meet his somewhere past the distant stars of a Kansas night.

"Get out of them britches, boy, or I'll think you ain't grow'd enough to know what yer aboot," she teased. He did not need a second invitation.

Claw removed the gunbelt first, placing it carefully on the back of a chair by the left side of the bed. That would be his side. For the rest of their lives, as long as a pulse beat in their breasts, the right side of the bed would be hers and the left side his.

The only difference in this arrangement would come on some far off someday when he did not wear his gun to bed.

On that day, he would no longer be a U.S. Marshal and she would be an absentee landlord.

The rest of Claw Kiley's wardrobe landed on the floor in a heap of shirt, boots, socks, trousers and long johns. She did not remember what happened to hers.

When Claw was beside her, they kissed while intertwining arms and legs. The struggle was awkward and natural, familiar and unknown. He tousled her long red hair, nudged her with his head, slipped his face between her breasts and drew in her scent, imprinting it in his makeup. She bit his ear and he made a low moan of pleasure.

With an easy flip of his body, he was atop her in a second, muscles hardened, breath hot. In a moment their rhythm raced with the pounding of their hearts, quickening, releasing, speeding off again with the intensity of time and present need pressing against their bodies.

Claw grunted in her ear and she held him, dug her fingernails into his flesh, tightened her buttocks and made him work for their pleasure. She guided him with sweaty thigh muscles, knocked his chest back with her shoulder, repositioned him then let his weight press her down into the bed.

Caught in the moment, he was frantic, eager to please and be pleased, listening to the bed creaks they made, the sound of flesh against flesh, using the sweet perfume of shared love to fill his head with joy.

They rolled together, now she on top and he, all six-foot seven of him, lost in a maze of urgency and togetherness. He bucked up, grunted with annoyance as a leg muscle cramped, worked though and forgot it. She dangled her breast into his mouth, felt the sharpness of his teeth, the sucking of his lips, then rapped him on the chin, driving him mad with desire.

"Cougar," he growled. "Cougar."

She was his world and until the breaking of dawn, there was no gun on the chair, no job, no one else in the world.

Love, she knew, was a cheat.

He knew no such thing and in his not knowing, she slept in his arms like a babe.

CHAPTER 6

"Claw."

Cougar shook him by the arm. When she got no more than a contented groan, this worldly woman dug her fingernails into the tender skin under the arm he had thrown around her shoulders.

"Claw! Are you going to sleep all day?"

His eyes flew open and he sat up in bed faster than if revile had been played in his ear.

"Where am I?" he gasped, pulling the blanket off her in his haste to cover his own bare chest.

"You get one guess, Giant, and if you get it wrong, your next stop will be the undertaker's."

Her voice was light and unconcerned, but her eyes were hard and meaningful.

"Good morning, Miss Bradburn!" he shouted. She just bet he made a good soldier. He had all the brains to be a successful private.

"Good morning, Marshal Kiley."

Sleep banished from his consciousness, Claw looked from her naked breasts to his own covered chest. He made a low noise which, on another occasion, might have been taken for a nervous laugh. The kind men make while standing on the gallows.

There was no way to gracefully return the blanket to the lady. Therefore, he did not.

"I have to get up!"

"Yes," she agreed. "I think you do. While you have been snoring the morning away, the bank has been robbed, three murders have taken place on Main Street, the livery burned to the ground and the cost of your buying a lady a beer went from five cents to ten."

"Really?"

"Really."

"What am I going to write to Hays?"

"Don't worry. When Hays comes to Hellhole, he always orders whisky."

Claw rubbed sleep from his eyes, ran largely unresponsive fingers through his unruly blond hair, then shivered.

"Don't look at me," she said as their eyes met. "You're the one with the blanket. If you're cold, I can only think of one remedy and if you take me up on that, you'll miss dinner. And probably supper."

He groaned.

"Who was shot on Main Street?"

Cougar, who was half turned away from him, froze. If she turned back and he was not grinning, she was in big trouble.

Big Trouble.

It took all the fortitude she possessed to face him and at that, it was only out of the corner of her eyes.

He was grinning.

God was still in His heaven.

"Get up!"

"Yes, ma'am." He did not move.

"Did you hear me?"

"Yes, ma'am."

"You're not moving."

"No, ma'am." His grin widened.

"If you don't get your long... legs... out of this bed within the next instant, you'll live to regret it. But not for long."

He moved.

"You'd make a good sergeant," he said as he performed the time-worn, ludicrous machinations of attempting to slip his legs through the unresponsive cotton material of his long johns while maintaining the slippery blanket over his "privates."

"Sergeant?" she replied with scorn.

"Lieutenant," he amended quickly.

"Lieutenant?"

"Captain."

"Captain?"

"Major."

"Major?"

"General."

"General?"

"Boss skinner!"

She was finally satisfied. It was all very well to be compared with military men, but the real figure of authority any denizen of a hide-town knew, was the skinner who could strip the leather off a carcass while it still quivered.

She might have let him go at "marshal," but he did not offer it.

Cougar wondered, where on his list of importance "marshal" fit.

She answered the unspoken question for him. Somewhere between "lieutenant" and "major."

Clad in long johns and trousers, he perched himself on the edge of the bed to slip on his socks. "Slipped" being rather more euphemistic than realistic.

They were stiff as a board and as dead as any ever interred in Boot Hill.

They were, Miss Bradburn decided, a good match for his shirt.

"Open the window as you leave."

He coughed. She presumed it was from embarrassment. Men were utterly incapable of using their olfactory senses against themselves.

And she did not smell.

Not enough for a gentleman to notice. Or cough.

"When was the last time you saw a tub?"

Idle conversation. To while away the minutes until he had dressed and disappeared.

"A what?"

Her heart sank.

"A bath tub."

"I saw one just the other day." He buttoned his shirt while she watched from the safety of the blanket. "Over at the barber shop."

"You 'saw' it?"

"Yeah. There was two years' worth of old newspapers in it. I was looking for something to read."

"When was the last time you ever sat in a bathtub - when there was water in it?"

"Can't rightly remember." And then the candle flame flashed bright before his eyes. "When I applied for this job. That was when. I took a bath before going up to fill out the application."

Cougar gave him a thin smile.

"Guess what?"

"What?" he inquired with all the innocence of a newborn calf.

"There's a tub in the Lowdown."

"Why?"

"Guess."

He tried. In fairness, she had to admit he gave the thought serious consideration.

"To make extra money?"

"Have you ever heard of a saloon offering baths?"

"Can't say that I have."

"Think again."

"For the girls?"

"You got it half right."

He gave her a half smile.

"What's the other half?"

"You're a big enough boy to figure it out."

"For the boys?"

"Right."

His face fell.

"I don't think I want a tub bath."

"Why not?"

"I don't fit in the damn things!"

If he had not flushed with his confession, she would not have believed him. It was just too convenient an excuse.

"You'll fit in this one."

It was a vow, rather than a promise.

Claw licked his lips.

"Duty calls. Will I see you tonight?"

"Unless you poke your eyes out between now and then."

He laughed. It was light-hearted and innocent. It made her want to cry.

"I'll see you," she said, dismissing him. He fingered his hat in his hands, tried to think of an appropriate reply, then compressed his lips together and backed out of the room.

As though she were his queen.

This time, the tears rolled freely down her cheeks.

Claw Kiley was half way across the street when he was hailed by a thin, frail-looking man standing by a buggy. The horse was lathered and heaving for breath, indicating a hard journey.

"Are you the law?"

Claw stopped and nodded.

"I'm the law."

"Been lookin' for you. Over at the Marshal's Office. Been waiting."

"It couldn't have been too long, by the looks of that horse," Claw replied tersely. Because his conscience was stung, he took it out on the man needing his help.

"I guess you was makin' rounds," The stranger stumbled over his words.

Claw did not know whether the man saw him emerge from the saloon or not. In either case, his temper was short.

"What can I do for you?"

"Not for me, Marshal," the man replied, eyes on the United States badge. "An' I dunno whether there's real trouble or not. But it felt like trouble."

"Come on over to the office."

There was no sense hearing the man out in the middle of the street. They crossed the hard-packed dirt thoroughfare, Claw opening the door to the office and entering first. The stranger followed, closing the door behind him. Both men left their hats on as an unspoken protocol attesting to the fact there was a real possibility of imminent danger.

"Let's have it," the lawman ordered.

"I saw a lot of smoke in the sky, like a house or a barn was burning. I was gonna go see, when I heard horses hooves. Men ridin' hard. I hid and they didn't come close enough to pay me no heed. But I seed them, a'right."

"How many men?"

"Four. Or mebbe five, one wounded an' leanin' down so's I couldn't see him too good."

"Where was this?"

"West. Mebbe five miles. Ain't fer certain. I followed the road in but I was off it a'ways when I seed 'em." He paused for breath, then wrung his hands.

When he could not meet Claw's eyes, it was a testimony to the fact he was not only scared from his own close call, he was frightened for the man he would indirectly send into the danger he had shirked.

A man did not like to admit cowardice. He especially did not appreciate owning up to it before one who could afford no such luxury.

"I'm sorry, Marshal."

"So am I. Appreciate you coming in to tell me."

It was a gesture not required by the badge he wore. Claw was reaching out, telling the drifter it was all right, he did not hold his running against him.

A promise that if things went badly for the lawman, he would not wish the stranger in his place.

"Thanks. Good luck."

Claw nodded at the dismissal, then remembered a detail.

"What's your name?"

He should have asked it before; when the man had no reason to lie.

"Leonard Cooke."

"All right, Mr. Cooke."

It sounded legitimate. He was grateful for that. If the man had said "John Tucker," or "Phil Bailey," Claw would have wondered. He had enough to ponder without damning himself for thinking of a lady and the night he had spent with her, instead of his job.

It would be a long, long time before he would forget again.

Not as long as the rest of his life, but a long time. Unless the men he went after shut his lights out prematurely. In that case, it would not matter.

Not to him.

Claw Kiley took his rifle from the rack, checked it to be sure it was loaded, which it was, then grasped a box of shells. A man who went after five outlaws did not expect to use his pistol.

Nor did he expect to bring them all back alive. That explained why he only put two pair of handcuffs into his saddlebag. No sense traveling heavy.

He had no one to tell and no reason to tell anyone he was leaving, but he crossed the street and headed for the doctor's office. Climbing the stairs one at a time, he knocked on the door and opened it, just as a gruff, "Door's open" rang in his ears.

"Oh. It's you," Fiz identified, as the shadow of the tall lawman fell across his floor. His words were casual, his voice guarded.

Shadows told more than whispers.

"I'm going out. Five miles west, maybe further. A ranch or a building was seen burning. Five men leaving the scene. What's out there?"

"The Duncan place. Or it might have been the Dryer place. Well named. Not a drop of water anywhere. Doubt anyone would bother burning it. It's empty."

"Who are the Duncans?"

"Man and his wife. No children. Been married thirty years. Older couple. They raise some fine horses. Live pretty much hand-to-mouth. Like the rest of us."

For once it did not sound like a condemnation.

"Listen..."

Fiz started to fuss with a bandage he had been rolling, then put it down with an annoyed gesture and looked up. The cloth unraveled and fell to the floor.

"I'm listening."

"I may be gone a week. Look after my cat, will you?"

"Your what?"

"My cat. Stray cat. She moved in with me at the Marshal's Office. Feed her."

"Why can't she live off mice?"

"I have milk and eggs brought to the office every morning. You can have them while I'm gone."

"I suppose I have to share the cream with the cat?"

"Do what you want. She won't tell on you, in any case."

"What's her name?"

"I didn't give her a name."

Fiz scowled. He knew a lie when he heard one, and worse, he knew he deserved it. He picked up the bandage and began rolling it.

"Be careful."

"Yeah. I wouldn't want to need that," Claw said, indicating the bandage. "Not after it's rolled on the floor."

He tried a smile. Fiz fluffed his feathers.

"Never had any complaints."

"Don't think you'd know one if you heard it."

"Why'd you come up here and tell me you were leaving?"

His head was turned and he looked at Claw out of one squinted eye.

Claw dodged the question.

"I'll be back in a week."

He turned to leave.

"Maybe."

Claw came to a dead stop so fast he might have been struck in the back of the head by a mortar and pestle.

"I came to tell you, so you wouldn't worry when you didn't see me around."

Fiz snorted, then immediately regretted his action. Taking a white linen handkerchief from his pocket, he blew his nose into it, then made a show of putting it away. Claw did not turn around to see the play acting.

When he was certain the older man was through, he opened the door and stomped down the stairs, taking one at a time. He was almost to the bottom when the physician called after him.

"Be careful."

The only two words a father could use as a benediction to his almost grown son.

"See you around," Claw replied.

Fiz did not wait until Claw was out of sight before turning and shutting the door of his office. Casting the cotton wrap down, he picked up his worn copy of the Farmer's Almanac and opened it. The small, paperback tome was dog-eared and stained.

One might have presumed he was checking the date. And perhaps he was marking off the seven days Claw Kiley predicted he would be away. It would not do Fiz much good, however, for the almanac was labeled "Boston" and the year was 1861.

Fiz Ward never was much for farming.

Or planting.

He was in the business of saving bodies, not resurrecting them.

Claw went to the livery stable, saddled his horse and rode out of town without looking back.

He hoped "Miss Cougar" would not miss him too much.

But then, she was a good mouser, and knew how to take care of herself.

Cream, it was said, always rose to the top.

The marshal was five miles out of town before he bothered to do any tracking. If the men he sought were wanted by the law, they would not take the road. And Leonard Cooke said they were off the road.

He smelled the burnt wood before he saw any indication of fire. Reigning the horse in, Claw rose in his stirrups and opened his mouth, the better to detect the subtle scent on the breeze. Whatever burned had been extinguished. It was odds on favorite the five men had not put it out. That increased the chances he would find Mister or Mrs. Duncan alive.

He hoped so. Taking time to dig a hole big enough for two bodies would put him a full day behind their murderers.

Rationalization was the tool a man used to bury his worries.

In another half an hour, the Duncan ranch came into view. The house was still standing, although the lawman could see from a distance the roof had been scorched. Wind must have whipped burning embers from the barn, for that structure was in ruins.

Claw remembered Fiz's words: they raised fine horses. Men who would burn a barn with horses in it were the kind he would take back over their own saddles.

"Hullo!" he shouted from a far distance. He did not want to be shot by mistake. "My name is Claw Kiley. I'm the United States marshal out of Hellhole."

There was no answer. He shouted again. No answer. The skin on the back of his wrists began to sweat.

"Mr. Duncan! It's Claw Kiley."

A man came to the door of the house, a rifle suspended from his right arm, as though it were a pistol.

"Come on up."

Claw rode closer, sorry he had not asked Doctor Ward for a description of Mr. Duncan. It would be easier when he had been around awhile. Then he would know the homesteaders and ranchers by sight.

It would simplify matters when they recognized him, too. When his name opened doors, rather than had them shut in his face.

"Lemme see the badge."

Claw drew back his vest. The man eyed the dull pewter symbol of authority for a long beat before beckoning the rider forward.

"Didn't know Hellhole had a new marshal. What'd you say your name was?"

"Claw Kiley."

"What's the doctor's name?"

"Ward."

"Who runs the saloon?"

Claw grinned.

"Man named Bix Bradley used to own it. He lost it in a poker game two nights ago."

"Bradley's gone?"

"Gone but not forgotten."

Duncan wavered.

"Man who won it from him must wear mighty big boots."

"Can't say I've ever seen the new owner in a pair of boots. Miss Bradburn, one of the saloon girls beat him."

"Ain't that sumthin'. What put you onto this?" he asked, indicating the barn.

"Man on the trail. Saw smoke. He came into town to tell me. What happened? Your wife all right?"

"Who told you I had a wife?" he asked, suspicion edging his voice.

"Fiz Ward. I spoke to him before I left. Wanted to know who lived out here."

"Lanky fella? With a scar on - which cheek is it?"

"Scrawny fella with a mustache and a black doctor's bag. No scar."

Duncan sighed audibly and sagged back against the frame of his house.

"Ma!" he called. "It's all right. This fella is who he says he is."

A stout woman Claw guessed to be in her late 50's emerged from the back of the house, covering her man with a shotgun. She gave the lawman an astute look-see, then shook her head.

"There was five of them, as ugly a bunch as you'd ever want to see, Marshal. They wanted fresh mounts. They had been ridin' hard and theirs was all tuckered out. No good to us. At first they offered money but when we wouldn't sell, they turned mean.

"They was in a big hurry. Scared-like. Kept lookin' over their shoulders. Real jumpy. We thought they was bank robbers at first. But they wasn't."

"What makes you say that?"

Mr. Duncan took over the story.

"I believe they would a kilt us, but one of 'em - a lookout - gave a signal and they went wild. Held Ma and me in here while they went to the barn and took fresh horses. Then they burned it, hopin', I think, to delay them who was comin' after 'em."

"Did you see who it was they were running from?"

He hesitated then shook his head.

"No, sir. But it was another bunch. Three. Mebbe four. Mebbe more. Couldn't tell. Only three came into the yard. Dirty lookin' fellas. Not from around here. Mountain men. I asked 'em to help me with the fire but they was in a hurry. Big hurry, Marshal. They was huntin' them others. Angry. Real angry they was."

"Help you, did they?"

"No." It was Mrs. Duncan who spoke. Her words were without bitterness. "One - the leader, I guess - he asked if there was horses or livestock in the barn. I told him they took all our horses." She pointed toward the back. "They shot their own mounts; wasn't no need to do that."

"So's them cumin' after couldn't take 'm," her husband replied. He carried the bitterness for both of them.

"What else did this leader say to you, Mrs. Duncan?"

"He asked if we was hurt. Said no. He sort of apologized, then, and they rode off."

The marshal digested this while repositioning his hat to keep the sun out of his eyes.

"Mountain men, you say? How could you tell?"

"Way they spoke. Way they was dressed."

"The others - the first men. Were they mountain men, too?"

"No. They wasn't. Looked like drifters, cowpokes. The kind what can't hold a job. You know."

"I know. How long ago was this?"

"This morning. Around nine o'clock. The mountain men come up not too much after they left. Hell bent for leather after 'em."

"You going after 'em, Marshal?" Mrs. Duncan inquired with a woman's fear.

"That's right."

"Don't know they done anything – them drifters, I mean."

"They burned your barn. Stole your stock."

"Seems a small thing for one man to go after five on accounta one barn an' horses."

"There's a law against stealing and destroying someone else's property."

"Might be them mountain men 'ill catch 'em first, save you the trouble."

"There's a law against taking the law into your own hands, too."

It was eloquently spoken. Jack Duvall would have been proud of his protégée. He had taught Claudius well. By the book.

Some called it the "good book."

Some, but not all.

The west was wide and wild enough for a variety of opinions.

Mr. and Mrs. Duncan would not hold it against Claw Kiley if he turned tail and returned to Hellhole. They had seen the men and made their own judgments. A barn was burned but no lives were lost. Horses had been stolen but they were practical people. Horses could be replaced.

Fiz Ward had said it. They lived hand-to-mouth.

"Living" was the key.

It opened some locks but not all.

Claw nodded his thanks.

"I'll be back this way. If I get the chance, I'll return your horses. If not, I'll send word for you to come into Hellhole and get them."

"Don't go on our account, Marshal."

It was Mrs. Duncan again. She remembered the way the marshal said, One of the saloon girls beat him.

She had heard that tone of voice before. A woman could do worse than marry a man who spoke softly about the woman he loved.

"It's the law, Mrs. Duncan."

"I reckon it is."

Claw tipped his hat to them and rode off into the afternoon light. They did not ask him to tarry the night.

They knew what he would say.

Something about the law not being kept waiting.

Chapter 7

The trail was not difficult to follow. There were two distinct groups of tracks: those from the five men who had threatened the Duncans and burned their barn and the second group, following them.

The rancher and his wife had not been certain how many men comprised the avengers. Avengers they were, the marshal had no doubt. Whether they were chasing the first bunch because of a deal gone bad or for other, unknown reasons, they were in holy pursuit.

That they would catch the drifters was not open to question. Nor did it tax Claw's imagination to guess what would happen when they did.

Bloodshed.

It was his job to keep the peace.

There were six in the second group. Four Mr. Duncan had guessed; maybe more. Two more to be exact. Three additional sets of tracks joined, merged, then traveled with the three who had ridden into the yard.

"Angry. Real angry they was."

Make that, "real angry they *are.*"

These six were on a mission; a vendetta. The most likely guess was anger over money, but Claw dismissed that probability. A man might be angry, even "real angry" over being cheated out of his cut, but he did not hate. These mountain men were seething with rage.

They were also careless. They did not care to cover their tracks. They rode together. The only time Claw knew for certain they had split up was when three approached the Duncan's. That was no more than common sense. If there was an ambush at the house, half would be waiting to offset the surprise.

Mountain men. That is how the rancher described them and Claw had no reason to doubt the man's knowledge. He had run across a number of mountain men in his day. They did not like to be cheated, but it would take more than money to draw them off their mountain.

That made it a vendetta of honor. The five they were chasing had either torn through a village, looting and burning, despoiling whatever came into their path, or they had disgraced a woman.

Depending on where they originated, these avengers had ridden nearly eight hundred miles on their quest. They had crossed two state borders and were likely to cross another before they caught up with their enemy.

The six had passed through innumerable lawmen's territories, probably bypassing twenty towns and cities along the way. He had heard of no major confrontations east of Hellhole. That meant both gangs had avoided trouble.

They were bringing trouble with them. Obviously, they were not looking for more.

This time, they had found it.

If one lone United States marshal on horseback could be considered trouble.

The five, mounted on fresh horses, pulled ahead of their pursuers, increasing their distance to half a hard day's ride. Claw noticed where one had lagged behind to drag brush over their tracks. He smiled grimly to himself.

That was about as effective as kicking trail dust over railroad ties.

Mountain men were the best trackers in the world. They lived a hard, harsh life, where game was scarce and existence eked out by selling moonshine. They were not Indians. They were the men and women who took the place of the Red Man as he was pushed westward.

The difference between Injuns and mountain men, Claw learned during the War, was that Indians had a conscience, while mountain men had none. No Union battalion willingly faced a company of Rebel mountain men. It did not matter whether these ragtag Confederates fought with army-issue rifles, home-manufacture muskets or sticks and stones. These men, with no stake in the larger issues of slavery and State's Rights, fought for the South because the blue-coated soldiers invaded their homes.

Had butternut-grey troops come into the mountains, the mountain men would have fought them, too.

One United States marshal was a match against five outlaws. He would have trouble against one mountain man.

Facing six, he was as good as dead.

Claw stopped when it grew too dark to ride and made camp. It took half an hour to catch enough fish for supper. He cooked them suspended over a fire, soldier fashion. He had no coffee and no means of making any, had he the beans. He cursed himself for not taking supplies from the Duncans and went to bed unsatisfied.

The night was not cold but Claw slept badly. He was bitten by mosquitoes and overrun by ants, finally being forced to move his bedroll away from where he had inadvertently set it down over an ant trail.

"A man ought to be like an ant, Claw," an old man had lectured him once. He was a drifter, a "good-fer-nuthin'," which meant, in the limited world of Claw's childhood, the individual had never been a lawman. "An ant don't never take 'no' fer an answer. You kin step on an ant and he don't die. You kin bury his trail an' he builds another. You kin squash his hill an' he's got fifteen other ways to git out. Kin a man say that?"

Yes, Claw learned, a man could say that.

He had seen men stepped on and live; he had witnessed men's houses burned and seen them rebuild. He had known men far from home look around themselves and see beauty in the strangeness.

A man was not an ant, but he was a survivor. And he had law to separate him from the insects and the beasts of his own kind. Law was the glue of society. It enabled men to put up their guns and live in peace with one another. Law required sacrifice from the few so the many could survive.

Could an ant say that?

As a child, he could not have asked that question. As a man, he lived by it.

It did not matter whether the Duncans understood his code. It made no difference if the townspeople of Hellhole appreciated his efforts. He knew what he was about. A man either lived by principles and had the right to hold his head up, or he shuffled about in darkness, hanging his head.

Principles, Claw, is the right and wrong a man holds inside hisself. Different men has different principles. As long as they abide by the law, you let them go in peace.

The six mountain men trailing the five outlaws held principles. Claw would like to have let them go in peace but he could not. They were acting outside the law.

The law, Claw, ain't always what's writ in books.

Claw had read the books. It would take long life for him to read what was not written in the books.

That kind of reading required experience.

That kind of literacy was called wisdom.

He was in the saddle at first light. Near noon, when the sun was at its zenith, he stopped and ate the remainder of the fish he had caught the evening before. He should have consumed it at breakfast. He rode the rest of the day with a sick stomach and the smell of fish permeating his hands and breath,

It was close to four o'clock when Claw saw the house. Tucked in between an identical pair of trees, the trunks were used to support the bowing side walls. The roof was thatched.

"Hullo!" Claw called. The stench of death was in the air. He did not give the owner time to respond, but rode into the yard and dismounted quickly. A dead dog, its skull shattered by a single bullet, lay by the hitching post. Flies swarmed around it.

On the frontier, nothing, not even death, was wasted.

The front door of the cabin was ajar. Kicking it in, then moving back against the wall, Claw waited. There were no sounds. He had not expected any, but he hoped.

"Hullo," he called again, this time fainter and with less enthusiasm. "My name is Claw Kiley. I'm a United States marshal."

Before the words were out of his mouth, Claw was inside the one-room cabin. The first thing he noticed was that the contents had been despoiled. Everything was upturned, broken into, smashed.

There was no method to the madness and he did not look for any.

The five outlaws had come searching for supplies. After they had taken what they wanted, they destroyed what they could never own.

The homesteader was lying, face down, on the floor. A pool of blackish, clotted, sweet-smelling blood had gathered around his head, like a perverted halo. Claw did not want to look at the face. The man was dead. Better not to be remembered at all, than be seen in the agonies of his final death throes.

Throwing a blanket over the body, Claw dragged him outside and dug a hole with a spade he found in the back. When the grave was deep enough for common decency, he rolled the unidentified body in, then started to cover it. Remembering the faithful friend, he returned to the hitching post, picked up the dog and brought it back. He placed the animal on top of its master with more care than he had deposited the body.

Claw got through the ritual of burial by concentrating on the mere physical task of shoveling. It was not until he returned to his horse and saw the remnant of the dog's ear lying on the ground, that tears came to his eyes. He turned away but not fast enough.

"Son of a bitch!" he cursed.

The act of speaking caused his stomach muscles to work backwards. He vomited bile on the dry earth.

"Son of a -"

He caught himself, realizing the inappropriateness of the statement and stomped the ground. His boot made a soft thudding noise, no more.

He knew he could not let it become personal. If his own anger and misery took over his brain, he would not think clearly. He had seen that happen before. Even to lawmen. Letting a death effect the heart was the one unforgivable mistake he could not afford. Vengeance made a man careless. He was already in enough trouble.

Swinging his leg over the back of the saddle, Claw remembered he should have gone through the dead man's possessions, looking for a name or an address for some next of kin.

Too late. Nothing would induce him to return to that scene of death.

He would have to pass the dog's ear.

He did not have the opportunity to camp by a stream that night and went to bed hungry. For once he did not mind. Though his stomach was empty, he could not face the thought of food.

Morning, however, brought with it a different story. He was starving. That meant, he would either have to veer off the trail, seeking sustenance from other travelers, like himself, or hunt for his meals.

Claw was not a hunter by nature. Odd, given his occupation, but the idea of shooting an animal, cleaning and dressing it, then roasting it over a fire did not appeal to him. The fact he had done it, and would do it, many times over the course of his life, never made the task easier. Nor did he necessarily relish the thought of fishing from necessity. Taking a day off to go fishing, knowing his saddlebags were full of food, should he fail to catch dinner, made the occupation one of pleasure, rather than necessity.

Make hunting or fishing a vital component of living and it became work. Onerous work. Work which entailed killing.

Sometimes, a man had enough of that to last a lifetime.

He did not come across a traveler nor did he find a cabin from which to gain supplies. That meant hunting or take the chance of further weakening himself by starvation.

Game was plentiful enough and by noon of the following day, Claw had shot two prairie chickens and two rabbits. He could have brought down more, but the idea of expending ammunition equally difficult to replace stayed his hand.

He cleaned his catch and cooked all of it, eating one bird before setting out again at a quicker pace. The mountain men, he observed by noting their divergent tracks, sent two of their party to hunt, as well. He came upon the carcass of a young buck and noted rabbit bones scattered around a still-warm fire. He was not far behind.

The five outlaws did not tarry long enough to hunt. That meant they had gotten enough food from the Duncans and the dead homesteader to delay the inevitable. They were probably eating light at any rate, knowing how close their pursuers were. There could be little comfort in the thought.

It was close to dusk when Claw heard the sound. Tossing aside a rabbit bone upon which he had been sucking, he reined in his horse and dismounted. The sound was repeated and his blood ran cold.

It was a scream.

A human cry for mercy. There was no answering word.

No mercy.

Taking his rifle from the holster attached to the saddle, he checked it again to be sure it was loaded, then ran forward. His horse took a step after him, swished its tail discontentedly, then began to graze.

The landscape had roughened considerably over the last day and a half. The level, undulating hills and clumps of brush trees and tumbleweeds had gradually given way to sharp rocks and patches of wood. The cry he heard had come from the lip of a vale, sharply studded by rock.

Even before he saw the men, Claw realized what had happened. The pursued had taken the trail down, looking behind themselves for the pursuers. But the mountain men had split up, only two lingering behind, while the other four had circled around. When the outlaws came out onto the flatter surface at the bottom, they had been attacked from three sides.

Moving swiftly from tree to tree, Claw made it to the edge of the valley and peered over. Three of the outlaws were tired to trees. One, the wounded man, had apparently died, for his body had been disposed of behind the trees. The fifth, stripped naked, was spread-eagled to the ground, hands and feet staked as far apart as they would go.

This man was covered in blood but he was not yet dead.

"Jesus!" he cried. "Mercy."

For his trouble, one of the mountain men kicked him in the face.

"Did I ask you to talk?" the tormentor demanded. "Didn't I tell you, iffn you was to open yer mouth, I'd go worse fer ya?"

"Please."

The mountain man turned angry eyes toward his fellows.

"This yahoo don't know no better'n to say please."

"'Please' don't mean nuthin', coming frum the likes a' you," a second said. "Funny, how you knows how to say the word, but you don't know what it means."

"Shoot him!" called one of the drifters bound to a tree. All eyes turned toward him in patient expectancy. "Shoot all of us. That's why you chased us halfway across hell. So, shoot us."

The leader of the avengers, whom Claw instinctively realized was not the man Mr. Duncan had referred to when speaking of he who had addressed him in the yard, was a small, squat man with a face full of black beard and shoulders wide enough to wrassle bear, spat on the ground, wiped his mouth with his hand, then crossed to the speaker. He stood a long time before disdaining to answer.

"No. You got it wrong, mister. That ain't when we want. We didn't cume all this way jist ta shoot ya. Iffn that's what we wanted, we coulda done that inny number a times. An' saved ourselves some grief."

"Just get it over with!"

The man smiled. From where he was crouched, Claw could see the mountain man's teeth shine in the fading light.

Teeth which would have passed for fangs at a gathering of foxes and wolves.

"It's the 'jist' part you got wrong, mister. We ain't aboot to 'jist' anythin'. Jist like you wasn't in no hurry to leave go o' that gal. You remember that, do ya?"

"We didn't mean nuthin' by it. We didn't know -"

"You didn't know she weren't knowd by a man? Now, didn't she tell ya?"

"No. She didn't say -"

The man did not have the chance to finish his sentence. The butt of a rifle smashed into his face, breaking his jaw and sending fragments of broken teeth three feet away. The rapist's head flew back, striking the trunk of the tree with such velocity, Claw could almost feel the ground shake.

"It don't make no diff'rence what you say. You done took her an' that's the whole story in a nut shell. Ain't it?" he asked, turning to his companions. They solemnly nodded.

The leader turned back to the man on the ground. Striding over to him, he drew a long, ugly looking knife from his belt and passed it before the victim's eyes.

"Know what I'm gonna do wid this pig sticker?" he inquired. The man's eyes opened in stark raving terror.

"No!" he gasped. "No. No!"

The mountain man tugged at his ear as though he could not hear.

"Say it ag'in," he cajoled. "Say 'no' ta me ag'in."

The man had learned his lesson, but too late. He could do no more than watch while the wielder of the blade slashed it across his exposed groin. His shriek was instantaneous and ear splitting.

"Now, ain't that music to my ears," the squat man sing-songed. He did not pause in his grisly task until the rapist's genitals had been removed, leaving nothing but a bloody stump, no more than a quarter of an inch high.

"See how you strut an' parade like a man, now. You feelin' like going fer a woman, big boy? Let's see how you's a gonna do it."

He cut the leather tongs holding the man down, then gave him a kick with his foot.

"Cume on. Let's see ya do a little dance, wigglin' them hips like I heard how ya done."

The man at his feet was incapable of coherent speech. His hands flew to his mutilated body, clutching at what was no longer present to be held, fondled, used as a weapon of attack and superiority.

"He ain't impressin' me none, Heath. Don't think no lady'd be interested in the likes of him."

"Don't think no lady'd be in trouble frum the likes a him," Heath corrected. "It's a bleedin' pity he didn't think on that befer."

"A cryin' shame," another of the onlookers agreed.

"Let's make 'em all cryin' shames."

The three men tired to the trees all twitched at once. There was no doubt they believed their destiny, if not their fate, had come calling.

"We didn't mean any harm! For Christssakes, you can't unman us for what we done! What kind of men are you, anyway?"

Heath shook his head while wiping the blade of his knife on his trouser leg in a sensual, sexually exaggerated motion.

"You have a lot ta say, mister. An' cume ta think on it, I don't want ta hear it." He looked around, giving his own hips a suggestive sway. "Inny of you boys want to hear him?"

"I cain't see my way toward havin' no pity on 'em."

"Like as if we could."

"Then I'll jest use this pig sticker to take yer tongue out, befer I do that other deed."

He laughed at his own joke.

Claw licked his lips and brought the squat man into the sights of his rifle. He had no sympathy for the outlaws. Hearing their crime did no more than confirm what he had already suspected. Nor did he question their guilt. But he was not a judge and he was not a jury. He was merely a man with a badge.

A man with the burden of civilization on his shoulders.

"Hold it right there!" he called. His voice sounded high and young. His face flushed.

If he thought his command would startle the mountain men, he was wrong. Heath, the leader, turned casually, bringing a hand up to shade his eyes as he squinted up at where the voice originated. There was no sun. His gesture was one of habit.

"Now, I don't rightly reckon I kin do that, mister. Who-ever you are."

"Name's Claw Kiley. Out of Hellhole. I'm a U.S. marshal. You're in my county."

"What county that be?" another called.

It seemed an odd question but Claw did not think to refuse him an answer.

"Ford County."

"No. We're outta Ford County," a third man disagreed, holding his hands out in a gesture of simple misunderstanding.

There was no aggressive action taken against the lawman, no anger. Claw had expected otherwise.

Raising himself to a standing position, he indicated with the rifle, still pointed at Heath's midsection.

"If you have a grievance with these men, present your evidence to a circuit judge. He can order them transported back to where you're from, so they can be tried."

"All the way back to Virginnie?"

"All the way back to Virginia, if that's what it takes."

"You gonna take them off our hands, Marshal?"

"That's what I had in mind."

"You know we cain't let you do that. We cume a long way ta see justice served."

"Do it the right way. Do it by the law. Then none of you will be held accountable for their punishment."

"State o' Kansas hang a man fer disgracin' a woman?"

"State o' Kansas cut a bastard's vitals off fer doin' what no man got a right ta do?"

"Let the law punish them."

"I'm afeered we cain't rightly do that, Marshal."

Those words were spoken from a man standing behind him and at very close range. Before Claw could turn, he felt the cold, deadly barrel of a rifle pressed to the small of his back.

"You been followin' us a long way, Marshal," the voice continued. "We wondered who you was. What fool you was. I reckoned you had to be some kind o' lawman."

"I'm not 'some kind.' I'm a United States marshal."

"I heerd you say it. Big man fer a big badge. Jest step out an' join the party, Lawman."

Claw flinched, hesitated. The gun was jammed into his back a second time.

Six against one. Claw knew the odds were against him when he started. He should have realized that five would keep him talking while the sixth crept around behind. He should have kept one eye behind, on his back. It would have made no difference. He knew it but it did not lessen his self-reproach.

"You know what you're doing is wrong."

His voice was low, meant only for the man behind him.

"I don't know it. An' what's more, you don't know it."

"You can't take the law into your own hands. That makes you just as bad as they are."

"I don't see it that way. You heerd them boys. We know about as much of law as you do, Badge. The law may hang a man fer murder an' it may hang a man fer robbery but it don't hang a man fer rape. Puttin' a feller in jail don't stop 'em frum gettin' out, do it? It don't stop 'em frum goin' after other gals, do it? You got a woman, Marshal?"

Claw did not answer. He knew what the man was trying to do. He could not let himself become involved. The Law had to remain above personal vendetta.

The mountain man behind Claw reached around and gently removed the pistol from his holster.

"Drop the rifle. Nice an' slow-like. I don't want to have to shoot you. In the back."

Claw dropped the rifle. He believed the man did not want to shoot him. In the back.

Heath had seen enough. Once assured the man trailing them was unarmed, he turned his attention back to those he had come so far to punish.

"Now, what was it we was sayin'?" He smiled broadly. "That's right. I was gonna cut yer tongue out."

The man with the big mouth clamped his teeth together then jerked in the ropes until he could see the tall lawman coming down the slope.

One man against six and he dared pin his hopes on him. His hopes for a trial and a jail sentence and the chance for life. Such was the aura of power the marshal exuded. And incidentally, the law he represented.

Claw was not afraid. Walking into a den created for retribution, inhabited by wolf-men seething with hatred, he held his head high, maintaining a clear, even expression.

"He's a young'un, ain't he?" one of the mountain men asked the man with the rifle.

"No more'n a pup with a lot to learn."

"It's a pity he won't live to learn it."

It was Heath who spoke. His meaning was clear. He meant to punish the outlaws like it said in the Good Book. An eye for an eye. There could be no witnesses to their deeds. Taking the law into their own hands made them guilty. Claw had quoted that from another book.

"Over there," the man with the rifle said. He was taller than the other mountain men, lean and muscular. His jaw was set, his eyes the color of gun bluing.

Claw followed his instructions. He came to stand by the three prisoners.

Increasing their number by one.

"Tie his hands," Heath ordered. The man with the rifle caught a piece of rope tossed him by one of the others and set to the task.

"Listen to me," Claw whispered. "You know what you're doing. You know what this will mean."

"I done had a lot o' time thinkin' on it, riding across four states, Marshal."

"You'll be a wanted man; a fugitive. An outlaw, no better than they are."

"I cain't see it that way. No use talkin' me outta it. You know what's gotta be done."

"Do it by the law. I swear I'll see justice done."

The man paused. It was not a hesitation but a wonder. Scrunching up one eye, he brought his face within spitting distance of the marshal's and stared at him, man to man.

"I ain't never seed the likes of you befer."

"I mean what I say. Give me the chance to prove it. Let me take them in and hold them in my jail. They won't get any special treatment. I promise you that. Your word will be listened to."

"What about that one?" he said, indicating the man rolled up into a ball on the ground. "The one what'll be squatting the rest o' his days."

Squint-eye was giving Claw the chance to make his own decision, take the law into his own hands, just as the mountain men had done. He was asking Claw to step out of his well-defined role to become judge and jury. To weigh what he might win against what he knew he would lose. It was the hardest, greyest choice Claw Kiley had ever had to make in his life.

It was a decision no one on earth had prepared him for.

Not even Jack Duvall.

"We'll take him to a doctor. Some small town. Leave him there. I'll tell the sheriff to jail him when he recovers. We'll take the other three on to Hellhole and have charges officially lodged against them."

"An' what will that sheriff of some small town ask you about how he cume to be half a man?"

"I'll say I found him on the trail like that."

It was as much as Claw Kiley, lawman, had ever offered. It was the first step he had ever taken outside the law.

He was learning judgment.

He had turned a page in the Good Book.

Started a new chapter.

Claw Kiley had gone after five outlaws and six avengers, with one set of principles and one job.

The job had not changed. The principles had.

Ada Duvall would have understood, where her lawman husband would not have.

It would have given her hope.

Small comfort, indeed.

CHAPTER 8

The mountain man Claw identified as Squint-eye tied Claw's hands behind him. There was no slack. He had said it.

You know what's gotta be done.

The lawman in Claw Kiley had tried.

Tried and failed.

Heath forgot about the marshal. His sole interest lay in torturing the four outlaws left alive. This is what they had come so far for; their crowning moment.

With the precision of a surgeon who had learned his craft at the slaughter yards, the squat outlaw inserted his knife between the mouthy outlaw's clenched teeth, slicing the lips apart as he did so. No need to worry. No one ever sutured up a cadaver.

Unless he needed the practice.

"No! No!"

One word, repeated twice. Fortunately, phonetically speaking, a man did not require lips to pronounce it.

Unfortunately, humanly speaking, no one with the authority to help was listening.

Holding back the man's hair with one hand so his head was in the proper position, Heath hacked away at his grisly task, severing the tongue near the root. Blood spurted in crimson jets, covering everyone within two yards of the operation.

Claw did not have to be reminded of the expression, the operation was a success but the patient died.

With eyes closed, he prayed he would never have occasion to hear Fiz Ward verbalize that medical conundrum.

"Lookie here!" Heath demanded, holding out the severed tongue. "What does it remind you of?"

"The horn you took off'n that other fella," one of the mountain men correctly identified.

"So it do! Never thought of it that way, befer. Now, we got two useless pricks."

"Let's make it three."

"I reckon that's what we came here fer, boys."

Heath gave a curt hand signal. The mutilated outlaw was untied and dragged to centre stage, where he was stripped and spread-eagled like his comrade before him had been. With tears of pain and misery streaming down his face, the newly muted man begged for his life with wide-open eyes.

"Ain't he got some nerve," a short, bow-legged mountain man observed. There was cruelty and harshness to his words. "I wonder if Mary Lou had that look in her eyes as he was stickin' his bastard 'gun barrel' into her?"

"No," the tall, squint-eyed man who had remained at Claw's side pronounced. "No, I don't reckon she did." All eyes turned to him. "I believe she had more dignity than that."

His words were spoken softly, betraying a deep-set emotion devoid from the voices of his five companions.

"Dignity. Now ain't that a pe-culiar word," Heath noted, eyes slanted with anger. "Take dignity frum someone, lose yer own. Ain't than what the Good Book says?"

The man with the squint-eye shook his head but made no other comment. Heath shrugged.

"That's what the preacher said as we rode out. I remember it clear."

Without waiting for further distraction, he drove the meticulously honed blade into the pinioned man's vitals, removing them to the tune of shrieks and incoherent pleas. When he had it in his hand, he squeezed the limp flesh then tossed it into a red-stained sack.

"Treasure."

And so it was. The kind spendable only in the Lower Regions.

When the remaining two rapists were emasculated in precisely the same manner, and their penises deposited inside the treasure bag, Heath approached the marshal. Wiping the knife on Claw's sleeve, he grinned wickedly up at him.

"You're next, lawman."

"How, in the name of your 'Good Book,' are you going to justify killing me? What have I done to merit the fate of those men?"

"Furst of all, bright boy, you're a lawman. That's reason enuf. Second of all, you cume after us. Third, when you seed what it was all about, you didn't ride off. That enuf reasons fer you?"

"No."

Heath spat in his face. Claw did not flinch. He was remembering the word, so recently spoken.

Dignity.

"No? Did you hear that, boys? The lawman says 'no' to me. That ought ta be enuf reason to bash his head in."

"Takes a brave man to beat a man tied to a tree. There's a lot of dignity to that."

Heath slapped Claw across the face, rattling the teeth in his gums. A small trickle of blood appeared at the corner of his mouth.

"Don't you be tellin' me a thing about dignity, blue belly. I know your kind. I know what you and them Union sodgers done to us. When they wasn't no menfolk abouts, you and them came an' done yer worst. You remember that, blue dog?"

"No."

For his trouble, Claw received another slap to the face, this one harder and with more intent.

"Was you one o' them what come into the mountains, Marshal? Wearing that proud blue u-ne-form an' burnin' everythin' in sight?"

"No."

This time, the blow was delivered to his midsection by a balled up, tightly clenched fist. The wind gushed out of the tied man like air from a shattered hot air balloon. Red-tinged spittle settled over Heath's grey-stubbled countenance.

"You stinkin' bastard! Untie him and spread him out like the others."

"No."

It was the tall, squint-eyed mountain man who refused the order. The leader stared at him through hate-filled eyes.

"I give you an order."

"You ain't givin' orders no more," he replied softly. There was decency in the voice. Decorum and a trace of some other emotion Claw could not place.

"How's that, ag'in?"

"I said you ain't givin' orders. We all set out to do a thing an' that thing's done."

Heath shook his head slowly.

"We cain't leave no witness. 'Specially not no lawman. You want this dog chasin' us all the way back home?"

The tall man turned to Claw. He was three or four inches shorter than the marshal of Hellhole, but in that moment, stood on an equal footing with him.

"You gonna chase us all the way home?" he asked. This time, the emotion was clear. It was hope.

That hope was dashed in one word.

"Yes."

"I tolt ya!" Heath exclaimed. "Think you know it all."

"I never said that."

Heath turned to his renegade army of four.

"Untie the lawman and spread him out like the others."

No hesitation. One man stepped forward, eyes gleaming. The game was not yet played out and they relished its continuance.

"Easy does it, Marshal," the mountain man warned. "We ain't gonna kill ya. We're jist gonna see to it you don't have no way to follow us home. That's fair, ain't it?"

Claw looked to the tall man by his side. He did not meet Claw's eyes.

"Go ahead, Hatferd," Heath ordered to one of the men by his side. "Untie him."

Hatferd cut the ropes restraining Claw's hands and pointed with his musket, while stepping back out of the lawman's way. Claw rubbed circulation back into his numb wrists but made no other attempt to obey the order to move.

"Git goin'. Make it easy on yerself," Hatferd offered.

"Make me."

Claw was ready when the man came at him. With a growl of animal rage, he had his arms up as the mountain man charged. With an act of prodigious strength, Claw grabbed him by the shoulders, raised him off his feet and flung him into the open space. Hatferd struck one of the pegs pounded into the dirt to hold one of the drifter's hands, screamed and leapt to his feet.

Before he could regain his balance, Claw pounced, like a cat, long arms extended. Having the advantage of length, he wrapped his biceps around his enemy's throat and began strangling, pent-up emotion driving him toward death. If he were to be beaten, mutilated then killed, he would not go without a struggle.

Not without taking one with him.

Growls of rage and hatred emerged through clenched teeth as Claw choked the life out of the man. There could be no thought now of bringing any of them back alive. Or of bringing them back at all. It was a struggle to the death and God help any who tried to stop him.

As Hatferd grew limp in his hands, Claw turned, a bloodied bull, eyes ablaze with death. Seeing none step forward, he flung the senseless body forward, propelling the lifeless arms and legs into Heath. Before the leader could raise his weapon, he was struck by the corpse and lost his balance. They fell together, musket flying from his hand.

There was no chance for Claw to retrieve the gun. He dismissed the idea and dove down, using the weight of his body to drive the breath from the living man on the ground. As Heath struggled, Claw punched him, first in the face, then kneed him in the groin. With a fist raised to deliver a blow, Claw was struck from behind by another of the mountain men.

This man mounted Claw from the back, wrapping an arm around his throat before driving the point of his own knife into Claw's left arm. As red fluid stained his shirt, he cursed and drove his right arm back, into his attacker's neck.

"Damn you, coward!"

The two men rolled off Heath and the dead mountain man, arms encircling one another in mortal combat. It was not to be a fair fight, however. That was not the deal. One of the remaining three mountain men raced to the struggling men, kicked Claw in the side of the head, then plunged his own knife into the marshal's back.

A cry of agony rent the air as Claw's strength failed. With one arm aimlessly flailing at the wound in his back, he was kicked again, this time in the chest. A sob, then another muffled scream as the hard, trail-dirt encrusted boot struck him once more in the face. His nose exploded in blood and mucus.

Seeing the fight well won, the last of the mountain men approached, trembling with excitement. As Claw rolled to the ground, eyes shut in terrible agony, he stomped him in the groin, once, twice, a third time, until Claw's world blackened and his arms refused to obey his feeble commands.

Jumping up and down in unsated blood lust, the mountain man licked his lips and kicked Claw one final time before drawing his knife. Dropping into a squatting position, he roughly inserted it between the edges of Claw's shirt front, then jerked upward, severing all the buttons. With his free hand, the mountain man ripped apart the shirt, baring Claw's chest.

"Ain't he purdy, ain't he purdy," he purred with licentious emotion. "Mebbe I'll jist teach you what it feels like to be a woman, Marshal. Then we'll see how brave you are."

The man was aroused and hard. They had destroyed five men and that was not enough. Here was a chance to strike back at the representative of another enemy; one who had left their home in ashes and their stills destroyed.

"You was a blue belly, Marshal. You was on the winnin' side. Remember how that felt? I'll give you sumthin' else to remember. So's you kin feel the same kinda pain we felt when we cume home. What'd you say to that, Yankee?"

"Go to hell."

It was all he could say. All there was left in him to articulate.

There were no dialogues in his Good Book to cover what he was experiencing.

It had been one against six.

Had it been one against twenty, he would have made the same choice.

The Law was the law.

The State of Kansas understood that perfectly. Which was why a lawman's salary was dirt cheap. Dirt was what he would be eating; dirt is what he would be buried in.

The Union Army, if so informed, would supply the flag.

Veteran's benefit. Along with wooden legs, black slings, eye patches, telegrams to widows and inexpensive wooden coffins.

Embalming cost extra and was not covered.

It was a price Claw could not pay. Which was just as well, for his body would never be claimed.

No sense spending good money after bad.

"Hold off."

It was the tall man, the squint-eyed man who had taken no part in the uneven struggle, who spoke. All eyes, save those of the marshal and the dead men, turned on him.

"Cain't stop me now," growled the man squatting beside the lawman.

The tall man ignored him. He turned his steely eyes toward Heath.

"We kill a U-nited States marshal, they'll cume after us. They'll catch us."

"There ain't no one -"

"They'll cume after us."

"We cain't leave him."

"No. We cain't. But there's no sense in all of us bein' hunted. You an' the boys ride outta here. I'll finish 'im off, then leave a trail, so the posse what cumes after the Badge kin follow. Let 'em chase me. I ain't got no wife and young 'ums. You do."

"No, Heath," the mountain man on the ground pleaded. "Let me have 'im. He's mine."

"Go now," Squint-eye ordered. "Go, befer I change my mind."

"You do this, you gotta run a long way," Heath remarked, eying Claw's prone form with regret.

"I know that."

"We cain't leave you."

"You go now an' don't leave no trail. Go up yonder," he said, indicating the rocks. "Cover yer tracks. I'll take them bastard's horses wid me, so they won't know you rode off the other way. Go home. We did what we set out to do."

"What about them?" Heath inquired, indicating the outlaws.

"We never said we was gonna kill 'em. We said we was gonna make 'em pay. They've paid. Leave 'em where they be. Iffn they die, they die. We didn't kill 'em."

"We killed one," Hatferd tried.

"That was what ya call 'self de-fense. No crime in that."

What Squint-eye asked was a sacrifice not easily made. The mountain men looked at their companion, weighing their options.

"We'll go," Heath decided. "We owe you."

"You don't owe me nuthin'. Now git."

"You'll cume back? When you shake them cumin' after?"

"I may. An' I may not. Cain't say. I'll be a long way off befer I kin figure that."

"We'll tell your kin. Tell 'em what you done fer us."

"You do that."

The mountain man squatting on the ground rose slowly to his feet. He shook his head angrily.

"I don't see it," he said. "I say we screw this Yankee bastard ten ways ta hell, an' then bury 'em far frum here."

"An' I say git goin' or I'll take back my words an' you kin all swing." There was a long moment of silence. "You know blue birds. They don't take kindly to one o' their own being done in like that. They'll know," he added menacingly, his eye squinted nearly shut.

"We're goin'," Heath declared. He held out his hand to the tall man. Without hesitation, they shook.

"I'll keep yer shack fer ya," Heath promised. The tall man shook his head.

"It's your'n."

The four men mounted and rode off, into the rocks. They would leave no trail. They would ride slowly, carefully, more mountain goats then men. When the new avengers came, and they would come, they would follow the lone mountain man with the riderless horses.

God took care of His own.

The tall man did not move until his kith and kin were well out of sight. Only then did he drop the rifle, cradled in the crook of his arm, and kneel beside the bleeding, half-stripped marshal.

He shook the lawman by the shoulder. Claw groaned and opened his eyes. He knew what had happened but not what it meant.

"Kin you ride?" Squint-eye asked.

"Where to?"

There was a pause before the mountain man smiled.

"Does it matter?"

There was a shorter pause before the lawman answered.

"No."

"Then I reckon we better git outta here."

"What about them?" Claw asked, indicating the four disfigured outlaws. None of them were conscious.

"What about 'em?"

"We can't leave them like that."

"They done disgraced a woman."

"They paid the price."

The mountain man considered. The corner of his mouth twitched before he spoke.

"They won't live without gettin' to no doctor an' there ain't no chance we kin git 'em ta one inny time soon. We're a long way frum town. Long way frum *yer* town."

"We can't leave them."

"Yer one ta be givin' orders, ain't ya?"

"You saved me. Why?"

Squint-eye grinned.

"What makes ya think I saved ya? What makes ya think I didn't mean jist what I tolt Heath an' them others? That I finish ya off here an' now."

"You asked me if I could ride."

It was not easy for Claw to talk. His jaw was swollen and his nose stuffed with clotted blood. One eye was plastered shut and his body was on flame with pain.

"I ain't got no reason a'tall ta save ya, do I?"

"None at all."

The man laughed. The sound was sharp and clear.

"You ain't got no sense."

Squint-eye gave Claw a hand and hoisted him to his feet. He swayed like an uprooted tree in a storm but kept his balance. His savior nodded approvingly.

"You been beat up some befer."

"Some," Claw agreed. He tried a smile. It was lopsided and ghastly. The mountain man took his meaning.

"Where'd you leave yer horse?"

"Over the ridge."

"You reckon its wandered back to Hellhole b' now?"

Claw looked surprised.

"No. I 'reckon' it's right where I left it."

"Tie it up?"

"No."

The tall man shrugged.

"Had it fer long?" Claw shook his head. "Didn't think so."

"Why is that?" There was pique in his interrogative.

"I watched you on the trail. I was usually the one who hung back. Saw you fightin' it some. It weren't no horse you was easy wid. Ycu gotta break it in, some. Or get another."

"Thanks for the observation. Coming from a mountain man who wouldn't know the hind end of a horse from a railroad engine, I take that kindly."

The man repositioned his hat while taking the opportunity to scratch behind his ear.

"What makes you say that?"

Claw coughed up blood but it came from his mouth and not his lurgs. He spat it, taking care to avoid the other's boots, a gesture that did not go unnoticed.

"I heard in the War that Virginians were called 'foot cava_ry.' No horses."

"Them was Stonewall's boys." He hesitated and then added, "I never did say I was in the War."

"Thought maybe you were."

The mountain man shook his head but it was unclear whether he meant to deny the charge or pass it off.

"Men have been killed fer jabberin' less than you're doin'."

"You wanted to see me dead, you'd have left me to your friends."

They stared into each other's eyes, looking deep. Neither blinked. It was another unwritten law.

Considering all the laws which went unwritten, it was a wonder legislatures bothered enacting any.

It was finally the mountain man who looked away. He did not blink. He turned his head. It was an acknowledgement of something young Claw Kiley could not grasp.

"Kin ya walk?"

"No."

There was a momentary hesitation, then the mountain man laughed. It was the second time.

"Ain't you the one," he marveled.

"That makes two of us."

"Git goin'. I'll join ya directly. Wid the horses."

"What about them?" Claw nodded his sore, painfully busied head in the direction of the outlaws. He could not let the matter drop.

"I gotta bury 'em."

"They're not dead."

"I'll ketch up ta ya. You won't be far."

Claw began walking. His legs were stiff and felt as though one was longer than the other. There was a searing pain in his back where the knife blade had entered.

He was just out of sight over the lip of the vale when he heard four, evenly spaced shots.

He shuddered and wondered if he had done the right thing.

Life was composed of such questions.

They were seldom answered.

The mountain man came upon him as the lawman was searching for his mount. It was nowhere in sight. When offered the reins of another horse, Claw accepted them. He mounted with difficulty. There had not been time for any of the bodies to be buried.

The two men rode in silence.

East.

Claw did not ask where they were going.

This, he supposed, was a question to which he would eventually have an answer.

They did not make camp until the moon arced high in the sky. While Claw made a fire, the mountain man removed saddlebags, emptying the contents on the ground. Frying pan, beans, coffee, a coffee pot, dried beef jerky and one large can.

Without bothering to search for water, a canteen full of brackish water was unceremoniously dumped into the coffee pot. The mountain man made supper. When it was prepared, they ate without exchanging one single word. It was not until they had consumed their fill that Claw indicated the can.

"Gonna open that?" he asked.

"Don't know how; lessen I shoot the top off'n it."

"Get it from that cabin?" His companion nodded. "I'll show you."

Claw removed his pocketknife, inserted it in the rim of the tin can, then painfully worked the blade around. When the top was two-thirds cut, he pried back the lid and showed the contents to his companion.

"Peaches."

The mountain man blew air through his nose in a gesture of wonder.

"Ain't that sumthin'. I cain't ever remember seein' nuthin' like this befer. Rumor had it them Blue-bellies ete peaches outta a can but I, fer one, never did see it. Me an' my reg--" He stumbled over his words as he altered the sentence. "Me an' my kin were more the green-apples kind. Know what green apples does to a man's insides?"

"Yeah; about the way I feel right now. Like you'd been punched in the gut ten thousand times. Not gonna stop me from eatin' these peaches, though."

Claw divided the contents and they ate the sweet fruit until there was nothing left. The mountain man drank the juice then wiped his face on his sleeve.

"A man could do worse than eatin' them peaches every day."

"I'm sure that dead homesteader would appreciate the fact his food was enjoyed."

"I didn't kill that fella."

"I know you didn't."

A silence grew around them as the stars straggled out of the night sky, dimly illuminating them as the fire burned down into embers.

As a coolness settled in over the land, the mountain man reached into the pocket of his jacket and removed a corncob pipe. He packed it with rough shredded tobacco, lit it with a stick caught from the fire and puffed until a bright orange covered the top. When he handed it to Claw, the lawman accepted it, drew smoke into his mouth, rolled it over his tongue, then handed it back.

They smoked in this manner until the bowl was nearly empty.

"I heered a story onest. Durin' the War. About a fella on Stonewall Jackson's staff. Young'un, he was, name o' Joshua. He seed a lot o' fightin' and even more dyin' in the time he rode with Ol' Blue Light. After a battle, he'd lie awake at night, listen' to the cries and the moans and the cussin' o' the dyin'. Got to him. So's it became his habit ta git up when everyone elst was asleep an' go out onto the field. They wasn't no medical men around ta hep' those sodgers. Jist wasn't enough ta go 'round."

"Yeah," Claw agreed, remembering.

"This fella, he was a different kinda boy. He didn't like to hear no kinda sufferin'. He'd see these men wid their legs blowed off, or their guts hangin' out and he felt bad. Real bad. Wasn't nuthin' he could do, save mebbe give 'em a drink o' water. Didn't have no doctorin' skills an' even if he did, they wasn't no way o' savin' those boys. They was dyin'. Know what this fella done?"

"Tell me."

"He's squat down next to 'em and talk. Git their name, iffn they was able ta give it. Tolt 'em he'd write ta their next o' kin. Then he'd ask 'em straight out: what kin I do fer ya? An' when the man'd say, 'put me outta my misery,' he's put a gun to his head an' shoot 'em. It were a mercy killin' he done."

"I heard something like that," Claw acknowledged. He was thinking about the War and about all the smaller wars he had lived through. He was thinking about the rapists left behind and the four, evenly spaced shots. "Whatever happened to this Joshua?" he asked, for the sake of having something to say.

"He died."

"Someone put him out of his misery?"

The mountain man took in a deep breath and let it out slowly.

"It were after Chancellorsville. Make it two weeks after, mebbe less. His body weren't found. No one never seed 'em dead. But he died. Mebbe he made a rush at some o' yer Yankee fellas. Or mebbe he jist pined away. I ain't never heard. But he died. He loved Ol' Jack an' he didn't want ta fight no more after the Genr'l was gone. I reckon he wanted ta follow 'im. Love's like that, sumtimes."

"He a mountain man, was he?"

"No. Never heerd that he was. Heerd some things. Mebbe they wasn't true. Mebbe they was. Don't matter. He made his decision. I reckon he was some kinda fella, all right."

"I reckon he was."

"He didn't like no unnecessary sufferin'. Didn't see no point ta it. Didn't matter to him whether the dyin' man was a Yank or a Reb. The dyin' don't have no more allegiance."

The last word was articulated with perfect pronouncement. It was an "Amen."

Claw bowed his head in acknowledgement.

When the fire burned down to a feeble warmth, the two survivors of a small skirmish settled in for the night. The moon was setting before Claw spoke again. His voice was low, almost a whisper.

"My name's Claw Kiley," he said. "What's yours?"

"Don't know as I got a name innymore," the mountain man replied. "I left it behind in that baranka."

"Man's gotta have a name... Guess Joshua will do."

The newly christened Joshua considered, then nodded. "Git some sleep. We got a long ride ahead o' us."

"Where we going?"

Joshua did not reply. He had said enough.

CHAPTER 9

Claw woke once during the night, his back and arm inflamed with pain. Sweat trickled from his overheated brow into his eyes, then ran down the corners, imitating tears.

In the distance, he could hear a man groaning. His heart caught in fear as his brain translated the sound. If the mountain man who rescued him had been hurt, that meant his friends had guessed what he was about and had come back to punish him.

Gathering his strength, Claw groped for his gun. Where there was life, there was hope. If Joshua No-Last-Name was not dead, only injured, he would do the best he could to save them both.

A pair of hands restrained the marshal just as he realized he had no gun; that he had failed to retrieve his weapon after riding away from the five dead outlaws. Shame burned in his breast but he had no time to contemplate that omission. He struggled, gritting his teeth. They would not get him without a fight.

"Whoa! Hold on!" came the command in Joshua's now familiar voice.

"You!" Claw gasped, relaxing his tensed muscles. "How? I heard groaning -"

Although his vision was cloudy, Claw saw the mountain man smile.

"So, you heard a man groaning an' you thought it was me?" Claw nodded. "It's weren't. It was you who was groaning."

"Me?" came the incredulous reply.

"But I rightly do appreciate you thinkin' about me."

Claw relaxed into the other's powerful arms, letting his head droop.

"I thought -" But there was no need to finish the thought. Joshua knew what he thought.

"Get some sleep."

Claw drifted off again, dreaming of men tied to trees, of blood and honor and pain. He awoke before dawn, confused and scared. Frozen into position, he lay on his back, listening to the stars, the whispering of the wind, the silent chatter between ants and bed bugs.

He dreamed again. This time, he was no longer scared. Nor was he alone. He was with her; with Cougar Bradburn. She was dressed in a flowing white gown, the long locks of her red hair piled high on her head. Around her neck she wore a silvery necklace, studded with charms and minute figurines.

Claw was not sure where they were. At first, he believed they were in the Lowdown, downstairs in the bar. During other moments, they were in some place he had never seen before. One thing was clear, however. She had the bluest eyes he had ever seen. And they were only for him.

Tipping his hat to her, Claw leaned down and whispered in her ear.

With all those trinkets around your throat, I took you fer an Indian or a riverboat gambler, ma'am.

Now there's a compliment to turn a lady's head, came the droll response.

The tone of her voice made it seem he had offended her. In his dream, Claw could not understand why. A squaw with that much silver would surely be a princess; a sharper bold enough to flash silver was a brave one, indeed.

Yes, ma'am. I thought it was.

She blinked at him, then smiled.

Just come in off the trail, Giant?

Yup.

I suppose you could use a drink. He nodded. You're buying.

She led him to the bar It was an unfamiliar place, one he did not recognize. There was no bartender.

Pay up, said the dream figure of Miss Bradburn.

Claw reached into his vest, searching for his money. The money he knew should be there. The pocket was empty. He searched his trousers, finding only one large key he took to belong to a jail cell and a small ball of twine.

I, I must have left my money in the office, he stammered.

No money, no drink. You gotta pay for my time, mister. She turned her back on him, waving familiarly to other men across the room. Belly up to the bar, boys! she sang in a sweet, compelling voice. Who wants to entertain a lady?

The men rushed toward her, one shoving Claw aside with a blow to the arm. Although the man had no weapon in his hand, he inflicted a tremendous hurt. Grimacing from both the pain and the slight, the United States Marshal moved away. His place was immediately taken by another. By the time it took him to reach the swinging doors, he was already forgotten.

Drinks all around! he heard a man call. Here's five dollars for a bottle of whisky.

I'll make it ten! another shouted.

Twelve!

Fifteen!

Twenty dollars for a bottle of whisky and the lady!

Hoots and cheers swelled the room, issuing the lawman out on the billows of his own sighs.

He would go to his office, get his money and come back. If it took twenty dollars, he would pay it. If it took twenty-five dollars, he would slap his money down on the counter. If it took thirty dollars, he would take out his gun and start shooting.

But he did not have his gun. Looking down at his side, Claw realized with a start of fear, his pistol was missing. He could not remember losing it, would never leave his office without it. What had happened to it? Where had it gone?

And then he remembered. The man at the bar; the one who had bumped into him. He must have taken it. Stolen it while Claw was watching Miss Bradburn. He could not go back without his gun. Not even with thirty dollars in his pocket.

A groan escaped his lips, then a sob, then a cry. His world began to spin. A great storm arose, covering him and all of Hellhole in one great cloud of dust.

He was falling, buffeted to his knees, groping around on all fours, lost in a maze. Blind, un-gunned, without a penny to his name, Claw crawled forward, unsure of the direction.

Above the keening of the wind he heard his name being called. He stiffened, listened, shivered. It was her voice, Cougar's voice.

Claw! Claw Kiley! Where are you?

I'm here, Cougar. Here. Hold out your hand.

He felt her hand grasp his, and he clung to it for dear life. Bringing it to his lips, Claw kissed it tenderly. As his passion mounted, he kissed her hand more fervently, until the shrieking of the dust storm was nothing compared to the pounding in his heart.

I thought - I wasn't good enough, he lamented. I didn't have the price of a bottle.

That was only a test, Claw. Just a way of seeing how you felt.

What do you mean? he shouted, praying she could hear him over the power of the Almighty storm.

There's lots of men who have money to buy me, Claw, but only one who loves me.

I love you, he avowed, holding her hand to his chest.

You heard them bidding over me, the lady continued. A man who loves a woman doesn't bid on her like she's prime beef on the hoof.

I didn't have any money, he replied, shamefaced.

You have something more precious than money. Look in your pocket again.

Claw did as he was ordered, bringing out the heavy key and the ball of twine.

This is all I have, he said miserably.

That's enough, she said. The key is to my heart and the ball of twine symbolizes our love. If we add a little bit to it every day, one day it will be a great big ball.

And then what?

Then we start another.

Claw grinned. He no longer felt the storm. No longer had to shout to be heard.

Hand in hand, they walked up the stairs. Looking around himself, Claw realized he did not know where they were, could only guess their destination.

Where -? he began, but was shushed by a squeeze on his hand. Her hand was warm in his. It made him feel tall.

Tall, in the sense of a man who did not need a gun.

They continued to climb. There were too many stairs to count. He abandoned the attempt. Where she went, he would follow.

It was a dream and not a dream. He saw faces of men he knew along the way. Some of those men were dead, touching off long-ago memories. Others were drifters, men who had passed through his existence. All had left their mark in one way or another.

He saw Marshal Duvall and his wife, Ada. Jack shoved a hand at Claw. They shook like friends rather as adopted father and son. It occurred to Claw he had never had occasion to shake hands with Jack before. It seemed odd to do so, now, when he was so happy.

He would have embraced Ada but she stepped back. When he made a move to follow her, Cougar held tight, restraining him.

You cannot touch her, she reminded him. He seemed to remember the reason, then lost it, just as a dreamer forgets the nightmare upon waking.

Hello, Ada, he called. Ada Duvall was not looking at Claw; she was staring at Cougar. Claw gently nudged the woman at his side. She's speaking to you, he said. You ought to say something.

I do not know her.

Her name is Ada Duvall, Claw introduced.

She is nothing to me.

Stung by her refusal to speak to the wife of his mentor, Claw tried again.

Marshal Duvall taught me a great deal about the law. I deputied under him.

You killed the man who shot him.

Claw started, nearly tearing is hand from her tight grasp.

How did you know that? he demanded. I never told you. Did I? Hesitation crept into his voice as swirls of trance-like fog filled his mind.

She does not exist for me, Cougar explained. Not now. Perhaps not ever. We are not the same. She is a widow and I am a bridesmaid.

Claw frowned, then looked down at his feet as he walked up the steps, which had suddenly become icy and treacherous.

But I just saw Jack. Why do you call Ada a widow?

Without bothering to reply, Cougar turned and wrapped her arms around his waist. Grabbing the long, slightly curling locks of hair at the back of his head, she drew his face down to hers and kissed him. What began as an entangling of momentary passion rapidly metamorphosed into one of desperate need.

Claw, she breathed into his mouth. My Claw. I've waited all my life to find you. Where have you been?

That question, so innocently asked, frightened him. Pulling away from her, he stared into her eyes, his once soft, engorged lips now set and taut.

Why do you ask that? he demanded.

Because I want to know all about you.

No one can ever know all these is to know about another person. I will not tell you. He was remembering her rebuke of Ada Duvall. What is a bridesmaid? he demanded suddenly. You said she was a widow and you a bridesmaid. I do not understand you.

Cougar broke his stare and started back up the stairs. Claw followed, trailing behind. When she reached the top, Cougar spun around, the flowing material of her floor-length shirt brushing across the top of Claw's boots. In itself, this action could not have caused him to lose his balance. It was taking his eyes off her which broke the spell.

With a grunt of surprise, Claw plummeted backwards, rolling down the stairs, head over heels. Before he struck the floor with murderous velocity, he lost consciousness.

When Claw awoke several seconds later, the scene had changed. He was no longer in a saloon, nor was he anywhere he recognized. The room he found himself in was huge, more like a barn than a house. The ceiling was high, with rafters one-hundred feet in the air. The floor was made of wood planking, but so tightly knit together, it resembled one solid plank of hard, highly polished marble.

The room was filled with people, all of them dressed for a party. The women had flowing white, pink and yellow gowns, while the men wore black suits with long, inverted pitchfork tails. They were dancing. Music came from somewhere.

A swirling couple brushed past him. They appeared not to notice his presence. When he tried to speak, no one responded. Feeling conspicuous and ill-prepared to attend so magnificent a ball, Claw attempted to leave, but his feet did not move. Try as he might, he was attached to the floor.

Fearing others would laugh at him, he pretended nonchalance, an opossum among a company of ruckus raccoons. His strategy worked. No one paid him the slightest regard.

He had almost begun to relax when she saw her: Cougar Bradburn. She was dancing with a man he had never seen before. With a jealousy powerful enough to uproot a mighty oak, he lifted his legs and walked over toward her. When she saw him, she smiled but gave no other indication of recognition.

Excuse me, Claw interrupted, addressing his comments to the gentleman. I would like to dance with the lady. The man ignored him. Claw persevered. I want to dance with the lady.

The stranger did not look at Claw when he spoke.

Ask the right way. Don't you have any manners?

Burning with shame, Claw stammered an apology then sidestepped as the couple danced past him. What was the "right way"? He did not know. Looking around for someone to ask, he realized, to his shame, he was the only man without a partner.

Working his way to the side of the room, he watched, eagle-eyed, for any dancers to break up or exchange partners. None did. He would have to wait for the music to stop, then ask someone.

The music continued without interruption. The longer he waited, the more agitated he grew. Seeing Cougar in the arms of another man did not aid his patience.

An hour passed. Two hours. He kept time by counting seconds.

After seven years had slipped away and he was in danger of becoming an old man, Claw walked back onto the dance floor, again approaching the couple.

I want to dance with the lady, he stated in his best marshal's voice.

This time, the stranger twisted around to face him, his expression cold and meaningful. Something had happened to this dancer while Claw waited. While the stranger appeared to be the same man, he was no longer dressed in party clothes. He now wore a faded checked shirt and dusty brown trousers. A low-slung gunbelt with a notched Colt dangled from his right hip.

I said, ask right.

I don't know how. Tell me. It was a tortured confession.

A man who doesn't know how to ask a lady to dance, doesn't deserve her favors. The word "favors" was spoken in such a manner as to incite rage in a lover's heart.

Step aside.

You are not a gentleman, the stranger spat.

Feeling his face redden in shame, Claw's eyes sought Cougar's.

I am a gentleman, he said.

Then do it right.

Tell me what to do.

Shoot him.

Claw blinked, swallowed, then let his mouth fall open.

The lady thinks you can beat me in a gunfight. Have the guts to try? Miss Bradburn's partner inquired.

It was then Claw recognized him. The man's name was Edward Coffin, stylized "The Undertakers Best Friend" by the newspaper writers Back East. Claw had not even realized Ed Coffin was a real man. Until this moment, he assumed he was nothing more than a made-up character to scare boys into going to school and girls into marrying bank clerks.

I have the guts.

Outside, then.

Coffin tore himself away from Cougar and worked his way through the crowded room, several times walking straight through dancing couples. They did not notice the intrusion. When Claw tried to follow, he continually bumped and jostled people, receiving for his trouble dark curses and obscene gestures.

It was pitch black outside as the two men emerged. Claw sought in vain for a street lamp, a patch of ground illuminated by some interior lighting. Nothing. Not even a moon.

I'm over here, lawman, Ed called. Can't you see me?

I can hear you, came the harsh reply. If Claw could not see the gunfighter, then logically, the gunfighter could not see him.

You're standing too close, Coffin warned. Back off.

Claw obliged him, a cold chill rising up his arms and into his chest.

On the count of three.

I ain't doin' no countin' wid you, Ed retorted, his voice heavy with sarcasm. Just as his appearance had altered, so too had his voice. He no longer spoke with the silver tongue of a suave gentleman, but now sounded like an uneducated trail hand.

I can't see you, Claw protested.

He was rewarded by a deep, grating laugh.

Well, I kin see you, an' that's all what matters.

Without help from his eyes, Claw placed the gunfighter's approximate position by the sound of his voice. Squaring off, he let his right hand drop to his side, seeking solace in the comfort of his pistol. Dire was the realization his holster was empty.

I have no gun! he thought, but did not say so. To protest now would be to act the coward. He would face the man without a weapon. If Cougar Bradburn were to see him gunned down in the street, she would have the consolation of knowing he died a man.

Despite his protest, Coffin began counting.

One. Two. Three.

Claw's hand went down by instinct. He drew his arm back as though he had a gun but could not fire. His opponent, whether or not he could see Claw was unarmed, rang off ten shots in rapid succession. The first bullet struck Claw in the right arm, shattering the bone. The second hit him in the leg. He crumpled, curling up at the edges like a charred piece of paper.

He was hit again, this time in the stomach. Without the ability to see, Claw knew instinctively the lead had gone through his middle, emerging through his back. Miraculously, he still breathed.

God worked in mysterious ways.

He was hit again, this time in the head. He felt his brains leaking down his forehead. He tasted blood on his tongue. It clotted in his mouth.

He thought inanely of sweetbread.

He heard footsteps, then felt dust, kicked up by a heavy pair of boots, in his face.

It was Ed Coffin standing over him.

You cain't kill a legend. Don't you know that, Marshal? No one can kill a legend. Claw tried to talk but no words issued forth. There was a hollow, sadistic, all-knowing laugh. But a legend can kill you.

Claw felt his life slipping away and he knew he was dying. The sensation was nothing he had ever experienced before; nothing he had ever imagined. Blackness swirled around him, the insidious fingers of eternal night working their way inside his body like grave worms.

There was pain. Agonizing, searing, unimagined pain, yet it was set off at a distance, away from his consciousness. He was aware of it, but able to endure because he knew he was dying.

A man can accept anything if he knows there is some final ending point.

He's dead.

Claw heard the pronouncement and accepted it. It did not surprise him that he heard the words. He did not have the ability to reason. Everything was as it should be because it was happening.

Are you sure?

Another voice. This, too, strangely familiar.

Dead sure.

Claw tried to smile. Lying on his back in a pool of his own blood, listening to voices consign him to the underworld, he appreciated the joke.

Why did he have to die, Fiz? He didn't even have a gun.

It was *her* voice.

Because he was a man, Cougar.

Gratitude swept through Claw's body the way blood used to fill his living veins.

And now he's a dead man.

You know what this means, don't you, Cougar?

Another grave on Boot Hill. Her voice was dull, leaden. Like the bullets which had deprived them both of life.

Claw Kiley faced a legend on the streets of Hellhole.

And that legend killed him.

Claw could hear Fiz Ward moving away. He tried to call, to explain that he was not dead, but his limbs did not respond. He tried to call out but his tongue clove to the roof of his mouth, plastered there by the blood and the brain tissue.

He'll become a legend himself, now. The man who faced a gunfighter he knew he couldn't beat. They'll write all about him. The whole world will know his name. They will speak of it with awe.

The whole world, minus one, she said. What good does a dead man do me?

Would you prefer to marry a coward?

There came a deep, harsh, grating laugh. It sounded like Ed Coffin's laugh but it was not a man who laughed.

I'm sure as hell not taking a dead man to my bed.

The cloud grew heavier, weighing on Claw's chest, slipping around his back, sucking the air from his lungs. He could no longer control his thoughts. He remembered pain.

Claw Kiley died in agony. His reprieve had been canceled at the last.

He was resurrected a legend.

"Claw! Claw!"

Claw heard the voice. It was one-thousand miles away. Someone was calling him, trying to rouse him from death. He did not want to wake up. Not to the horror of a bullet ripped through his innards. Or the top of his head blown away. Not to the memory of she who did not want to love a dead man.

He felt himself struggling. His arms were paralyzed. He remembered one of them was shattered. He tried to kick then recalled a bullet had broken a leg bone.

"Cougar!" he sobbed. "Don't remember me this way. Please. I only wanted to..." But what he wanted no longer mattered. No one listens to the desires of dead men.

Ada Duvall was a widow and Cougar Bradburn was a bridesmaid. He knew what she meant, now. Too late.

"Claw! Open your eyes."

He fought against the order. He was no longer bound by earthly rules. No one had the right to command him.

"Cougar. Come back."

Come back. Where? To his grave? It seemed a pitiful request.

"I never wanted to be a legend. I just wanted to keep the law."

Let your legend keep it.

He did not understand.

He was twenty-three years old and he was dead. Those who perish do not have the same understanding as those who live.

They do not have the right.

"Claw!"

It was not her voice, but another's. Claw listened, trying to place the speaker. The pain came upon him again, swirling like death but it was not death. It was another type of suffering. One reserved for the quick.

Morning came into his eyes like a slap in the face. The marshal of Hellhole took a deep breath and screamed.

"Yer all right now," came the same voice. "You were havin' a nightmare. Are you awake, now? Kin you see me?"

Claw saw him. It was the mountain man. Joshua, No-Last-Name.

"Am I dead?" It was not as foolish a question as it sounded.

"No. Yer alive. Shot up some but still kickin'."

Joshua rubbed his leg where Claw had landed a blow.

"Where am I?"

"Out on the prairie. You git some coffee in you, you'll feel better."

Coffee was the universal panacea. No doctor had better medicine. Get some hot, stout coffee in your stomach and a man could face almost anything.

"Here. Take a sip o' this."

Joshua put the cup to Claw's lips. He took a drink then gagged, tasting blood and brains. Joshua wiped the patient's mouth with a red neckerchief, then offered more. This time, the lawman kept it down.

"Thanks."

He did not know whether he meant it or not but it seemed the right thing to say.

"That's all right."

Joshua helped Claw into a sitting position, chaffing his wrists to restore circulation. The action made him nauseous but he did not complain.

"Try some more."

Claw obeyed. He was alive again and therefore bound by the old rules.

"You was callin' fer some woman," Joshua observed, retreating a step to rekindle the fire. "An' she was callin' you." The image was so vivid, the mountain man saw it through Claw's eyes. "Callin' you Claw."

"That's my name," came the weak response. "Claw Kiley."

"Reckon it is." Joshua stirred the contents of a pot he had simmering over the fire. "Git you back to Hellhole, the doc there can patch you up. Nuthin' too bad." His back was to the marshal. "You ever read the Good Book?" he inquired softly.

"No."

"Heard some preachin'?"

"Some."

"Claudius was a feller in that book."

"I heard about him."

"A good feller. You named after him?"

"No one told me, if I was."

"Them folks in Hellhole - they call you Claw?"

"That's right." It tired him to talk.

"Wonder if they know." It was not spoken as a question. Claw did not have the strength to answer. "I got a ways to go wid you –" He hesitated and did not finish the sentence.

There was a long pause.

"You can call me 'Claw,' too."

"No, don't reckon I can. I ain't your father an' I ain't yer town friend. Iffn you had tangled up wid ol' Stonewall's Foot Cavalry, I mighta shot you. Not that I'm sayin' I was one o' his boys." The word "his" was spoken with reverence. "I weren't no reg'lar sodger."

"That's all right. Irregular 'sodgers' fought, too."

"We done it in our own way; danced to our own tune, you might say. What was you in the Army? A lieu-tennent? Captain?"

"Private."

Joshua blew air through his front teeth.

"Iffn you'd a been a Reb, you'd a been a major."

"That's because the attrition was so high." He did not ask if Joshua knew the meaning of the ten-dollar word. "What rank was this Joshua fella?"

"Heerd he worked his way up to lieu-tennent."

"Then you outrank me."

"No, sir, never that." He stroked his beard that had just a tinge of grey to it. "You're a U-nited States marshal, now. That's a heap of a promotion." He winked and stared away. "You'll grow into it, sir."

"Your calling me 'sir,' makes me uncomfortable."

"I 'spect that's the way it's gonna be, Marshal."

"Why is that?"

"Guess that's fer me to keep inside m'self', sir."

That handle sounded just right on the tongue of mountain man Joshua No-Last-Name.

He had never met a legend but he knew a good man when he saw one.

A man worth dying for.

Had Claw known what Joshua was thinking, he would have corrected him.

A man worth living for.

CHAPTER 10

Breakfast consisted of a mash of corn meal, brown sugar and flour, fried in bacon fat. Served with coffee, it made an admirable start to their day's journey.

"So, what are your plans?" Claw asked as they rode. He was unable to sit the saddle at a fast clip. The mountain man, comprehending without being told, had kept their pace at a slow, steady walk. The comfort level of the night before had worn off, some, leaving the depth of their relationship something they would have to work through.

"Gittin' you back to Hellhole in one piece is as fer as I got," Joshua admitted.

"Alive, you mean?"

Joshua snorted, rolling back his blue eyes in cheerful amusement.

"You reckon the state o' Kansas pay a mite ta git you back?"

"No. I don't reckon they would."

"That makes you a heap more worthless than me."

"How do you figure?"

"By yer own words, you ain't worth a lick. But iffn them boys I was with ever git wind o' the fact I brung you back - alive - and didn't have no 'gitimate 'cuse like a re-ward, they'd be after me, next."

"Offering money?"

The answer to Claw's question was a laugh. They rode in silence before Joshua continued.

"I said 'worthless.' They's other things in life worth sumthin' other'n money."

"I guess I could agree to that. Like this badge I'm wearing."

Joshua scratched his two month growth of beard, keenly appraising the man before speaking.

"That supposed to mean sumthin' to me?"

"I thought it might."

"Cain't say it does."

"You're not like those others, you know."

"What others? Them outlaws?" There was an edge to his voice but not for the reason Claw suspected.

"No. They were bad apples, no argument. I meant those men you were with. Those mountain men."

"I ain't like 'em, huh?"

"That's what I said."

They rode for an hour before Joshua reined in his horse and pointed to a shade tree.

"We'll rest the horses here."

Coming first to the tree, Joshua dismounted then wandered off into the bushes, leaving Claw to fend for himself. With the ache in his back and the throbbing from the wound in his arm, it took him several minutes to negotiate the distance without falling on his face. He was seated under the tree, fanning himself with his hat by the time his companion returned, ostensibly fastening a button on his fly.

"We got time fer a pot o' coffee, if you've a mind."

"Sounds good."

Joshua gathered dry twigs, started the fire with a match he kept tucked into the band of his hat, then dumped a handful of grounds onto the pot. He brought the water to a boil, simmered it for a precise but incalculable time, then poured two cups, handing one to Claw.

"Thanks." The gratitude was meant to convey appreciation for more than the coffee. Joshua gave no indication he understood.

"Think nuthin' of it. I like a cup o' coffee about this time. It keeps man's thoughts straight." He stirred the embers of the nearly consumed fire, then looked over at the lawman. "How is it you see I'm different frum them others?"

"They'd have killed me."

"Yer right aboot that, Marshal. A badge don't mean to us what it means to you."

"What does it mean to you?"

"You sure are the talkin'est fella," Joshua complained. "You could make a man's ears sore."

"So answer the question and shut me up."

Which was the same as saying, "Tell me it's none of my business and I won't ask anything else."

"A badge means the 'thority to string a man up after a judge an' jury done sentenced him fer sumthin' he didn't do."

Claw fussed with the bandage on his arm as he talked. It prevented eye contact.

"You wanted?"

"Yeah," Joshua agreed, boring a hole into Claw's boot. "There was a gal I'd say wanted me. Right purty she is, too. Nice gal. Not fer me, though."

"Why not?"

Before his boot was set aflame by spontaneous combustion, Claw moved it out of the line of fire.

"I ain't the settlin' down kind."

"Maybe you just never found a place worth settling down in."

"I git itchy. I git to wonderin' what's over them yonder hills."

"I get like that myself," Claw admitted. "You know what's beyond those hills?"

Joshua grinned. "More hills."

"Empty hills."

Joshua got up and walked away, his back to Claw.

"I ain't wanted by the law, iffn that's what you were askin'."

"That's what I was asking."

"If I was, what would you do?"

"Guess we'll never know."

Joshua cursed under his breath. His discretion was not lost on Claw who understood respect as well as, or better, than the next man.

"You ready to git goin'?"

"Yeah. The sooner we get back to Hellhole, the sooner I can go back to work."

Joshua' right arm jerked in a spasmodic motion and he turned back to face the lawman, face scrunched in annoyance.

"What in Sweet Marie are ya doin' now, if it ain't workin'?"

"Sittin' around, looks like to me."

Joshua rolled his eyes.

"How long you been a lawman, pup?" Claw rose awkwardly to his feet, ignoring the question. Joshua inched closer until he was cheek to jowl with the "pup." "I asked you a question."

"Were you talking to me?" Claw inquired innocently.

"Course I was! You did you think I was talkin' to?"

"Some pup."

"You see one around here?" came the exasperated demand. Claw's eyes opened six feet, seven inches wide.

"Nope."

With the realization he had been set up, Joshua withdrew his face, cleared his throat and spat on the ground.

"So. What's the answer, Marshal Kiley?"

"Seems to me, I been a lawman all my life. I was raised by lawmen, weaned on lawman's wife's milk. That good enough for ya?"

"Yer pa was a marshal?" Joshua busied himself repacking the coffee put and cups in his bedroll. The task was an arduous one, requiring all his physical attention.

"Never knew him. Never knew my ma, either."

"You raised ya, then?"

"Already said."

"Kinfolk of your'n?"

"Nope."

"Then why they'd take you in?"

"Guess they figured no one who wasn't raised to it would want to be a lawman. There's no - percentage in it. And since these men were dedicated to bringing law into this country, they raised me to take over."

"When they got shot," he completed the sentence.

"That's about right."

"Who takes over when you git shot?"

"Haven't figured that out, yet."

"You told that gal of your'n? That one you was dreamin' aboot?"

"Told her what?"

"'bout you needin' a replacement when you git shot."

"Wasn't planning on getting shot right away."

"Never knew a feller who was."

Without waiting to be asked - or of having his offer declined by a stiff-necked U.S. marshal - Joshua crossed behind Claw, placed one hand on his shirt collar and the other around his belt. With a heave and a grunt of effort, Claw was vaulted into the saddle.

"Hey!" he called in genuine irritation. Joshua glared at him, expecting to be chastised for his act. Establishing eye contact, they counted off a dozen blinks between them. As the challenger, Claw fired first. "Next time, be a little less rough, will ya?"

Faster than a man could wink at a pretty girl, Joshua slapped his hand down on the rump of Claw's horse.

"Git!" he ordered.

Ears back, nostrils flared, man and beast took off in the general direction of Hellhole. Followed at a more leisurely pace by the guardian. It would take him a long while to catch up. He would take as much time as he needed. It would take that long and longer to wipe the grin off his face.

"Fiz! Fiz!" the red-faced man hailed the conservatively dressed man in the buggy. "Fiz, I gotta speak to you."

The stableman's troubled face cut off the physician's hopeful query about whether he had hailed him to finally pay off the bill for services rendered, issued when the last of the Claudians held the reins to the Roman Empire. It was always said Fiz Ward had a long memory.

It went back to the days when he had first entered the healing profession.

"What is it, Bark?" he asked, "Bark" being short for "Barker."

"The marshal's horse just wandered in. Still saddled, the reins hangin' loose on the ground."

"Any sign of Claw?" Bark Barker shook his head. "Did you see blood anywhere?"

"Didn't think to look. And then I seen you."

"What in thunder do you expect me to do about it?" Fiz snarled. "I don't suppose you need any help unsaddling the poor beast. Give it a good rubdown and some oats. I'm sure the marshal's good for it."

Bark winced from the barb.

"What if he's not coming back?"

"Then, I suppose you can always sell the horse and take what you have owing out of that."

"You know what I mean," Bark whimpered, wringing his hands.

"No. I don't know what you mean."

"Won't you come over and see?"

"Unless the horse has suddenly developed the astonishing ability to speak, I don't know what good I can do, looking at it."

Nevertheless, Fiz laid a gentle rein on his own horse's back, and it moved forward, toward the stable.

"Where is it?" he demanded, descending from the relative protection of his buggy.

"Over here."

Bark led him through the dimly lit stable to a stall in the back where Claw Kiley's horse, still saddled, awaited.

"Am I supposed to see in the dark?" Fiz groused. "Bring a light."

Bark disappeared, to return moments later with a lantern. He held it up as Fiz inspected the saddle. When the physician angrily shooed him back, Moss dared to inquire, "What'd you find?"

"A horse and saddle. What'd you expect me to find?" Fiz rubbed his hand over his mustache then shook his head and walked away.

"What'll I do, Fiz?" Bark called after him.

"I told you what to do. Unsaddle him, curry him and feed him. Then wait."

"What are you going to do?"

The answer to that was not so easily brushed aside.

"I'm going to buy myself a drink."

It was a five minute walk from the livery stable to the Lowdown By the time Doctor Ward reached his destination, a new decade had begun. Looking around himself, he noted the emptiness of the place. It was early. If she saw him come in, she would know he had not come to buy a drink. Her suspicious would immediately be alerted. She would think the worst.

The fact that he came bearing bad news did not alter how he handed the situation. There was a right way and a wrong way to do anything. If he put it to her correctly, he would spare her a night, possibly a night and a day's bitter agony before harsh reality set in.

It was not that Fiz believed Claw was dead. He was just not sure the marshal was alive. There was a difference. About as thin as the band of a wedding ring. And far less substantial.

"Afternoon, Fiz," a friendly voice hailed him. For a moment, Fiz did not recognize it. Turning, he faced the smiling countenance of Frankie MacPhearson.

"Howdy, Frankie. What are you up to?"

"Just helpin' out a friend," he smiled shyly. "Miss Bradburn doesn't have a bartender, so I said I'd help out."

"Tending bar?" Fiz's voice betrayed more skepticism than he felt.

"Oh, no," Frankie reassured him. "Washin' bottles, sweeping the floor, that sort of thing. She can't ask the girls to do it and no one would want Miss Cougar to stoop to such an undignified task."

Fiz started to reply then clapped his mouth shut. He had started to ask where the drunk had learned the five dollar expression, "undignified task," then changed his mind. Perhaps Frankie had heard it enough, directed his own way and remembered it. That was the easy answer. Fiz was in no mood for anything more complicated at the moment but that did not assuage his conscience. It was a question he ought to have asked.

"Everyone's entitled to their own secrets," he growled, startling Frankie with his unexpected vehemence.

"What do you mean, Fiz?" He hiccupped at the end of the sentence, further irritating the medical man.

"I said, everyone's entitled to their own secrets. I was referring to you." Which was only half true.

"I don't have any secrets, Fiz," Frankie protesting, thus matching the physician's veracity half way.

"Where is Miss Bradburn?"

He had already made up his mind she was gone, shopping or out to eat or on a long visit and would not be back before evening. He therefore reacted with more than a little consternation when Miss Bradburn answered the question for herself.

"Right here."

She straightened from her squatting position behind the bar and faced him. He had not seen her, failed to sense her presence. His feathers ruffled.

"What were you doing back there?" he demanded in an accusatory tone, as though he were the proprietor and suspected her of pilfering.

"Taking inventory."

If she detected anything amiss, she did not betray it.

"With him helping you?" Fiz growled, glowering at Frankie. "I don't imagine he can count past five. Can you read?" he pursued, leaning forward, head shoved into Frankie's face.

"I dunno," the man stammered. "It's been a long time since I tried."

"Frankie," Cougar interrupted. Both men turned to face her. "Never mind. Go and bring me one of the crates from down stairs. The one labeled 'Betty Roderick.'"

"Who is Betty Roderick?" Fiz demanded as Frankie hurried away.

"I have no idea. The name was scribbled on the side of one of the whisky boxes."

They waited until they heard the shuffling footsteps on the stairs, then saw the torso of a man, with a wooden crate for a head, emerge from the cellar.

"Here, Miss Cougar," Louis said, offering her the box. "Is this the one you wanted?"

The words "Betty Roderick" were clearly written on the side. Cougar nodded.

"That's the one. You can put it down right there," she indicated. He did so and she dismissed him with a friendly wave of her hand. "Once you finish cleaning the bottles out back, empty the tub water and call it a day. There's coffee, bread and jam in the back room. Help yourself."

"Thank you, ma'am." Frankie made a slight bow, then backed away. Fiz waited until he was gone before continuing.

"What else are you paying him?"

"My body," Cougar replied casually. "We had a quick romp in the back before we got down to work."

Fiz coughed discretely into his hand.

"How did you know he could read?" he asked into his still cupped fingers.

"I asked him. He can also perform higher mathematics, speak French, recite poetry by heart and he has better table manners than you do. Or at least, better than you display."

"Thank you."

"You're welcome. What's the bad news?"

He should have expected her question but he had not. He should have answered her but his own ears were not ready to hear what he had to say.

"What makes you think there's bad news?"

She might have answered that it was written on his face but did not.

"I've never seen you pick on Frankie before."

"That's because I've never seen him do any work."

"The same could be said of you and no one picks on you."

He bristled. In his annoyance, the depression which had weighed his footsteps, dissipated into a defensive optimism.

"Claw's horse came in... without him. Still saddled and bridled."

"And looking for oats," Cougar guessed. "Did you tell Bark to feed him?"

Fiz nodded. "How did you figure?"

"I know the horse. It originally belonged to a tinhorn gambler. He lost him in a game and the fellow who won him sold him to Bark. It's got one *penchant,*" Cougar underscored. "It likes to eat. If you don't tie it up or hobble it, it'll pull up stakes and trot for home. Unless Claw finds another horse along the way, he'll be pretty foot sore by the time he walks all the way back to Hellhole."

Cougar smiled, replayed the thought over in her mind, then laughed.

"You think that's all there is to it?"

"Yup. You didn't find any blood on the saddle, did you?" He jerked his head with a negative answer. "Was his rifle missing?" Fiz nodded in the affirmative. "So. We wait. You know," she continued, looking around. "This place has mice. I could use a good mouser. If I find one, I think I'll name it 'Marshal.'"

Fiz stared at her, furrowed his eyebrows, hunched his shoulders then turned and walked out. He had no business being in a saloon in the afternoon. Not when he had work to do. There were bills to be written and sent out, letters to compose, magazine articles to read. Bandages to roll.

He was always busy. So busy, there was never any end to the work he had to do. Anyone who said he was not busy was a liar.

Or, in the case of Cougar Bradburn, simply mistaken.

The other alternative, of course, was that she was simply teasing him.

It was all very annoying. By the time he reached his office, climbed the steps and put a pot of coffee on to heat, he had forgotten all about the riderless horse. There had too many real problems to worry about.

CHAPTER 11

"I reckon you kin git the rest o' the way back to Hellhole by yerself," Joshua said, casually slinging his leg over the side of the saddle in an attitude of restful wariness.

The two men were perched atop a long hill, looking down into the distance. The city lay before them, spread out in haphazard fashion, two winding streets serving as the main business section of town, with individual dwellings scattered hither and yon around the perimeter in an elliptical pattern.

"Don't know that I can," Claw grimaced. He flexed his wounded arm but it was the pain in his back which worried him. He could feel the wound had begun to bleed again because his shirt was plastered to his skin. Ripping it off would be almost as painful as the original incision.

"It ain't more 'in a mile, mebbe two, Joshua observed casually. He was staring into the distance but his concentration had never left the man at his side.

"You can do better than that," Claw complained. "Mountain man like you; man who could track a cat over hard rock."

A smile curled around Joshua' heavily whiskered lips, raising his cheeks into what another man might have considered a challenge.

"You think?"

"Yeah."

The mountain man scratched his chin, then pointed with his left hand, as though marking off the distance in feet. With his right, he drew his gun and leveled it at Claw.

"You're goin' the rest o' the way in by yerself."

"You going to shoot me, are you?" There was not the faintest trace of surprise in the marshal's voice.

"I will if I have to."

"Well, don't bother burying me deep. Someone'll be out this way in a day or two. Probably the town doctor. He'll see the grave and have someone dig me up. They'll move the body back to town. He'll check it over, determine how many slugs it took to finish me, then bring me up to Boot Hill. There it is, up thataway," Claw indicated.

Joshua' eyes did not shift from Claw's face.

"I know Boot Hill."

"This one in particular?"

"Nope. But I figure you seed one, you seed 'em all."

"Oh, I don't know," Claw drawled. "This one can boast... let me see. Two sheriffs, one United States marshal and a passel of deputies."

"Rough place."

"Yeah."

Silence resumed. One horse swished its tail, the other flicked an ear, then bent its head down to graze. Flies settled in over men and beasts. The sun burned hot.

Claw could feel the trickle of blood, like perspiration, crawl down his flesh. He twitched his shoulders to alleviate the feeling. It did not work. He was tired and wanted to sleep.

"I ain't goin' down into yer town," Joshua said softly.

"Want to tell me why not?"

"Yer friends see you comin' in wounded, they'll figure out what happened right quick. Never knew a town fella to ask questions."

"I told you." Claw's words were terse, clipped. "I'm new there myself. You could count my friends on one hand."

"It onlyest takes one. With a rifle."

"Well," came the resigned sigh. "There's Fiz Ward. Never seen him use a rifle. He has better accuracy with his tongue. Can't kill a man more'n two steps from him, using a weapon like that. Then, there's the lady. She'd shoot you, sure enough, but not until I was out of range. You stick close, you'll be all right. There's also a fella named Frankie. He drinks more'n he should. He might hit you over the head with an empty, but I figure he'd apologize to you before he did it. Give you the chance to step aside."

"That's three," Joshua counted. "You got two more comin' to ya."

"I got a cat," Claw conceded. "She might scratch you, but I doubt it. She took to me pretty quick. I guess that makes her a good judge of character."

Joshua flicked away a fly which had settled on his face.

"Name the last," he demanded.

"That last one. Now, he's a tough one, all right. Given to a temper. But I'd say he was a fair man. A good man. You might like him, once you get to know him. He's not easy to know, mind. But I'd trust him with my life."

"Who is he?"

"Fella goes by the name of Joshua. Named after the boy who followed Old Stonewall."

The so-named man gave a snort, shifted positions in his saddle, then jerked on his worn, sweat-stained hat. It was an act more of nervousness than of irritation.

"I'd say you was pretty hard up fer friends."

"It only takes one for a man to feel needed. Wanted. Good friends are hard to come by."

"What are you sayin'?" Claw did not reply. Joshua tried again. "I ain't yer friend."

"Saved my life."

"I'd o' done as much fer a dog."

"For a dog, mebbe. But not for just any man. You sized me up, took a chance you didn't have to. I've been giving that a lot of thought."

"Man does too much thinkin', it gits his brains to hurtin'."

"Man finds a fella he can trust, a man he owes, he doesn't want to lose him."

"I ain't no town man. I'm a mountain man. Give me claustrophobe to live down there. Besides, a fella needs money to live in a town. I ain't got nary."

"Thinking about giving you a job."

"What job?" The interrogative was half disdain, half joking.

"Deputy."

"Deputy? Sun git to you, did it? I cain't do no deputyin' fer you, ner fer no one else. I ain't no lawman. I done lived outside the law all my life."

"No," Claw remarked, turning to squint into the sun. "You've lived without law. There's a difference."

"None that I ever reckoned mattered."

"I'll pay you ten dollars a month plus keep."

"I ain't listenin'. You better git that horse o' your'n movin' or that lady wid the rifle'll get trigger happy."

Claw chuckled under his breath, nodding agreement.

"I've been gone long enough, she might shoot me, at that. Might give you a reward, too."

"What fer?"

"For putting her out of her misery."

"You got queer ideas, Kiley."

"It was 'Marshal' back on the trail."

"I ain't feelin' friendly toward ya jist now."

"You going to put up that pistol? Or you going to use it?"

Joshua hesitated, clearly torn, then slowly holstered the gun.

"You're what I'd call an odd duck, sir."

"I've been called worse. By friends," he added with a grin.

"I don't doubt it."

"Then how 'bout coming into to town with me? At least get a bite to eat."

"I ain't hungry."

"Sleep in a bed."

"Now, why'd I want to go an' do that?"

"You can't go back, you know. So, if you don't come with me, where will you go? Fella gets mighty lonely out in the baranka all day."

"I'll keep busy."

"Just so you don't get any ideas about robbing the bank."

"I ain't no bank robber. Never took what weren't mine."

"Man like that'd make a good deputy."

"I put a badge on, I'm a dead man. Them boys I was wid, they git wind o' what I done, they's take it upon themselves to cum an' shoot me themselves."

"I won't tell 'em, if you won't."

Claw grimaced as a sudden, sharp pain shot through his back. The movement startled his horse. It danced a step, fattened its ears to its head, then lashed out with a hind leg. If Joshua had not anticipated the action, his own mount would have received a kick to the thigh.

"I'll take you down into yer town an' I'll see you brung to the doc's. But I ain't interested in nuthin' more, save mebbe a hot meal an' a drink."

"Way I'm feeling, better make it two drinks."

Claw spurred his horse and the two animals began the slow journey toward Hellhole.

"It's the Marshal, Miss Cougar! The Marshal's coming in!" Frankie called, his voice raised an octave in excitement. Cougar looked up from the book she was reading, nodded an acknowledgement, then rose to a standing position. She crossed to the bar, took a bottle of whisky from underneath and set two glasses out.

When Cougar was satisfied all was in readiness, she walked with deliberate slowness to the swinging doors and looked out.

What she saw told her two things: Claw was not alone and he was hurt.

"Frankie," she ordered. "Go get Fiz."

"Yes, ma'am."

He scurried off in the uncoordinated shuffle, developed over the years, from moving on the constantly shaking ground of his own hell.

Once he was gone, she parted the doors with her hand then stepped out, letting them swing shut behind her. She caught Claw's eye as he passed, a quick, silent communication between them.

"No," his look said. "I'm not in any danger. This is a friend."

And so Joshua No-Last-Name-At-The-Moment would be forever more. Cougar did not have the name but she had the reassurance. That was enough.

The horses stopped at the hitching rail in front of the Marshal's Office. Joshua dismounted first, crossing behind the horses to Claw. He did not offer a hand but as the marshal reached out, gave his arms gladly. By the time he was on his two feet, Cougar had joined them.

"Fiz's coming," she informed the two men. Claw grimaced, then nodded.

"I'm all right," he said. "A little pain never hurt anyone."

"I'll remind you of that, sometime."

Miss Bradburn ran a critical eye over Claw's body, assured herself he was in no imminent danger, then turned her sharp appraisal to the stranger. She conducted the scrutiny with undisguised interest, challenging him to earn Claw's unspoken regard.

"This is Joshua… Jackson," Claw introduced. "He saved my life."

"Did he try to take it before he decided to save it?" she asked. The question was astute, uncompromising. She was a woman of the world and wanted to have the score without fabrication.

"No."

She nodded. "How do you do, Mr. Jackson?"

Joshua was not above his own blatant appraisal of the Marshal's woman. He liked what he saw. A lot.

"Ain't no 'mister,' to it, ma'am. 'Joshua' will do, jist fine."

"Step aside! Move, will you?" came Doctor Ward's irritated command to the crowd which had gathered to see the blood on Claw's shirt. It was not an uncommon sight but always stirred interest. The scene was free of charge and permitted the man - or woman - witnessing the actual event, to spread the news.

Knowledge, as they say, is power.

"Can you make it up to my office, Claw?" he asked after seeing the lawman on his feet and making his own judgment about the blood.

"Yeah. Nothing too bad, Fiz. I made it this far. With a little help." Claw indicated the mountain man with a jerk of his head.

"Who are you?" Fiz demanded.

"Jist passin' through." Fiz accepted the statement at face value.

"Get a move on, Claw," the healer ordered. There were those in the crowd who suspected he had dinner on the table and did not want it to get cold.

Claw walked in the general direction of the doctor's office, speaking to Joshua as he went.

"Stick around. I'll be back in an hour and we'll talk. Buy him a drink, will you, Cougar? On my charge. I'll pay you later."

"Sure thing."

She waited until she was certain Claw would not require help getting to the office, then held a hand out to Joshua as an invitation.

"You heard the Marshal. No one in Hellhole goes against his orders."

He remained rooted to the spot. "I ain't likely to take no drink on his charge an' I ain't got no money to pay fer a drink on my own."

"Then you'll have a drink on me," she said meaningfully. "No one refuses Cougar Bradburn without a good excuse."

"Like what?" he asked, arching his left eyebrow.

"Like it bein' Sunday before noon; he's gone on the wagon and he isn't drinking anything stronger than mother's milk; or he's dead. It isn't Sunday, you don't look like a man who has a wagon, let alone gets up on one, and you're not dead. That's it."

"Yes, ma'am," Joshua responded, licking his lips and tipping his moth-eaten, trail-worn hat. "I guess I could use a drink, at that."

"Glad to know you're going to be sensible."

Cougar led the way across the street, then entered the saloon ahead of the mountain man. Joshua paused before the doors to dust himself off, then wiped his feet on the edge of the building before entering. Realizing her eyes were on him, he grinned apologetically for keeping her waiting.

"It's a poor man what brings dirt on his boots into a room with a dirt floor. Befer ya knows it, the corn'll sprout between yer legs while yer sleepin' and then where'll ya be?'"

"The Lowdown has a wooden floor."

He winked. "I guess ya won't have to worry aboot the corn, then."

"But I may have to worry about you. What're you drinking?"

"Beer'd go down fine."

She poured him a beer, then motioned to a table. They went and sat at it.

"Ain't you drinkin'?"

"I did my drinking waiting for Claw to get in. Now that he's back, I'd better save the rest of it for the customers. I'm Cougar Bradburn," she reiterated in introduction, offering her hand. "I own this place."

Joshua took her hand, shook it, then brought it to his lips and brushed his whiskered lips over the back of it.

"Your ma teach you to do that?" she asked in some amazement.

"Nope. Figured that was the onlyest way I was gonna git to kiss you, the way you an' the Marshal are."

"I don't know if me and the Marshal 'are' anything, exactly. And if you get yourself cleaned up and shaved, I might just let you kiss me somewhere else."

"Miss Bradburn, if I wasn't a-lergic to water, an' if I owned myself a razor, I'd take you up on that mighty kind offer."

"It's 'Cougar,' to friends."

"Don't know that I'd be here long enuf to be a friend, ma'am, but I do rightly appreciate it. I don't suppose it's so easily offered as you made it sound."

Cougar started to nod her head, then changed her mind. "Thank you."

He drank the beer, started to wipe his mouth with the kerchief around his neck, then decided against it and used the back of his hand. It was a deception she was not unfamiliar with. As such, it bore no comment.

"Claw says you saved his life. I'm beholding to you." She waited for the count of three before continuing. "How'd you happen to come along?"

"Wasn't like that. He was trackin' me an' my kin, who was trackin' some fellers who needed killin'."

"Did you kill 'em?"

"Yes, ma'am. They was killed."

"And Claw wanted to stop 'you and your kin' from doing the killing?"

"That's about the way of it," Joshua agreed, not even slightly surprised at the depth of her perception.

"He didn't."

"They was only one o' him, Miss Cougar. Don't hold it a'gin him "

"Oh," she laughed. "There's a lot I'd hold against him, but that's not one of those things."

Joshua leaned back in his chair, took in the room with a long, steady glance, then ran his eyes up the stairs, one by one, in a shufflingly slow pace. When he reached the top, he made a rapid survey of the closed doors strung out across the hall, then sighed and settled back down into his seat.

"That marshal's a lucky man; havin' a town like this."

"You think so?"

"Yup."

"Mebbe you could share it with him."

"I ain't much fer settin' down."

"You're not going back the way you came." It was a statement, not a question.

"Don't reckon so."

"Need a job, I can always use a good man around the place."

"Now, that's the second offer fer a job I done got in one day. It's twice more'n I got in a lifetime."

"What was the first offer?" She was almost too quick.

"Marshal Kiley done asked me to deputy fer 'em." If he had any qualms about telling her, Joshua did not reveal them.

"Claw asked you that?" He nodded. "What did you say?"

"Same thing I tolt you. I ain't the settlin' down kind." And then, "How much are you offerin' me?"

"That depends."

"On what?"

She let the question hang.

"How much did Claw offer you?"

"Ten dollars a month, plus victuals an' a bed."

"I could offer you more."

"Reckon I kin handle myse'f wid a gun. Don't know aboot wearin' no badge, though."

"A man wearing a badge's been known to get a hole or two in his shirt," she agreed. "But there are other considerations."

"Like   what?"

"When the time's ripe, you can have the State of Kansas pay to have someone dig a new sink hole for you."

Joshua went over the chair backwards and did not stop laughing, even after he gave his head a hard clunk on the wooden floor. Cougar laughed with him, giving him a hand up after he caught his breath.

"Ma'am, that's the best reason I ever did hear tell to git myself a job!" he admitted. "You dern near talked me into it."

"That was my intention."

"Sweet Jesus," Joshua swore.

"Amen," Cougar agreed.

Ruefully rubbing his head, Joshua accepted another drink, downed it for "medicinal purposes," then yawned.

"Excuse me," he apologized. "I ain't had much sleep. The trail ain't 'actly a bed o' roses, an' the Marshal snores."

"I'm sure Hellhole has better accommodations than either the trial or a 'bed of roses,'" Cougar offered, then added, "I know."

Joshua blew air through pursed lips, shook his head, stretched and stood.

"Miss Cougar, iffn he don't marry up wid you soon, he's a damn fool."

"Oh, he's ten times a fool," she readily agreed. "But then, I don't know if I'm the marring kind." She lowered her voice for the last sentence, causing both the grin at the oft-expressed male sentiment. "Besides," she pursued, eying him suggestively, "I'm for sure not through looking around. When it comes to some things, Claw's more boy than man. Sometimes, I woman wants a fellow who's been around."

He grinned, made a noise by swinging his right leg back and forth, then appealed to her with dark, sobering eyes.

"Miss Cougar, you don't know me. You don't know where I've been, or what I've done, yet yer askin' me, widout sayin' so, to take that job Marshal Kiley offered me. You wanna tell me why?"

"He can't do it alone. He needs a good man to help him."

The mountain man shook his head slowly, with a noncommittal gesture which spoke more of his own low opinion of himself than hers.

"I never said I was a good man."

"You didn't have to. I said it."

"An' how do you know?" It was a challenge, stated with a defiant lilt of the chin.

"I'm a woman who's been around. You're a man who's been around. If we can't size each other up, then there's no hope for anybody."

He hesitated, then bared his teeth without realizing it. Cougar waited, hands on hips. When their eyes met, she lifted hers toward the stairs with a calm offer. Had it been a "whatever it takes," he would have turned her down flat and been out of Hellhole by nightfall. But it was not. The offer had more friendship than bribery, more desire than gift. Claw Kiley was a *boy* and she never *did* say she was the marryin' kind.

"Miss Cougar, I better go look after my horse. I gotta bed 'em down fer the night. Then I gotta git me a place to sleep. Cheap," he added. "Somewhere a fella won't git hisself in trouble. You reckon the stableman'd let me crawl into the straw? I'd pay 'em back by doin' some cleanin, that sort o' chore."

"Joshua Jackson," she said, her face calm, set in stone, her words deliberate. "You come here as a friend. You saved Claw's life. That has a value to me. You turned down an offer I meant more than I thought I did. That has another value. You understand?"

"I'm listenin'."

"I've slept in barns, before. I've slept in alleyways. There were times I'd have been glad to sleep on the bottom of a river. You're not going to sleep in any damn stable. I suppose Fiz will keep Claw up in his office tonight. Go over to the Marshal's Office and sleep there. Then the two of you can work something out in the morning."

"I don't know, Miss Cougar. This ain't what I want." She made no reply. "I ain't got no feel fer the law."

"You think I do? I'm not asking you to love the law. I'm asking you to love the man."

There was a long pause.

"Well," he signed. "I ain't never turned down a lady, yet."

He tipped his hat, made a slight bow, then walked out of the Lowdown Saloon, whistling a jaunty tune. Joshua Jackson had come to Hellhole.

CHAPTER 12

"Where's Joshua Jackson?" Claw asked. He was lying in the bed of Doctor Ward' "rest and recovery" room and was not happy about it. "There's nothing wrong with me. I want to get up and get out of here."

"That's one question and two statements. Which do you want addressed first?" Fiz asked, stroking his chin in a manner suggestive of thoughtfulness.

"I want my trousers back, I want my boots back and I want -"

"Now," Fiz interrupted. "You're making demands."

"If I don't get what I want," the prone-positioned marshal threatened, "I'm going to lock you up."

"On what charge?" There was more amusement than seriousness to the question.

"Endangering public welfare."

"Yeah," Fiz agreed. "Thought out to get me five or six years. I'll be out just in time for the State of Kansas to get around to paying me for treating your very serious wounds."

"Is that all you ever think about?" came the exasperated query. "Getting paid?"

"No," Fiz assured him. The silence at the end of the one word sentence, "no" was pregnant.

"What else do you think about?" Claw asked. Fiz noted his patient has regained a more respectful tone of voice. Which was as well for him, or he might have been told exactly what else Doctor Ward thought about and how he intended to inflict it.

"Cougar Bradburn is in the outside office. Do you want to see her?"

Claw demurely pulled the blanket to his chin and nodded. Fiz made low, inarticulate noises in his throat as he turned his back on the patient and summoned the lady.

"Good to see you back, Claw," she greeted him. "And in one piece."

"He is not in one piece!" came the loud, irritated voice of the physician who had remained behind.

"Good to be back," the patient agreed, trying a smile. The fact he succeeded was testimony to his lips being the only part of his anatomy which did not hurt.

"When your horse came in without you, we sort of thought maybe we'd be looking for a new occupant in the Marshal's Office."

"You weren't far wrong," he admitted in a low, rueful voice. "Did Joshua come over for a drink?"

She nodded, stepping away from the bed, so she might have a better view out the window.

"He's an interesting man," she observed carefully.

"What did you think of him?" There was more to the question than a casual inquiry. Claw Kiley's stock rose considerably in Cougar Bradburn's portfolio.

"I liked him and I trust him," she replied, back to Claw. "I liked him enough to offer him a job, but I see you got to it before me."

"He tell you that, did he?"

"He mentioned it."

"What did he say?"

"Just that you thought he might make a good deputy."

"And?" It was like pulling teeth, an apt analogy considering where he found himself.

"He thought he might take you up on it."

Claw heaved a sigh of relief, then rested back on the coverless pillow. The shaft of a chicken feather poked through and scratched his cheek. With an annoyed grunt, he punched the offending feather back inside and turned the pillow to a more comfortable position. This time when he rested his head down, it struck the mattress with a soft thud, the feathers having gathered on either side of his ears.

"I have a better pillow than this in the Marshal's Office," he complained.

"That *is* the pillow from the Marshal's Office," Fiz's voice informed him.

Claw prudently let it ride.

"What else did you talk about?" he asked, turning his attention back to Cougar.

"Where he was going to stay. He offered to ask Bark to put him up at the stable, but I told him since you weren't coming back tonight, he might as well use your bed."

He thought about that one.

"Yeah, well, I suppose that won't do any harm."

Fiz moved into the doorframe, wiping his hands on a towel.

"I suppose he has more discretion than to read all those important papers you get from Hays."

Claw rolled his eyes.

"You ought to run for mayor. I don't see how you could be any more irritating as a politician than you are as a doctor."

"Just might do that."

Claw groaned.

"Does he get supper, Fiz? I can bring some up," Cougar offered, before Fiz attempted to entertain them both by outlining his political strategy.

"He does. You might order some for me, too. Federal government ought to subsidize physicians. Might improve the quality of care its citizens get."

"There's a novel idea," Claw agreed.

"But I guess it does the best it can," Fiz pursued, "paying the doctor bills for United States marshals."

"Keeps a roof over your head," Claw agreed. Then added dryly, "Invite Joshua up and we'll have a picnic."

"There's an idea."

After ordering dinner for four from Ma Smitt's, Cougar walked to Claw's Office, opening the door quietly as she entered. Joshua was standing by the wall map, studying the extent of Ford County and the marshal's jurisdiction. He was so intent on his observations, when she made a point of shutting the door with a bang, he nearly jumped out of his skin.

Spinning around, hand to his gun, he saw her, registered the fact there was no danger and landed, like a cat, on his feet, chagrined and apologetic.

"Ain't used to bein' in no public place," he explained, re-holstering the pistol with conspicuous calmness. "The onlyest time I ever been in a jailhouse was when I was in the jail."

"That's a lot of territory to cover," she said, indicating the map. He turned back to it with a nod.

"I cain't see how inny one man kin cover it all. Ner inny two men. It's like openin' up the door to the safe, but warning the robbers beferhand they's a combination lock on it."

"I like that," she said with simple sincerity. "A lot. It says it all, doesn't it?"

"He's a young'un, Claudius Kiley. I reckon you have to be young to take a job like he done. Befer you learn how to figure the odds again' ya. Onst you reason it out, it gits to be too much."

"I don't think he'll ever figure it out."

"He's a smart'un, Miss Cougar. The kind this land's lookin' fer."

"You like him," she marveled.

"I cain't say I ever seed anyone like him befer. I'm thinkin' on what you said to me in the drinkin' parlor. An' I'm thinkin' aboot the offer he made me. He ain't gonna git no ten dollars a month fer no dep'ty."

"Then I'll pay you."

"That wouldn't sit wid him an' it wouldn't sit wid me. No, sir. No, ma'am," he corrected with a grin. "Ain't no mistakin' yer a lady."

She accepted the compliment without haranguing over the word.

"I told Claw you'd be sleeping here tonight and he thought it was a good idea. We're having supper up at Fiz's. It's already been ordered. Enough for four. That's Claw and Fiz and you and me," she clarified.

His jaw worked a long time before he finally spoke.

"I thank you."

"We're even. The doctor's office is across the street and up. You'll see the sign."

"Well, aboot that, Miss Cougar, I ain't one fer no readin' and writin'." It was an awkward, embarrassed admission.

"I wouldn't know how to read and write myself, if someone hadn't taught me. No one comes into this world knowin' readin' an' writin', Mr. Jackson."

"I never thought on it in jist that light, ma'am."

"Welcome to Hellhole - where anything can happen - and usually does."

"I may like this place better'n I thought."

"You might come to, at that," she grinned. "Why don't you follow me? Once you've found the doctor's office, you'll never forget where it is."

He matched her grin and they marched off, two soldiers recruited into the Hellhole deputation for law, order and the preservation of Marshal Claudius Kiley.

Cougar directed Joshua to where "Phillip Ward, M.D." hung his shingle, then gave orders for him to get the feast, while she arranged for the "liquid refreshment."

Turning "this way, that way, through the alley, and back out, two doors down," Mr. Joshua Jackson arrived at what he hoped was the correct destination. Knocking tentatively on the door, he removed his hat as the perpetually middle-aged proprietress answered his summons.

"I don't have any rooms available," she snapped in her finest, most self-righteous and matronly manner. "And I never accept borders without a recommendation. If the Hellhole House is full, I suggest you try -"

"'Cuse me, ma'am, but are you Ma Smitt?"

"I am," she admitted. "I don't know who sent you, but I only accept gentlemen of breeding and culture."

"Now, ma'am," Joshua began, politely positioning his foot so she could not slam the door in his face, "where I cume frum, 'breedin' is done by cows an' horses an' 'culture' is what yer grandma tolt you of her grandma an' of how yer one grandpa fought in a mighty War fer Independence, an' how the other done cume acrost the great ocean, all my hisself. An' how he cume to make a fiddle an' brung music frum his pappy's land to the mountain people, what never heard nuthin' like it befer, an' who paid good money to listen to it.

"I wonder, kin you say you got better 'culture' than that?"

"Who are you?" she demanded, as though a name would explain everything.

"My name's Joshua… Jackson an' I'm the one who brung the marshal in this mornin'. He's over at the doc's right now, an' the victuals I've been tolt to fetch frum you are goin' to him. An' to the doctor and to 'select guests,' of 'breedin' and culture.'"

Ma gave him a venomous stare then pointed a finger in his face.

"Wait here."

"Ma'am, I don't believe I'd step inside iffn you invited me."

The door was slammed, striking his opportunely positioned foot and bouncing back.

"Well, I never!" Ma exclaimed.

"Cumes a first time fer everythin'." Joshua reopened the door and nodded politely. Ma disappeared in the back.

She returned directly with a heavily-laden basket, covered with a red and white checkered cloth and a loose-fitting wicker top.

"Now, boy, when the doctor is finished with the food, you bring the basket and the dinnerware back here to me. If it's after ten o'clock, it can wait until morning, but see you come by straight away. I'm up at seven o'clock. And come 'round to the back door."

Joshua' hands remained stiffly at his side.

"What's the matter?" Ma demanded.

"Ma'am, I ain't no 'boy.' Now, I don't mind bringin' yer basket an' yer plates an' cups an' saucers back to you cume mornin', but I ain't no servant, neither, an' I'll jist drop by yer front door an' knock. Iffn you don't choose to open yer door, it's all the same to me."

"I shall most certainly complain to Marshal Kiley about this. Imagine - talking to me that way."

"Yes, ma'am, you do that. I'd be right interested to hear what he had to say."

"I know where you come from," Ma pursued, unable or unwilling to let the matter drop into the hands of the law. "You're a mountain man; one of those men who distill spirituous liquor for a living and would steal an honest woman's possessions for a drink of whisky in a saloon."

Joshua shook his head in a slightly confused manner, to indicate he did not quite understand her analogy.

"Ma'am, I sure don't care to git off'n on the wrong foot with you," he said, nudging back the door with his boot, "but iffn I was one to make my livin' distillin' spirits, why'd I go an' spend my hard-earned money in a saloon?"

"You know what I mean."

"I'm afeared I do, ma'am. An' it's likely true I've made my livin' in an assortment o' ways, but right about now, this very minute, you could say, I'm deputyin' fer Marshal Claudius Kiley."

"Where's your badge?"

"I guess you could say, I'm deputyin' in a spiritual sort o' way; the marshal took me on faith, an' I'm takin' the law on faith. He does the badge-wearin' an' I do what he says. Now, iffn you don't mind, I'll take that basket an' be on my way."

Ma Smitt hesitated, clearly torn, then thrust out the willow basket.

"We shall see what the morning brings."

"Where I cume frum, the mornin' brings a new day. Obliged, ma'am."

So saying, Joshua Jackson tipped his hat, turned his back on Ma Smitt and disappeared into the growing darkness of a Kansas night.

Joshua was the last to arrive at the "picnic" and the most welcome, for he brought with him the food basket.

"You were gone a long time," Cougar said, relieving him of his burden. "Did you have any trouble finding the place?"

"No, Miss Cougar. But I had some jawin' to do with Ma."

Fiz grunted, indicating Cougar place the food out on a table he had cleared for the occasion.

"I don't doubt it." Then, looking at Joshua for the first time, added, "Don't mind her. She heads the unofficial 'Morals Gang' in Hellhole. Even duly elected sheriffs have been known to quail at the sight of her."

"Which is why we gave up on sheriffs and got a Federal marshal," Cougar added. "One who can't be run out of town after every election. Don't let her bother you. She runs a respectable boarding house and a small eatery. She's cheaper than the Regent and makes chicken pie once a week for those who don't mind her sermons."

As they removed the woven cotton coverings from the still-warm dishes, Joshua made an observation.

"I onest heard a preacher give a mighty fine sermon. He was talkin' aboot the evils of 'gluttony,' an' how a feller wid en' empty belly was more likely to git into heaven than was one wid a full belly. It went over real well, 'cause he was a jawin' to a company o' Rebel sodgers what ain't ate a meal in three days. An' was like as not to cume face to face wid their Maker inny moment."

"His name wasn't Ward by any chance, was it?" Claw half teased as he hobbled out to join the company.

"I cain't remember his name, but he was a big, tall fella. The kind what lets his nose lead him to a cabin four miles off."

"I don't doubt it."

"Sit down and eat," Fiz ordered.

The fixings of fried chicken, boiled potatoes, gravy, grits and corn bread were served, consumed and fingers licked clean before anything else was said to spoil the supper.

"I'm feeling better," Claw declared. "It's a wonder what a good meal will to."

"But before you ever got to that 'healing meal,'" Fiz snarled, "you had your wounds cleaned and bandaged. To say nothing about a hefty dose of laudanum and several hours sleep."

"He's afraid with any more testimonials like that," Cougar joked, "Ma will hang out a shingle and go into competition against him."

"She might just do it, too," Claw agreed, elucidating Joshua. "Like a certain doctor we all know, Ma has a taste for the finer things in life."

"Is there a 'Pa'?" Joshua inquired.

"None we've ever known."

"Then," the mountain man declared happily, "They outta quit their grousin' and git hitched up. When he's out fixin' up broke bones or collectin' fees, she kin treat whoever comes in all bust up."

"Now there's an idea, Fiz. Ma's not a bad looking woman... if you like that sort."

"We all know the 'sort' you like, Claw," Fiz hissed in an unfriendly manner. He was ignored.

"Better yet," Cougar pursued, "Fiz, you ought to tend to the doctoring and let Ma do your bill collecting. I never knew anyone yet who stiffed her out of her room rates or failed to pay for a home-cooked meal."

"O' courst," Joshua joined in, thus forever casting his lot on the wrong side of Phillip Ward, "If she's Ma, an' they ain't no young'uns around, people will git to wondering. Better see what you kin do aboot that, right quick."

Fiz's hand slapped down on the table, spilling a glass of wine. The red liquid immediately stained the tablecloth. A gasp of horror escaped the lips of all picnic goers.

The wrath of Ma Smith was renown throughout Ford County and reputedly as far away as Hays and Topeka.

"I'm going back to bed," Claw announced.

"I have to go to work," Cougar remembered.

"I have a baby to deliver," Fiz declared.

"I'll soak it," Joshua decided. "My own ma a'ways said, 'they's onlyest two sure cures in this world for the ills of a body: soakin' an' drinkin'. If soakin' don't work, try drinking a barrel o' water.'"

"And if that doesn't work, try drowning yourself in the barrel. Never known a patient to rise from the dead and complain about anything," Fiz sourly observed.

"Which is why us mountain folks gits to be so long-lived," Joshua concluded.

"Which reminds me," Cougar shot back over her shoulder to Claw as she hurried away from the scene of the crime. "I had the tub in the Lowdown emptied and scoured. You might just take a tip from Joshua's ma and come on over for a bath."

"Yeah. I might just do that," Claw promised through lying lips.

The marshal retired, the saloon owner went to oversee her business, the physician departed, bag in hand, for place or places Unknown, leaving Joshua Jackson alone with the remnants of supper. He did not mind cleaning up, nor did he shirk from the nearly impossible duty of attempting to get a red wine stain out of a cotton tablecloth.

Alternately humming and whistling, he cleaned the dishes, wrapped the leftovers in a cloth then set them by the window to keep cool. The tablecloth he duly soaked, with calm expectation of success.

Had any of the three asked him why he was so inexplicably happy, when they had mercilessly abandoned him to mess duty, his answer would have been simple and straight forward.

"Well," he would have drawled, blue eyes sparkling with intensity, "I never done minded payin' fer what I get, an' I done ate good. But what makes me feel like hummin' an' whistlin' is that you all left me alone in the doc's office. They's a heap o' things a feller could take an' mebbe git some money fer. You three done left me an' never onest reckoned on me stealin'. If that ain't a vote o' confidence, then I ain't a Virginian an' that ain't a R'publikin in the White House."

His astonishing and totally unexpected knowledge of politics would obfuscate the more important sentiment he had expressed: they trusted him. The three most important people he would ever meet; the three people Mr. Joshua Jackson would grow to love more than any blood kith and kin he left behind in the Allegheny Mountains, had accepted him into their family without ever questioning his credentials as a friend.

Without knowing, the marshal and the lady and the doctor has paid the mountain man the highest compliment in the world.

CHAPTER 13

The marshal was released the following morning. The explanation for his dismissal came in the following statement: "I need the room."

Claw knew better than to ask, "Need the room for whom?" and made good his escape. Freedom was never sweeter to a man released from prison.

He tried the Marshal's Office and found it empty. His bed did not appear to have been slept in. He did note, however, the pillow was missing and was thus forced to reconsider Fiz's statement that the pillow in his back room had come from Claw's own bed. He resolved to retrieve it the moment he was certain the physician had departed on some long, complicated case.

Attempting a rescue while Fiz was within striking distance did not strike Claw as a particularly good idea.

He was glad to note, however, that his feral cat gave him a loud welcome home and a flick of her tail as a hello. He stooped, taking care not to aggravate his injuries and summoned the cat by rubbing thumb and forefinger together.

The cat stared at him with a look straight from the pages of a Gothic novel. He abandoned the attempt to appear charming.

"Come over here, cat," he growled, forgetting, for the moment, what he had named her - and why.

The feline hissed, arched her back and disappeared, to reappear a moment later with a mouse between her teeth. The tiny rodent was still alive and struggling, apparently no worse for its ordeal than a nip in the skin behind its neck.

"I see," the wise old lawman observed from his lofty height. "All business until we get reacquainted again. All right."

This time, he held out his hand without gesturing with his fingers. Miss Cougar surveyed him long and hard, finally deciding in ancient wisdom and shared feline consciousness he was harmless. She stepped forward, one paw inching along behind the other. When she was within a half foot of him, her jaws parted and the terrified mouse was dropped into his hand.

"Thank you. Good job!" Claw praised.

Her work for the day complete, the cat turned, crossed the room, leapt up onto the neatly made bunk, curled into a ball and promptly went to sleep.

"Out of the mouth of babes," Claw unwisely quoted.

He was young and it was problematic which would be his undoing first: a gunfighter's lightning-fast draw or his own sharp tongue. With wisdom would come the savvy to turn faster guns than his away from Main Street; with age would come a blunting of his wit.

The odds were stacked against him.

Taking the mouse to the door, Claw held the creature up to the bright morning sun and inspected it for damage. He wiped the bit of blood off the fur with fingers wet from his mouth. Then, checking to be certain Miss Cougar was not watching, he bent over and released the mouse.

"Let this be a lesson to you," he warned in his lawman's voice. "Don't come back." Then, with more mischief than sense, he encouraged, "Go across the street. That's where you belong." He might have added, "If the Lowdown is overrun by vermin, my cat and I will both be invited over," but did not.

Thus proving the odds could sometimes be beaten.

Temporarily, at least.

"Howdy, Marshal," sang a familiar voice. It was too friendly to be anyone he knew intimately, which shortened his list of possibles considerably. Turning, he saw the jaunty walk of Joshua Jackson coming toward him and grinned.

"Howdy, Joshua."

"The doc sprung you, did he?"

"He did. How'd you do last night?"

"I made out fine."

"Find the bed comfortable?"

It was a casual question, meant to sound no more like an interrogation than a man wishing another good day. Claw knew however, by a quick observation of the tight corners at the foot of the bed, no one had drawn down the blanket. Even if Joshua had bothered to straighten the bed clothes upon rising, he could not have duplicated the marshal's military corners in exactly the same way as they had been performed more than a week gone by.

Joshua had been given permission to sleep in the Marshal's Office and it would be logical, even practical, for anyone to assume he had slept in the marshal's bed. Only Claw could know he had not. He therefore challenged Joshua to offer an easy, convenient lie. Whether he opted for the truth or not would tell the tall lawman a thing or three about his new deputy.

In the eyes of the law, a lie was a lie, on the same order as a man's word was his bond. If one were given easily, than the other was equally suspect.

"I ain't much fer beds, one way or t'other, sir." He paused a moment as if contemplating the quality of the mattress, then continued when the marshal made no immediate reply. "One sagged in the middle, one sagged at the foot an' the third had a board removed from the head."

"What beds are you talking about?" came the exasperated question.

"The ones in the jail cells. What did you think I was talkin' aboot?"

"I thought you would sleep... in my bed. In the bed in the corner."

"Pshaw," Joshua muttered through playful lips. "I weren't gonna sleep there."

"Why not?"

"I reckoned that was Miss Cougar's bed."

If a hole had opened up on Main Street, Claw Kiley would have jumped into it with no regrets.

"The cat's bed," Joshua clarified with undisguised glee and a wicked gleam in his eyes. "The other Miss Cougar told me the cat's name. She seemed real tickled aboot it."

If a volcano had begun spewing forth lava over Hellhole, the Marshal would have volunteered to take a closer look at the red eye.

"What'd you say we get some breakfast and then I'll show you around?"

Joshua accepted and ordered flapjacks at the Regent without ever once pausing to consider he had already eaten six fresh eggs and drunk half a pail of milk this morning before the sun had risen.

"This here is Joshua Jackson," Claw introduced John Walker, the 14-year-old waiter, to the mountain man. "He'll be working for me, so if you see him around, feel free to call on him for anything."

"I'll surly do that, Marshal," the boy acknowledged. "And I'll tell cook an' the others, too."

"Be obliged if you did that."

As other citizens drifted in and out of the restaurant, Claw introduced Joshua, and occasionally himself, never failing to use the word "deputy" in the introduction of his partner. When they had nearly finished eating, Joshua wiped his face with the napkin provided and shook his head.

"I never said I was gonna wear that deputy's badge o' yourn."

"No," Claw agreed. "You never did."

"I know what yer doin'."

"Is that a fact?"

"That's a fact."

"Gonna enlighten me?"

"If I go to work fer you an' don't wear that badge, I'm still free to leave inny time I choose. But you tellin' all them folks I'm yer deputy puts a different light on it. You know I cain't go home knowin' there's them what knows what I was here. Shoot, if my kinfolk git to know I was actin' as yer deputy, they'd string me up, jist fer the principal o' it."

"Yeah. That's so. So that makes us even. You were one up on me this morning, you know."

"No," Joshua drawled. "I figured I was two up on you."

"The day's early."

Which came as close to evening the score as the annals of Hellhole were ever likely to see.

Claw paid for their meal and they left, he first, Joshua following.

Neither man had a complaint in the world.

They walked the town, Claw pointing out places of interest, spots of concern.

"I make rounds in the morning and before I go to bed."

"That's twice a day?" Joshua asked, making a valiant effort to comprehend all he was being told.

"Generally," Claw admitted. "Over here is the bank. Check the front door, then walk around the back. As you're walking, look up and be sure the windows are closed. I've had the owners place bars there, but you never know when some damn fool'll take 'em down - to air the place out."

Joshua snorted in due appreciation.

"I always keep my eyes open for horses saddled nearby - or fresh dung outside the bank. Bank closes at four. Shouldn't be anything fresher than five or six hours old by the time I check. If I see anything newer than that, it makes me suspicious."

"Good thought," the new, badgeless deputy agreed.

"When we get 'round to the side streets, I'll show you where Herbert, the bank president lives. Anything goes wrong, he gets hauled out of bed. He'll bluster a lot but don't stand on ceremony with him."

The absent "Mister" before Herbert was not lost on the listener.

"He rub you wrong, did he, sir?"

"He's all right, for a banker, I suppose. It's just that those types don't see things the way you and I do. Sometimes they have to be jostled a little."

"I expect that makes you a popular man."

Claw could not tell in the mountain man's voice whether he meant he had made an enemy out of the banker or if Hellhole's citizens appreciated his efforts.

"Lowdown generally opens its doors around ten in the morning. mebbe sooner. Miss Bradburn doesn't have a regular barkeep at the moment, so it might be later until she hires one. There's been some question about how late the law allows saloons to stay open." He paused to catch Joshua' eyes, then grinned. There was about his expression both school boy and rogue. "Some say ten o'clock, some say later. I expect Miss Bradburn'll close up when business gets thin. The last couple of lawmen were accustomed to getting a little something on the side from the previous owner of the Lowdown, allowing him to keep the lights on. We don't have any of that around here, now."

The last was spoken with ominous warning, but it was not directed at Joshua as much as any listening spirits.

"What's good for one is good for all," Claw continued as they resumed their walk. "No favorites. There's another saloon in town - the Wolf Pelt - I'll show you where it is. It's rough and it's dirty but Blade is all right. You'll get along with him. He'll call if he needs you. If he doesn't call, that means he or one of his regulars can handle it.

"I don't interfere where I'm not needed. Don't see a point to it. This is a tough hider town, Joshua, and men are used to wild ways. Long as they keep the law, I'll keep the peace. They start getting vicious or breaking things up - or too loud to let a decent woman sleep - an' I lock 'em up.

"Those that can't pay off the damages they inflict, work it off next morning. Or as long as it takes. They sleep in the jail at night. They hurt someone bad, I hold 'em over for the circuit judge."

Joshua raised an eyebrow and stared up at the tall youth.

"You ain't got no book nor some rules a feller could bone up on?"

Claw took his meaning.

"Yeah, there's lots of books filled with laws. We got one or two lawyers here who can probably quote each one, chapter and verse. We got a circuit judge by the name of – Jackson – like yours, come to think of it - who comes by this way every so often - or if I wire him to come down. He's got an assistant I haven't met by the name of Brookstone. Either can sit a case. Don't know about Brookstone but Judge Jackson's a good man. It wouldn't surprise me that if I threw a lawyer in jail for spittin' on the boardwalk, he'd give him two years up at the State Penitentiary."

Joshua' eyes shifted down to the dirt street.

"Ain't got no boardwalk," he observed. "I'd say, charge 'em wid exposin' themselves in publik. Wouldn't want 'em gettin' off on no tech-no-kality."

Claw laughed in agreement.

"Where'd you pick up that word? It's a good one. I'll have to remember it."

Joshua accepted the compliment but declined to answer. They moved on.

"I like to make rounds," Claw continued. "It gives me a chance to get the feel of the town. Gets to be I can sense when something's wrong. You'll get that way, too. Not first off," he added.

"I don't know," Joshua demurred, scratching his chin. "Yer a town man, sir, an' I'm a mountain man. Don't know that I ever will git a sense o' what's right and what's wrong."

"You already have that sense. It's a feeling about the town I was speaking of."

The deputy turned his back to Claw to tip his hat to a lady walking by. She nodded politely and hurried on.

When they had finished walking the streets, the law men returned to the office.

"Here's where I keep the key to the gun rack," Claw demonstrated. "They're here for you to use."

"Got my own rifle."

"The government pays for the ammunition. I'll introduce you to the shopkeepers. You get what you need and I'll mark it down on my expense account."

"Gov'ment squawk about it?"

Claw sat at his desk, flipped through some wanted posters then looked up.

"Does a bird have wings?"

"'bout what I thought."

"They pay for the coffee, too, so I always keep a pot on."

Joshua considered a moment, then crossed to the pot-bellied stove and stared at the coffee pot with knowing eyes.

"I'll take over the chores o' makin' the coffee, sir." Claw started to protest then decided better of it. "You like it stout. I'll make you 'Jackson'-style coffee you can stand a spoon up in."

"That's what I'm afraid of."

"Which 'ill make it more drinkable than what's been in this pot befer."

"You think so?"

"Does a duck like water?"

"Since I'm only paying you ten dollars a month, I don't see any harm in your taking on odd jobs here and there, if you've a mind," Claw continued along his original line. "Just run it by me before you go off on any long trips. Two days off a month. If it's not busy, I won't look for you. When the hiders come to town, we sleep standing up."

"How many days off a month do you git?" Claw started to reply, then said nothing. Joshua nodded. "'bout what I figured."

The mountain man waked around the room, getting the feel of the office now that the homeowner had returned. Where last night he has slept among ghosts and creaks and half-dreamed conversations between men he did not know, the presence of Claw Kiley chased them all away. Had he been blindfolded and did not know better, Joshua Jackson would have sworn he had been in two different locations.

It was a lesson and he marked it well. Claw Kiley belonged here, and Claw Kiley was the law. But without Claw Kiley, the haints returned and the law dissipated like swamp gas with the rising of the sun.

Without Claw Kiley, Joshua Jackson was an interloper.

"I'll make us some coffee," he announced suddenly, startling himself as well as Claw.

"The well's out back. And so is the privy."

"Found 'em both last night, thankee, sir."

Hellhole was home for a time. Whether those days and nights would stretch into months, then years, only the fates dictating fast draws and outlaws knew.

They drank coffee together then admitted the hair on their chests had grown an inch for the partaking of the hot beverage. That ritual complete, Claw settled himself down to write reports and Joshua went for a "stroll."

The first place his wandering boots took him to was the stable. Whistling as he approached, Bark Barker heard the music and came out to greet him. There was a momentary period of appraisal before the newcomer spoke.

"I'm workin' fer Marshal Kiley an' he tells me the State o' Kansas will put up my horse."

"If what you say is so, then I expect the State of Kansas will do just that. But I don't have no dealings with the State. I give the marshal a bill end of every month and he pays it. I never asked him where the money came from. That's his business an' I don't go pokin' my head in anyone's business save my own."

"Friend, that's a powerful fine way fer a man to live. My name's Joshua Jackson."

He held out his hand and the two men shook.

"Barker's my name; people just call me Bark. You be deputyin' some, then?"

"I will. When I'm needed. But I'll keep my eyes peeled fer inny odd jobs what comes along. Legal ones," he added with a wink. The humor was lost of the stableman.

"I hear of anything, I'll let you know. You want I should give your stable bill to the marshal, end of every month?"

"What's it run to?"

"I give him a break, he being the law. Five dollars a month. That includes stall, feed and some rubdowns. He comes in all tuckered out, I'll rub the horse down, clean 'em up. He has time, he does it himself."

"How much off iffn I do all my own rubdowns an' I hep' ya out around here doin' chores? I'll clean the stalls an' do the exercisin' of them what needs it. Been known to do a little horse doctorin', too, if that ain't steppin' in on Fiz Ward's territory."

Bark snorted and shook his head.

"Fiz Ward don't do no horse doctorin'. I've seen him deliver a foal now an' again but I don't call him regular."

"He's too good fer it, ugh?"

"He says he's too busy. I suppose he is. He's a good doctor, though."

"Where's he frum?"

Bark paused to consider the question.

"I never asked. He's not one you sit an' jaw with. It ain't that he's unfriendly. Calls a mighty good square dance." At which Joshua' eyes sparked.

"That a fact?"

"It is."

"How long he been here?"

"Drifted in after the War sometime. He musta had some money 'cause he bought that building right off and set himself up in business. Bought a horse and buggy, too. Paid cash. Didn't argue none on the price. He puts the horse up here and pays regular on it. Complains some about it. I learnt not to pay him no mind. We git along fine."

"Who's his friends?"

"I don't know as he's got any close friends. Seen him eatin' at the Regent a time or two with the marshal. Them both bein' educated men, I suppose they find things to talk about."

"You say he knows his doctorin'?"

Bark weighed the question.

"I heard it said.... Now, who was it? Oh, that's the fella. He was passin' through. Name was Joe Morgan. Tradesman. He went up to see ol' Fiz and tried to sell him some of his wares. Fiz wouldn't have none of it. Said what he had was no better'n what he could make himself. Looked at Mr. Morgan's catalogue, though. And bought some 'instro-ments' even that tinker didn't know what they was for. Expensive, too.

"That fella, he asked Fiz what he was buyin' 'em for, since he was the only doc around and he said he got a lecture for his trouble and almost lost the sale. He come by once again, last year. Had a cart full of books. Found them back east, I guess, an' had 'em shipped to Saint Louie. Peculiar thing, that."

"What's pe-culiar?"

"Joe said Fiz's name was in some of 'em."

"You mean, they was his books to begin with?"

"That's what I thought he meant, too, but it weren't. He said Fiz had writ 'em. I thought it must be some other fella by the same name."

"What'd this Joe fella say to that?"

"He said he thought it was the same one, all right. Why you askin'?"

Joshua wandered away to stare at the animals Bark had out in the corral. He pointed to one at the furthest end of the enclosure.

"How old's that paint horse?"

"Two years, no more."

"How much I git back iffn I trade you my horse fer that paint?"

"In cash money?" came the suspicious query.

"I was thinkin' o' stable rent."

Bark ran his hand over his sharply-chiseled and well-stubbled chin, considering the proposition.

"You trade me fair, horse for paint, 'an do the chores, like you said - when you have time - make it three or four days a week - an' I'll put your animal up fer - make it two dollars a month."

"Cain't ask no fairer than that. I'll jest take a looksee at that critter befer I make up my mind."

Joshua slipped under the lower bar and walked toward the paint. The animal eyed him placidly, swishing its tail with unconcern. When the man was within kicking distance, it laid back its ears and lashed out with a rear leg. Having anticipated the action, the deputy deftly avoided the kick.

"Well, I ain't askin' to git friendly on the first date," Joshua crooned gently. "You mind iffn I jest take a look at yer feet, young'un?"

When the brown-and-white made no further attempt to fight, Joshua lifted up one leg after the other, inspected the frog, ran his hand up the leg bones, then stared, eyeball to eyeball with the horse.

"I 'spect you never cottoned to do no deputyin', so that makes us even. We start out on the right foot wid one another, you figure we kin git along?"

When the paint dropped its head for a scratch behind the ears, Joshua accepted the proposal.

"I treat you right an' you do the same fer me. I ain't never not got along wid none o' yer kind. Generally find 'em better company than the two-legged variety."

Reluctantly leaving the horse behind, Joshua returned to Bark.

"I'll do 'er. Here's my hand on it, an' I'd appreciate you writin' on a piece o' paper I done bought 'er frum you, fair an' square."

"I'll have the bill of sale writ up for you next time you come by. You got papers on the horse?"

"There ain't no one lookin' fer that horse." Joshua hesitated then added, "You kin ask Marshal Kiley iffn you want."

"I'll ask him and if he says it's all right, we got a deal."

"I'll jest do some cleanin' in the stalls now," Joshua decided. "I a'ways said, 'they's no time like the present' to git a job done."

"Pitch fork is in the rear. Soiled hay goes out back. You'll see the pile."

"My nose'll take me right to it," Joshua agreed. "Cain't never complain aboot the work or the smell, 'cause it means a man's livin' wid creatures what'll give its heart to ya fer a kind word an' a soft saddle blanket."

To which Bark agreed and made himself a new customer and not incidentally, a friend.

CHAPTER 14

When the shooting began at 9:30 P.M. neither the marshal nor the deputy had to be summoned. Both jumped up from their chairs in the Marshal's Office and headed toward the door. Joshua was closer and went out first, Claw right behind him.

"Lowdown!" he said.

Claw passed Joshua on the run, not because he had longer legs but because the shorter man pulled up and let him by. It was the marshal's job to lead. He had earned that right. No words were necessary to explain that unwritten law.

Bursting through the swinging doors, gun drawn, Claw looked around with his eyes, but his head was already facing the direction in which the gunfire had come. Two men were standing in the rear of the saloon. Both were strangers to him. One had his arm around the waist of a saloon girl.

"Stand back," the outlaw ordered. His words were garbled, for a portion of his jaw was missing. An old, ugly scar replaced the area where bone and live tissue had once made him a handsome man. His clothes were dirty and he wore a sun-bleached kepi, which might once have been either grey or blue, pulled low over his eyes.

"Let the girl go," Claw ordered. There was no room for compromise, no possibility of misunderstanding his intent. "What happened here?" he asked of Cougar, who stood behind the bar.

"They came in through the back," she explained, her own voice calm and even. It was the voice of experience, rather than unconcern. "I caught them trying to open the safe."

"We want money," the second outlaw warned. He was dressed like his partner, though his coat bore dull embossed "U.S." buttons. Two were missing, giving him an unbalanced look. "Give us two hundred dollars and we let the little lady go."

"My name's Claw Kiley. I'm a United States marshal. I don't bargain. Release her. Now."

"U.S. marshal? I didn't know there was a U.S. marshal in Hellhole."

"You do now. Let her go or I'll put a bullet between your eyes and you'll have a scar that'll have to do its healing under Boot Hill."

"You'd kill me, Marshal?"

"Soon as look at you."

"We mebbe served together, Marshal," the man with the kepi offered. "Chickamauga? Nashville? With General Thomas?"

Claw's face remained immobile.

"So?" he questioned. "What's that got to do with this?"

"Thought you might... have some understandin'."

"The only thing I'm understanding right about now is that you've got your arm around a woman. Let her go. Then we'll talk about old times."

"We made a mistake... didn't know there was no law hereabouts. We'll jest step back the way we come an' you fergit all about it. How's that, now?"

Claw considered the request. His face twitched with concentration. His hand wavered. He appeared to be reliving old battles. He had been called upon by one of his own. Forgive a minor transgression. Let them go and forget he had ever seen them. It did not seem too much to ask. Not for old time's sake.

When the man with the U.S. buttons on his coat made his move, Claw was ready. It required no more than a jerk of his wrist to point the gun in the right direction. He fired without hesitation, the bullet striking the outlaw high in the chest. The body hurtled backward, crashing into the wall with a thud as definite as the gates of Kingdom Come slamming shut.

Claw did not see the man fall, though his mind registered the fact. His attention was turned to the first outlaw, the scar-faced man with the kepi. The lawman had threatened to put a bullet between the abductor's eyes A promise spoken was a promise kept. He squeezed the trigger, feeling the familiar, reassuring jerk of the pistol as the projectile exploded from the short barrel.

Two events transpired almost simultaneously. The saloon girl held hostage screamed, and the outlaw behind her fired his own weapon. That bullet went wide of the marshal, striking something metallic and pinging off it, the nearly spent lead embedding into the base of the bar.

As the hostage crumpled, the outlaw, whose own face was covered in blood from the bullet that had slashed the woman before striking him, was unable to hold her. He dropped the dead weight, paused to look over his shoulder at his potential escape route, then took the third bullet from Claw's pistol in the shoulder, spinning him around. Another bullet, this one from Joshua's pistol, struck him in the spine, just below the base of the skull. He staggered, stumbled forward from the force of the blows, then crumpled into the sawdust on the floor of the Lowdown.

"Someone call Fiz!" Cougar ordered. She was closer and faster than either of the two lawmen, reaching her girl and scooping the body up in her arms before Claw or Joshua reacted.

"Get Fiz!" Claw repeated. One of the men by the batwings nodded and disappeared. Motioning the rest of the onlookers to stand back, Claw crossed to the women, kneeling down beside them.

"Is she hurt bad?" he asked.

"She's bleeding."

Dead bodies did not bleed. That was one of the first and most bitter lessons a man who carried a gun learned. If the woman's wound bled, then she was alive.

"Let me past, you damned ghouls!" Fiz snarled. A narrow opening was made, allowing him through. Wielding his black bag like a club, Fiz reached his patient. He stared at the woman, then lifted his eyes only far enough to meet Cougar's. When he spoke again, however, it was to the marshal.

"Clear this place out. You - Joshua - give me a hand. Let's get her into the back."

Claw raised from his knee and turned to the crowd with a threatening look. The taste of death was in his mouth. It would take very little provocation for him to add to the number of graves required on Boot Hill.

"Break it up; clear out. All of you."

The men moved. Fast. Only one lingered long enough to take a bottle of whisky from the bar. He was almost out the door when Claw's long strides enabled the lawman to catch up with him. Ripping the bottle from the man's slack hand, Claw raised it to the level of his own shoulder then smashed it against the wall. The glass scattered, some broken chards embedding themselves into the wood, others slashing the thief's face and neck. Droplets of whisky rained over his coat, catching the sparkle of reflected light from the inner room, as though a swarm of fireflies had descended upon him.

"Next time, you'll remember that when I say get out, that means without helping yourself to anything."

Holding his profusely bleeding head with his hand, the man sniffed a frightened apology and scurried away. It was as well he did, for death attracted death and Claw Kiley was, at the moment, the living, breathing personification of the Grim Reaper.

His chest heaving for air, the lawman took two more steps to the doors and stared out. There was no one in sight. Finally satisfied, he turned his back on Hellhole and hurried into the rear room of the saloon.

"How is she, Fiz?" he asked. Had his anger and his blood not been aroused, his voice would have quavered. There would be time for that later.

This time, the physician met the marshal's eyes.

"She'll be all right. It's a face wound. I'll get the bleeding stopped, then take her up to my office."

Had the woman been dead, Fiz Ward would have said the same thing. Only one person in the room did not comprehend that truth, which was as well, for it was to him the sentence had been addressed.

"I kin carry her, Fiz," Joshua offered.

"Yes," came the considered reply. "You can." And then to Claw, "Get out. Can't you see I have to get this dress off her?"

Claw nodded and backed away, pistol still clutched in his gun hand. Breathing hard, he crossed to the dead men, kicking each in turn to assure himself they were no further threat. Neither body exhibited independent motion. Both were bathed in crimson and bone. Neither bore any relationship to the human race. Both had grown considerably smaller in death.

When he heard the soft scuffling sound behind him, Claw whirled, eyes blazing, nerves jangled, mind praying for the opportunity to vent his pent-up emotion on a third, fourth, fifth outlaw. The scene was not through; the tension remained, like the tautness in a hangman's rope while the body hung, suspended, in mid-air.

The interloper onto the lawman's space was Cougar Bradburn. She faced him, stolid, quiet, unemotional. While he burned hot, she was cold. Not from indifference, nor from horror at the carnage.

She was his equal, his counterbalance.

"You saved a lot of lives by doing what you did," she said.

"It was my bullet which hit the girl."

"She'll be all right."

He hesitated, clearly torn. The room reeked from the sickly sweet stench of blood. The acrid scent of gun smoke burned the nostrils, stung the eyes. His nostrils flared, his blue eyes did not blink. Cougar watched his chest move, in and out, up and down. She knew he had seen death on small scales and in massive confrontations, yet never did a man, could a man, become inured to the sight of an injured woman.

"Fiz says she'll be all right." She silently thanked God that was so.

"I heard."

He was wounded inside, frightened, scared. Not for himself, but of himself. It had been a grandstand play, a foolish move, a threat carried out. He knew better than to shoot for the head. He had been carried away by the moment, by the time and the place and the badge. Right had been on his side. Wrong was the result.

"Get that riffraff out of here, will you?" Cougar asked, nodding toward the bodies. "It's bad for business. A lady has to make a living, you know." He nodded stiffly, yet did not move. "Next time," she said, "if you're going to get fancy, blow the bastard's balls off, will you? The girls could use a good laugh."

He stared at her. Slowly the color came back into his face. As sweat trickled down his forehead, a mighty roar worked its way up his throat. In a moment, both Claw and Cougar were convulsed with laughter. It was a good joke. One they would share more intimately and far longer than any physical encounter.

When the corpses had been removed and the saloon refilled with men eager to share their opinions with others of like mind, Claw and his deputy returned to the office. There was silence for a long, long time. Finally Joshua stretched, then yawned wide enough for the muscles in his jaw to crack.

Taking that as his cue, Claw rose to his feet and spoke. It was the first time he had addressed Joshua since the shooting.

"You handled yourself well back there."

"Twern't nuthin'."

"I have something to ask you." Joshua waited. When no question came, he raised an inquiring eyebrow.

"Ask away."

"Later."

"I 'spect I'll be around later," he admitted. "You want me to make rounds?"

"No." And then, "I'll talk to you in the morning."

"I reckon I'll be here then, too."

"For how long?"

In the distance a dog barked.

"Fer as long as you call Hellhole home, Marshal."

"What have I got to do with it?" There was an edge to his voice.

"Everything."

"I want you to make friends here; settle down."

"Oh," Joshua agreed, readjusting the neckerchief around his throat as though the task could not wait one more second. "I reckon I'm aboot the most friendliest Jackson they is, Marshal. Folks see me cumin', they jest a burst out grinnin'."

"I mean it."

"So do I. Now, my namesake – that would be ol' Blue Light – they say he were a right quiet man. Never spoke lest he had sumthin' to say. Rest 'o the time he clammed up like an oyster. But when he spoke, men listened. He knew the Good Book, too. Did a lot of prayin'."

"You follow his example, do you?"

He did not answer the question.

"He said – or so it's tolt – that the Genr'l believed the enemy couldn't kill him; that he could walk through the battlefield while the fightin' was fast 'n furious an' never git touched. An' you know sumthin', sir? That were a fact. No Yankee bullet ever touched him. It was whispered among the boys – that'd be the grey an' the blue boys – that God watched over him. He had a cause. It weren't slavery an' it weren't what you'd call States' Rights. It were defendin' what was his. An' you know what was his'n?"

"Tell me."

"The whole state o' Virginie. Where he were born. Where was you born, Marshal?"

"Out here somewhere."

"You an' Stonewall both have yer pe-cul-iar ways an' they's good ways. A man's ways."

"You're a Jackson, now."

"By adoption."

"Seems to me what was said of the General could be said of you. This state isn't Virginia, it's Kansas. But it's yours, now. Yours to defend."

"That's what I been tryin' to tell you, Marshal. I'm here fer as long as you are."

"What if someone shoots me tomorrow?"

The answer to that was self-evident.

"I'll find the feller and make him wish he were never born. Then I'll bury you both." He looked at Claw. "Innythin' else you want to ask, 'cuse iffn they is, we might as well set down ag'in."

"You do talk a lot," Claw agreed, putting on his hat. "We'll pursue this in the morning."

"I'll make the coffee."

Claw timed his return to Main Street to coincide with the closing of the Lowdown. Cougar was just latching the inner doors when she heard his familiar footsteps and paused for him to approach. He respectfully tipped his hat to her.

"All quiet?" she asked. He nodded.

"Got a minute?"

"I got all night."

She stepped back to let him through, then shut the doors. A single lantern was placed on the bar.

"Want a nightcap?" He shook his head.

"I've been doing a lot of thinking." Again, the silence punctuating his sentence. When he did speak again, it was not to express what was on his mind. "What's an oyster?"

"It's a shellfish, about this big," Cougar demonstrated with her hands. "It has a hard shell. You generally find them off the coast, in warm water, mostly Southern. They cluster in oyster beds. Take a knife, open it up and you can eat the flesh. They're considered a delicacy."

"Ever ate one?" She nodded.

"Lots of times."

"Any good?"

"You have to develop a taste for them," she admitted. "You can eat them raw or fried in batter."

"Where do they come from?"

"Sea coasts; New Orleans. Atlantic coast, too. Why?"

"Joshua spoke of one."

"Why didn't you ask him what it was?"

"Didn't have the chance." She nodded sympathetically.

"What do you really want to ask me?"

"Those two fellas tonight. They got in the back way?" She nodded. "That happen often?"

"I'll put a new lock on the door -"

"No," he said quickly. "That wasn't my meaning. A man wants to get in, he'll get in."

"So?"

"Comes Saturday night, I'll probably have a jail full of drunks and cowboys."

"Probably."

"That makes a problem for me."

"You want to keep some of them in cold storage in the Lowdown?"

"I was thinking about Joshua. Where he's going to sleep. You might do me a favor by putting him up nights. He could sleep in the cellar. We could rig up a bunk, whatever else he needs. I don't imagine he'd be any trouble to you."

"I don't imagine he would be. So. You want to get him out of your way by having him sleep here. In the cellar."

"Yeah."

"And I suppose he sleeps with one ear open, too. It might just be handy to have a man around. In case someone gets in the back."

"Hadn't thought of that."

"Joshua hears someone break in, he tiptoes up the stairs and stops him before any shooting starts. Before anyone gets hurt. Of course, we'd have to ask him what he thinks."

"I wanted to run the idea by you, first."

"That was wise. I appreciate it."

"What do you think?"

"I think you must trust him one hell of a lot, Claw Kiley."

"I'd trust him with my life," he said. Which was the same thing as saying, "I'd trust him with your life."

"Just how well do you know this Joshua Jackson?"

"I know he's named after Mighty Stonewall."

"Recent acquisition? The name, I mean? Didn't see any family resemblance."

Her remark took him off guard.

"You know what General Jackson looked like?"

"Every house in the Confederacy has his picture mounted on the wall."

"Kansas," he elucidated her, "went for the North."

"Do tell."

"You'll have to show me sometime. What he looked like."

They had taken the conversation as far as intended.

"See what Mister Jackson says." Then, impishly, "Will I be expected to feed him, too?"

"No," came the hurried, innocent reply. "I'll feed him."

To which Cougar laughed and bade him good night.

The proposal was put to Joshua the next morning. He readily agreed.

"You couldn't guess it to look at me, but I ain't never had no reg'lar place to rest my head befer. I take to the idee right kindly."

"I was hoping you would."

"I ain't got much gear. I kin move in there tonight."

"Wouldn't be a bad idea. You come back here for your meals."

"I'll do 'er, sir."

"I'll be... riding out this afternoon," Claw continued, the tone in his voice shifting to one of somber reflection. "Be back by supper, most likely."

Joshua wisely did not offer to accompany him.

"I'll keep an eye on the place. Hellhole'll be here when you git back."

"Thanks."

Claw's trip to the dry goods store did not go unobserved. Joshua watched from behind a building across the street. His keen eyes saw the marshal buy four boxes of ammunition for his pistol. It was as well to confirm his suspicions. If he were really going to be a deputy, he would have to read Claw Kiley like a fresh trail. Only that way would they both live to see the town grow around them.

Joshua noted the exact time Claw left on horseback. He just happened to be in the rear of the stable, cleaning out the stalls. When he was sure the marshal was gone and noted the direction he took, the mountain man cleaned his hands and went for a walk. He had his orders. Something about making friends.

It was past noon by the time Claw got where he was going. It was not a specific destination. The area he chose had no name, no spot on any map. He was not looking for *somewhere;* he was seeking nowhere.

A place of hiding; of solitude. A location where a man could scream his frustrations to the sage brush and the jack rabbits and have his one-sided conversations go unrecorded by posterity.

The area he chose was flat, but bordered in on two sides by rolling hills. It was not physical privacy he carved, but rather emotional. Within this small space, alone on a dry, worthless sector or prairie ground, destitute of human companionship, he could vent his frustration.

Perhaps more importantly than that, Claw Kiley could admit his guilt. The sage brush and the jack rabbits and the high-flying scavengers did not care that a United States marshal, in a moment of weakness, a second's indulgence to vanity, had come within a hair's breadth of killing a woman.

The outlaw with the scarred face had mocked him, challenged him. It had been a calculated gamble. He knew and the lawman knew the difference between life and death was one bullet between them. Goading Claw into firing at his head, rather than his body, increased the odds of the lead going wide in his favor. In the split second it took Claw to fire again, Scar Face could have issued him a ticket to the Pearly Gates.

Scar Face knew Claw's town was watching. The good citizens of Hellhole were standing behind the lawman. Not with him - behind him. They were judging, appraising, issuing their own silent ultimatum.

If you're so good, Marshal, accept the challenge.

You came to Hellhole to prove something, Claw Kiley. Here's your chance.

You're young and you fought on the wrong side of the War. If you want to be accepted, if you want to be one of us, put on a good show.

Any gunfighter can shoot an outlaw in the chest, Marshal. It takes a man to put a slug between his eyes.

It was not a contest between a lawman and an outlaw. It was a showdown between those who could never fire a gun in violence and he who made his living with bloodshed.

The irony which Claw Kiley never saw, never would see, was that he could face one hundred gunfighters, track dozens of bank robbers, jail innumerable drunks, break up thousands of fights and never be accepted. Not as long as there existed in the world another hired gun, one more boy seeking a reputation, a group of violent hide cutters.

Yesterday's fight was buried and forgotten. It was the moment which counted; the ever present now. Prove yourself today, Marshal Kiley. And tomorrow and the next day. The approval of the townsmen was hung, like a carrot on a stick. The lawman could snatch at it, even grab it but he could not hold it, never sup from it.

That was his destiny and his fate.

The man who wore the badge was doomed to be an outsider, an alien. An outcast. Dwell with us, these citizens invited. But not as one of us. Keep the peace, protect our lives and our property, even look upon us as friends. But never, ever mistake your place. When you stand on Main Street, you are alone, Marshal. Those are the terms of your employment, the lot you cast for yourself. Hellhole was here before you came and it will stand after you leave. Live with that knowledge or go away.

Dance alone or die.

Claw dismounted and tied his horse to a stunted, sun-dried tree. He paced off twenty feet, then set out empty bottles he had retrieved in the early morning from a refuse pile in a nameless, deserted alley behind a shuddered store. The bottles became his enemy, standing before him, mute testimony to the innocence of youth and the hurt pride of inexperience.

Six times he fired, until his gun was empty, hitting two. He was angry, his passion working into bitter fury. The man with the kepi mocked him. Claw reloaded and fired again, missing all but once. He swore at the bottles, glowered at their outline against the backdrop of sand and baranka then fired a third barrage, blasting four to meaningless bits.

Claw took a dozen more bottles from his saddlebags and set them up, then retraced his steps. Twenty strides, then he turned and fired. Two shattered, giving up their ghosts without a cry of protest. He reloaded and fired again. Nothing else mattered in his world but striking his targets. He would eradicate the memory of the bleeding saloon girl by killing the memory of her abductor's faces; the scar and the kepi and the leering, challenging eyes etched in brown, beer-bottle glass.

An hour passed, and then a second. His anger honed into hot fury and his aim steadily worsened. With each shot, Claw imagined the woman jerk back, drop onto her face, die in a pool of bright red blood. His arm twitched from weariness. The gun had become unaccustomedly heavy.

As he stood, man against memories, for another round, a voice spoke to him out of nowhere. Claw jumped, badly spooked, and spun around, face a mask of fury at the unwanted intrusion.

"Ghosts can't die, mister, because they aren't alive."

The speaker was a tall man with jet black hair. He was broad shouldered, a face scarred from life. He was alone, without a horse. A narrow, meandering track led off to the left where he had walked down into Claw's sanctuary.

"Where did you come from?" Claw demanded.

The man shrugged.

"Over the hill."

"I didn't hear you."

"You wouldn't have heard a company of cavalry coming."

"Don't know what you mean."

"Didn't expect you to."

"Who are you?"

"Who are you?" the stranger asked, answering a question with a question.

"I'm the marshal of Hellhole."

The man looked from the face to the badge, then nodded understandingly. He did not have to ask why the lawman was out alone in the desert. It was written on his sleeve.

"I've been watching you shoot. You're good," the man observed.

Claw snorted. "If you've been standing there watching me, you know I've missed more than I hit. How's that good?"

The bitterness was as palpable as the hot sun.

"You didn't want to hit those bottles. You wanted them to hit you. They can't, of course, but if the effort made you feel better, then it was worth it. Here," he offered. "Let me show you how it's done properly."

The unknown man held out his right hand. For the first time, Claw realized his companion was not wearing a gunbelt.

Rather than comply with the request, Claw hitched his own belt and squinted off into the distance.

"Where's your horse?"

"I don't wear a gun because I'm too good."

Claw jerked as though his head were on a string and an invisible child were playing with him.

"What do you mean - too good? Are you a gunfighter? I don't recognize your face." He peered closer but recognition did not come. "What's your name?"

"It wouldn't mean anything to you. No," he continued after a thoughtful pause, "I'm not a gunfighter. I've never shot a man in my life."

"Then what do you mean, you're too good?" There was irritation, challenge. Without realizing it, Claw was casting himself in the part of a townsman.

"Give me your gun and I'll show you. If you trust me."

"Why should I?"

"No reason."

Claw tried to dislike the man but could find no basis for hate. He dropped his hands to his buckle, but was shaken off.

"Just the gun." To the lock he received, the man replied, "I didn't say I was a fast draw. I'm not. I don't have to be."

The admission shot warning bells in the lawman's brain, but he disregarded them. In another place, at another time, that foolishness would have cost him his life. It did nothing now but bring a smile to the other's face as the lawman held out his pistol.

"Thank you," he said. "For trusting me. Trust is hard to find. It's an unusual - commodity." He accepted the gun, examined it minutely then nodded in satisfaction. "An efficient killing tool," he said, then added, "Note, I did not say, 'An efficient killing machine.' You, sir, are the killing machine. This is only the tool you use to perform such a job."

"My job," Claw gritted through clenched teeth, "is to keep the peace. I don't kill unless I have to."

"That is a lie."

Claw withdrew a step, his face a sweaty pale mask of anger.

"You think so, do you?"

"No. I know so. Any man who carries a gun knows that's a lie. If he doesn't, he dies fast and ugly, face down in a dusty street. You said you are a United States marshal and the badge you wear attests to the truth of these words. You've probably worn a gun since you were old enough to hold one. The fact you're still alive tells me you're a killer."

"Now, wait a minute -"

A hand was held up for silence. Claw obeyed it without question. Even in his anger he understood wisdom.

"I didn't say you liked to kill. You're being out here tells me that. If it hadn't, I wouldn't have stopped."

"Who told you to?" No answer. "Are you a lawman?"

"No."

"Ever been a lawman?"

"No."

"Then who the hell are you?"

The newcomer heaved a sigh and turned his attention to the bottles. Without warning, he raised the gun and fired. He neither took aim, nor did he hesitate until all six bullets in the gun had been fired. He hit six out of six bottles.

"Set them up again," he commanded. Claw did as he was told.

This time, the gunman stepped back five paces and fired again. He hit six out of six.

"That's pretty fancy shooting," Claw admired, handing six more bullets to the man. When the pistol was reloaded, the sharpshooter spoke.

"Got a coin in your pocket?" When he received an affirmative, he made a motion with his hand. Claw took a silver dollar from his pocket, fingered it a moment, then tossed it into the air. Before the sun had a chance to glint its rays off the shiny metal, a slug of lead was placed dead center. The marshal retrieved it, then looked questioningly at the shooter, clearly in awe.

Before he could speak, the man turned, pointed to a tree and fired five more times. Each shot hit a limb of the tree, knocking an inch off with each blow, until five inches were severed as neatly as though he had performed the operation with a scalpel.

"Is there anything you can't hit?" the townsman asked with respect.

"I couldn't hit you from where I'm standing," came the quiet reply.

"What do you mean? I'm no more than five feet away. No one could miss at that distance."

When the gun was reloaded, the man pointed the weapon at the marshal. His hand shook, then began to tremble. It required his left hand, clasped over his right wrist, to steady it.

"You asked who I am, Marshal. It's not the 'who,' but the 'what' I am which counts. I'm a sharpshooter. A circus performer. I've made my living doing gun tricks for the last - three years. Made a good piece of change doing it, too."

"You're the best I've ever seen."

"I'm not the best there is," he admitted. "But maybe close to it."

"How'd you learn to shoot like that?"

"Practice. Hard work. Like you're out here doing."

"Then why aren't you carrying a gun? A man with your skill -"

"I showed you why. And I told you why, if you were listening." The gunman held out the pistol, butt first, to Claw. "Take it back. I don't want it. I'm through with hand guns."

"I don't understand."

"I don't suppose you would. But maybe if I say a man gets tired of showing off his skill, that'd make more sense to you."

There was a silence as deep as the sky.

"Yeah," Claw agreed finally. "That makes more sense."

"A man doesn't make a living with a gun; he makes death. A man carries a gun, he's bound to use it. A man shows off in front of other men, they want to challenge him. Shooting at a target is one thing. Shooting at a man is another. I was never meant for that. It takes a... different calling."

Claw's face flushed red.

"I killed two men yesterday," he said suddenly. "They needed killing; I don't regret it. They were robbing a saloon; held a woman hostage. One of my bullets grazed her in the face. If I had better aim, she wouldn't have been hurt."

"That's why you're out here?"

Claw nodded hesitantly.

"That's part of it," he replied slowly, the words dripping with self-recrimination.

"What's the rest of it?"

"Will you teach me how to be a sharpshooter? Teach me the skill you have."

"Marshal, I don't know that it can be taught. Practice. I told you that. I also said you were good. You are. What's more, you know it. It's a common misnomer that gunfighters are sharpshooters. They aren't. All a gunfighter needs is a modicum of accuracy and a reputation; it's fear scares men off. And the soulless ability to shoot a human being without giving a damn whether he lives or dies.

"Do you think you can match that, even if you could hit a silver dollar on a cowboy's hat from twenty feet?" The sharpshooter waited for an answer which never came. Claw did not have to answer. The shame was written in his sad, yet defiant eyes. "Think again. Think real hard, because I'll teach you something even more important than fancy tricks.

"A man who uses a gun with dead-eye aim isn't a man at all. He's a cold blooded snake. A man who can perform as though he's in a circus with nothing more than applause to lose, has no right being a U.S. marshal. He's not a lawman, he's a performer. You take my meaning?"

"I take it," came the sullen reply.

The stranger suddenly laughed. Claw was so startled, he took a step back from him for fear of contagion.

Wiping tears from his eyes, the man held out his hand.

"I'm pleased to make your acquaintance."

"Why?" demanded the youth, suspecting the stranger was making fun of him.

"Because you care. Men who care about their actions are about as rare as hen's teeth out west. Where I came from, the only things which matter were a share of the gate and a reputation. I had a contract which said that as long as no one ever beat me in a shooting contest - shooting at brightly colored bottles and coins tossed into the air - I'd have a job.

"The most I had to risk was some pride and money. What do you have to risk?"

This time he waited, forcing Claw to speak. The words were begrudged.

"Getting shot. Having one of my people hurt."

"Killed," came the correction.

"All right. Killed."

"I wouldn't have your job - I *couldn't* have your job. No one could. No one but you. That makes you a unique man."

"One who almost got a woman killed."

"All right. You know what they call that in show business?" Claw shook his head, clearly puzzled. "Live and learn. Next time, you'll shoot for a target you can hit."

"Damn."

"Better than being damned."

"Where you headed?" Claw inquired in an effort to save face.

"I'm looking for a place to settle down. A place where my daughter and I can live in peace." At Claw's raised eyebrow, he added, "I'm part Indian."

"You don't look it." It was meant for a compliment and taken as such. "What's your name?"

"Never had anything but a stage name. Went by the handle of Sharpshooter Steve. The crowds liked the alliteration. 'S' in sharpshooter, and 'S' in Steve," he explained easily. "What do they call you?"

"Marshal Claw Kiley. I liked the alliteration. 'C' in Claw and 'K' in Kiley." He dared grin and Sharpshooter Steve matched it with a large, wide smile. "If you're planning on settling in Hellhole, you might think of taking a different name. If you plan on hiding your past, that is."

"Hadn't given it much thought," the former circus performer admitted. "What do you suggest?"

"Well," Claw wondered aloud, "I have a friend who'd be glad to help out. He's had recent experience adopting names. But the ones he suggests will likely either be Virginians or out of the Bible. Or both."

"Not sure I could handle either."

"You'll like him, anyway."

"I already do."

"Hellhole could be a good place to settle. Bring your wife with you?"

"My wife's dead. But I have a daughter sitting in a buggy behind that hill. She's a good cook."

"We could use that in Hellhole. Ever do any bartending, Mr. Steve?"

"No. But I can learn. Is there a job open?"

"Might require you to hold a shotgun, now and again."

"I'll fill it with rock salt."

"Lady owns the saloon. Her name's Miss Bradburn. I'll put in a good word for you."

"Appreciate it if you don't tell anyone about what I told you."

"I'll walk back with you to the buggy. Show you the road into town."

"I'd be obliged."

Claw got his horse and walked with it over the hill, the sharpshooter beside him. A young woman looking eighteen or nineteen years old watched as the two men approached. As they reached the wagon, Claw noted the striking resemblance she bore to her father.

"This is Marshal Kiley, Mary. He says there's a job for me in Hellhole."

"How do you do, Marshal," Mary said, extending her hand. Claw accepted it, then tipped his hat. She had wise eyes and a no-nonsense attitude he responded to. They were the kind of people who reminded him why he wore a gun. And a badge over his heart.

The ride back was far shorter than the ride out. When Claw had them settled at Ma Smitt's, Claw took the man to the Lowdown.

"This is Steve, Cougar. Steve Sharp," Claw introduced. "Mr. Steve, this is Miss Cougar Bradburn. She owns the place."

"Pleased to meet you, Mr. Sharp."

"Make it 'Steve,' please, Miss Bradburn." He smiled. He had a soft, gentle look she liked.

"I will, if you make it 'Miss Cougar.' Claw tells me you're looking for a job."

"Yes, ma'am."

"He says I can trust you. I'll make up my own mind, but I'll hire you on his word."

She smiled and Steve smiled. Hellhole gained three new citizens, a bartender, his daughter and a wiser lawman.

The frontier was settling down.

CHAPTER 15

"How's the new man working out?" Claw inquired, pushing back his Stetson and leaning against the bar. Cougar nodded agreeably to his close presence.

"Better than I could have hoped. He deals, too. Or says he's played cards 'some.' From what I've learned about Mr. Sharp - which isn't much - I'd say that meant he's either never touched a pack of playing cards in his life, or he's a pro. Where did you say you knew him from?"

Claw shook his head. He understood she was not asking for past history, but rather, for present impressions.

"New man comes to Hellhole, I keep an eye on him. But this one seems quiet."

"Oh?" The question was only half serious. Claw arched his brows and rolled his eyes.

"Especially when I find out he has a daughter who's making fried chicken this evening. You're invited to dinner, by the way," he added suggestively.

"By whom?"

If he laughed at her question, Claw Kiley would have been dead before he hit the sawdust on the floor.

Feigning innocence was an equally dangerous road to walk.

"Miss Mary came over to invite me. Seems she and her father found a small place to buy."

"Where?"

Claw knew perfectly well Miss Bradburn was in possession of the address. If Steve had not told her, any one of a dozen men could have supplied the information. There was little need for a telegraph within the confines of Hellhole. All a man need do was make casual inquiry in the Lowdown, and whatever he sought would be his.

The proprietor of said Institution of Higher Gossip and Communication did not even have to ask. She was easy to talk to and had been known, on occasion, to reward the bearer of news with a free beer.

Next to discovering the Mother Lode, receiving a free beer was all most men could hope to aspire to.

"Over on Dry Street. At the end, on the right. The one with the tree in the yard."

Hellhole had no church, no school, six respectable women and ten trees. If Claw had simply described the abode as "the one with the tree," she would have known exactly where he referred.

"How much he pay for it?"

Between the federal lawman, the town physician and the lady saloon keeper, it was a toss-up who knew more about what. The possessor of information was necessarily an important person. Knowledge was power in any rural town.

Two years ago, a man had been shot for holding out when asked about the cost of a freight shipment.

That was before Kiley's time. The doctor had pronounced the man dead and the circuit judge had declared the shooter innocent by a point of law referred to on the books as "unavoidable homicide."

"Twenty dollars for the house and thirty dollars for the tree," Claw informed her. He had not known the clerk but legends were larger than life in Hellhole and he did not want to become one posthumously. Cougar nodded thoughtfully. She was confirming her own information. "Give him an advance for it, did you?" the marshal pursued, hoping to gain something by the conversation other than a free beer.

"Not likely."

"Just wondered."

"If I had that kind of money to throw away, I'd buy a roulette wheel." Claw yawned and nodded his head, feigning indifference. "What would the law say about that?"

"The law would say a roulette wheel was a much better investment than a tub."

"Don't think I've forgotten."

"Forgotten what?"

"Dinner is at four. I'm supplying the wine. What are you bringing?"

"Thought I'd take you along."

Cougar made a low comment under her breath which he was not meant to hear. Nevertheless, it stood as a warning.

"Stop by the Regent before you come to pick me up and buy a loaf of bread."

"Then what'll Fiz bring?"

"Who invited him?"

"No one."

She pretended to consider the statement, but her mind had already jumped to other things.

"He's got a warehouse full of canned goods and preserves. Some strawberry jam wouldn't be a bad idea."

Here was a new piece of information. Claw turned to her with interest.

"What warehouse?"

"Don't you know?" Claw shook his head slowly. It was not good to appear too excited or it would spook off his informant. "In the lower level, below his office."

"Is that his, too?"

"Yup."

"Does he own the whole building?"

"Are you going to buy a drink?"

Few things in Hellhole were completely free. Claw poked through his vest pockets, finally retrieving two nickels. She did not speak again until he had placed them on the bar.

"He does. The ground level is unoccupied."

"Why is that?"

"I don't know. Heard he was going to rent it out to a tinware dealer, but he never did. I suppose he held it too dear."

"Where'd the tinware dealer go?"

"To Caldwell."

"Can't say I blame him. I wouldn't want a shop under the doc's myself. I don't suppose he wanted any blood dripping down into his goods."

Cougar agreed sympathetically.

"Blood rusts tin pretty badly. From what I hear."

"So what's Fiz got in that empty lower level?"

"Look for yourself."

"The windows are boarded up."

"That's because he doesn't want anyone to know."

"How did you find out?"

"Oh," she laughed. "I know a lot about Dr. Ward."

"Talks when he's drunk, does he?"

She gave the marshal a quizzical glance then moved behind the bar.

"You want that beer now?"

"I'll take a rain check if you don't mind."

She grinned and pulled the spigot. Nothing came out.

"Don't generally put a keg in until late afternoon. If I do, it goes flat by quitting time."

"I'll keep that in mind."

"Never spent much time in saloons, did you?"

"Never saw the need. Until now."

"I'll keep that in mind."

"See you later?"

"You better. And Claw?"

"Yeah?"

"I wouldn't go poking around Fiz's lower level."

"I might say the same thing to you."

Cougar picked up a beer mug and contemplated tossing it at the offender. Fortunately for the marshal, the effort would have cost her ten cents to replace the broken glass, and she forbore.

"See you later," he said with an ill-advised grin.

Miss Bradburn pocketed the ten cents and the information, then went upstairs to take a nap.

At three-fifty in the afternoon, Marshal Kiley presented himself at the Regent and ordered a loaf of bread. He did not have to wait more than a minute for a still-warm loaf, wrapped in a red-checkered cloth to be delivered.

"How much do I owe you?" he asked John Walker, surprised at the service. He had forgotten to order the bread earlier in the day and had anticipated a wait of over half an hour while the dough was prepared, had risen and was baked.

"Compliments of the house," came the reply.

"You mean, I don't owe you anything? Since when has the Regent started giving out free meals?"

"It's meant as a present for the new bartender over at the Lowdown."

"A present from who?"

"From 'the management.'"

"I'll be darned. Word travels fast. Thanks. I'll be sure and tell Steve."

"No, sir. No call to do that. Just enjoy."

Claw nodded his thanks and left, neither considerably older nor wiser than when he entered the restaurant.

Walking down the street with his precious gift, Claw made a valiant effort to avoid the ruts. He was less than successful with horse manure, much of it being hidden under an accumulation of dust. If Hellhole had few trees, it more than made up for that omission by covering each building with a quarter inch of dirt. While dirt did little in the way of providing shade, it was as much at home in Hellhole as were the six hundred and thirty-three unlicensed dogs roaming the streets.

If either dust or dogs were counted as "heads" in the upcoming 1870 census, the city could be incorporated as the most populous in Kansas.

"Afternoon, Sally," Claw acknowledged as he marched through the swinging doors of the Lowdown. "Miss Cougar around?"

"She told me to tell you she'd be down in a minute."

"I hope she's not taking a bath," he grumbled. Fortunately, his breach of etiquette was ignored by the saloon girl.

"It'll be nice to have a bartender," she replied, instead. "Steve seems like a nice man. I met his daughter this afternoon. He came to show her around."

"Oh." Then, upon consideration, Claw inquired, "He brought her inside the Lowdown?"

"Sure. Miss Cougar gave them both the Grand Tour."

"What did Miss Mary say?" He was more curious than he could account for.

"That as far as 'Grand Tours' went, while most girls would prefer Paris or London, she was right proud to be shown around the Lowdown Saloon."

"That must have surprised Cougar some."

Sally nodded. "She said *she'd* rather be in Paris or London."

They laughed together. It was a shared secret, although what they thought the other was thinking was as far off the mark as Hellhole was from the Continent.

"I see you picked up the bread," Cougar remarked from the top of the stairs. Claw looked up, took in the tall redhead's shapely figure, attired in a new red dress, and whistled appreciatively.

"Yes, ma'am."

He did not take his eyes off her as she descended. He did not breathe until she was beside him and only then to gasp a brief, "You look fine."

"Thank you," the proprietress responded with veiled amusement. "You don't look so bad yourself - for a man who hasn't yet made the acquaintance of Mr. Bathtub."

"Who's he?" Claw asked innocently as Cougar slipped her arm through his and they turned toward the door.

"Someone coming in on the stage," was all Sally caught before the two disappeared.

The walk to Dry Street took ten minutes and might have been accomplished in five, had not they been followed by a pack of hounds nipping at their heels. Claw made a gallant effort to keep them from sinking their teeth into his date's long dress and subsequently ripping the fabric. Failing in that, he resorted to a violent explosion of hand waving and threats.

"I'm sorry," he apologized as they hurried on before the canines could regroup.

"You heard the expression, 'it rains cats and dogs'?" Cougar asked, sidestepping to avoid a hole deep enough to hold one dead horse, two lawmen or thirty-six dogs. "It's true enough, I guess. The only problem is, when the cats and dogs sink into the ground, it doesn't do much for the water table."

"Neither do the privies," Claw sniffed. "Anybody ever heard of filling some in?"

"In Hellhole?" Cougar snorted. "That takes effort. No one thinks the town will be around long enough to bother."

"That being their attitude, why do they dig holes in the first place?"

"Who said they dug holes? Way this place was set up, the outhouses were positioned around the most convenient depressions and the buildings were placed by them."

"Never thought about it like that."

"You ever been to any place different?"

Claw hesitated, then shrugged.

"I don't know. You?"

"New Orleans is more than a sight different than Hellhole," she admitted, shifting the weight of the wine bottle from one hand to the other.

"You miss it?"

"Do I miss New Orleans?" Cougar thought a moment, then hitched her shoulder. "I miss what I never had. Does that count?"

"What is it you never had?" he probed, steering her across the street and through a narrow alley.

"A chance. Respect. Someplace I could call my own. Money. Clothes. A family. Want me to go on?"

He stopped and looked down into her deep blue eyes.

"I wouldn't have asked if I didn't want to know."

Cougar hesitated then resumed her walk.

"An education. A chance to travel. Good friends. Money. I miss the food; I miss chicory in my coffee. I even miss the smell of the river, the water birds, the big steamboats coming and going along the Mississippi. I guess a girl could stand on one of the piers and do a lot of wishing about foreign places.

"There was always something happening in New Orleans; bands playing on the wharfs, men dressed in top hats and silk vests; men in sheepskin or covered in buffalo robes. People coming and going. There was both a sense of newness and oldness there. Tradition and..." She paused, tried the word on her tongue, then added, "Innovation." They walked another moment before she concluded, "No. I can't stay I miss it."

There was a sadness in her voice, a sense of longing which did not match her words.

"What about you, Claw? Is there anything you miss?"

"Maybe I haven't lived long enough to miss anything," he mused thoughtfully. "I've spent so much of my life looking forward, I can't say I rightly miss anything. I want what I have now. To me, that's something new. It's exciting. I want to grow with Hellhole; to watch others grow around me. To take a stand and see it mean something."

"If someone gave you one thousand dollars," she demanded suddenly, "What would you do with it?"

"Put it in the bank."

"Why?"

"To prove I had faith in my own ability to defend it from any who would try and rob it." She made no reply. "What would you do with that kind of money?" When her silence persisted, he prompted her. "Fix up the Lowdown? Put on some permanent siding? Shore up the cellar with cement? Buy a roulette wheel?"

"No."

"Well?"

"I'd put a bounty on a man's head."

"What man?"

"I don't have one thousand dollars, or I might tell you."

The couple emerged from the alley and resumed their walk on an even more poorly constructed street.

"You want me to kill a man for you?" Claw asked as they walked.

It was not an idle question and she appreciated his sincerity.

"Would you?"

"Not for money."

"For what, then?"

"Maybe because you figure he needed killing."

"What if I wanted him shot in cold blood? Shot in both knees, then gut shot? What, then? What if you couldn't kill him legal?"

"This fella you're talking about. Is he in New Orleans?"

"Maybe he doesn't exist at all."

"Then maybe I'd shoot him twice - in the belly."

Cougar Bradburn stopped, looked south for a long moment, then let out a deep sigh.

"Thanks. Maybe if he existed, he's dead now."

His hand found hers and they continued their journey.

The new home of Mr. Steve Sharp and his daughter Mary was located on a lot filled with sand, scrub grass, broken wagon wheels, dog droppings from time immemorial, and one tree. The few windows which still held glass were aglow with a party atmosphere. With "Welcome" in the air, the marshal and the saloon owner squeezed their hands together one last time, then skipped merrily into the yard.

"I count three panes of glass," Cougar remarked as Claw knocked on the door. "That's two more than I expected. I guess he got a bargain, after all."

"How long had the house been vacant?"

"'Bout half a year. The former owner was a merchant from Back East. He came out west because he was tired of 'conventional attitudes,' whatever that means."

"What happened to him?"

"A drunk shot him dead. Oh, he lingered awhile, then went out with a whimper. The bank bought the house for taxes owed and we shipped the body to Philadelphia."

"That what he wanted?"

Cougar shrugged and adjusted her bonnet.

"Who knows? There was a freight wagon heading that way with room enough for the coffin. The price equaled what was left in his estate, so off he went."

"Was he from Philadelphia?" Claw inquired with just a trace of exasperation in his voice.

"I don't remember him ever saying."

"Then why did you send the body there?"

He knew the answer before his interrogative had passed from his lips. He mouthed silently with Cougar.

"Because that's where the freight wagon was going."

"Bury me on Boot Hill," he muttered, speaking in a low enough voice to obscure the words. He need not have exerted the effort.

"Oh, I don't intend on burying you anywhere. Someone shoots you in the street, we'll just drag you into an alley and let the dogs have at you. If you're considerate enough to get yourself ambushed on the trail, that's where you'll stay."

It was party time and Miss Bradburn was in a festive mood. The fact she dampened Marshal Kiley's enthusiasm seemed lost on her.

"Welcome!" Steve greeted as he pulled back the thin door. Like a gentleman, he had waited until the conversation lulled before welcoming his guests. "Come in."

He bowed at the waist, then stepped back, a large grin on his handsome face. The lady, then her escort obliged him by entering. They were immediately joined by Mary. Attired in a new calico dress and simple moccasins, her large-boned frame, open, honest eyes and bright smile transformed her easily into a feminine version of her father.

"How kind of you to come."

"The pleasure is ours."

"Please sit down. May I take your cloak, Miss Bradburn?"

"Certainly."

Cougar handed over her outer wrap, then sat in the one chair of honor, so designated by its high back and two solid oak arms. Not only was Cougar the one woman invited and so entitled to the best seat, she was also Steve's employer. As such, it behooved her to accept that which was her due.

"Would you like some coffee, Miss Bradburn or a glass of water before dinner?"

"I'm fine, thank you."

"And you, Marshal?"

"No," he declined, making an obvious sniffing noise through his nose. "I'll wait for that chicken. It sure smells good."

"Yes," Cougar agreed. "Did your mother teach you how to cook?"

"I never knew her," Mary replied gently. "She died two days after I was born."

"How sad. I'm sorry."

"Would you care to see her likeness?"

Encouraged by their enthusiastic nods, Mary took a small cameo from the mantle and handed it to Cougar.

"She's lovely."

The late Mrs. Sharp had indeed been a beautiful woman. Her jet black hair, sharp features and dark complexion, which the artist made no attempt to hide, were softened by her kind, wise smile and intelligent eyes.

"Very beautiful," Claw agreed, making no allusion to the woman's ancestry. If the daughter or the widower cared to elaborate, that was their choice. If not, then they were entitled to their secrets. Hellhole was not Boston. Who a man consorted with held far less importance than how he conducted himself.

Much could be forgiven in the name of westward expansion.

The arrival of Fiz and Joshua was the occasion of much loud welcoming, matched by their hosts upon entering. Neither the physician nor the deputy were quiet men by nature. Their close proximity to one another brought out their vociferous tendencies, as though they were in a shouting match, each vying for the title, "Hellhole Welcoming Committee Chairman."

While Fiz was demurely kissing his hostess' hand, Joshua plopped himself in the second place of honor, the matched, tall-backed chair without arms, but amply supplied with a hand-stitched cushion on back and seat. Claw had respectfully left it for Fiz, preferring to remain standing. Joshua, however, appeared to have no such consideration.

Had Dr. Ward been less well breed, he might have bitten the slender fingers of Miss Mary from sheer shock.

Dropping her hand faster than he would a hot potato, the elder statesman crossed to the mountain man and poked him with a stiff finger.

"Get up," he demanded.

"I jist set down."

"Get up, I tell you. That's my chair."

Joshua appeared greatly surprised. His brows furrowed together in the middle.

"I though you jist tolt me you had never been here befer."

"I haven't."

"Then how kin this be yer chair?" It was beneath Fiz's dignity to reply. Joshua pursued the point. "Does it have yer name on it?"

"No. Of course not," Fiz snorted.

Joshua made a point of settling in, then flashed his teeth at Miss Mary.

"Sure is a right comfy chair yuh got here, ma'am. I'm right honored to be settin' in it."

"Not *settin',*" Fiz corrected irritably. "Chickens *set*. Men *sit.*"

"An' I'm plum ol' glad to be doin' jist that," Joshua agreed.

"Dinner is served," Steve announced, thus sparing Doctor Ward a further grammar lesson.

As the gentlemen led the way into the dining room, Mary politely put a hand on Joshua' arm.

"If you do not mind, sir, my father does not allow firearms at the table."

Joshua immediately unbuckled his gun belt, but Claw hesitated. Seeing the marshal's dilemma, Steve quickly interceded.

"We must make an exception for these law officers, Mary," he explained in a low, half apologetic voice. "They may be required to leave suddenly and we would not wish to stand in the way of the performance of their duty."

"I don't mind, Miss Mary," Joshua began, but Claw interrupted.

"I appreciate that, sir. Joshua, it's all right for you to leave your gun in the parlor, as the lady requested, but I cannot remove mine."

He stole a glance at Cougar but she did not meet his eye. He accepted that as a tacit if reluctant approval, which it was.

Around the small wooden dining room table were placed three chairs. Steve brought in the chair with arms for Cougar, then went back for the other. That left the company one chair short.

Joshua stamped his foot on the floor, then shook his head ruefully.

"It's this bum knee I got, Miss Mary. Iffn I set too long, it gits to botherin' me. An' I a'ways digest my food better standin' up."

"There is no need for sacrifice, Mr. Jackson," she began, understanding his ploy before the others had considered the plight. "I will serve you and then -"

Before she had completed the sentence, however, the shattering shrieks of red-hot rage pierced the warm glow of the Sharp's home. Claw's shoulders sagged a moment before he responded to the summons.

"Sit down, Joshua. I'll see about it. Excuse me."

With a nod of his head to the gathering, Claw slipped away.

"For a big man, he can disappear faster than anyone I ever knew," Cougar observed.

The meaning of her sentence, referring either to a short or a long departure, was left uncommented upon by the gathering.

CHAPTER 16

The disturbance was on Main Street and it took Claw no longer than one minute, at a full gallop, to arrive. Gone were thoughts of fried chicken, warm bread and the pleasure of sitting beside the lady who had so suddenly become important to him. The sound of men's voices raised in accusation and curse, the smell of sweat and the threat of gun smoke and blood were enough to dominate any lawman's mind. In actuality, they were what he lived for: what outlined to him, in stark reality, the worth of his profession.

Any man may eat, and most men loved, but not one in a million could keep the law in Hellhole.

"What's going on here?" he called from a distance of two hundred yards. Unwilling to use his own weapon as a deterrent, Claw froze the fighters with the authority bred into his voice and instilled into his confidence by those who had put the law above their own lives.

"Who the hell are you?" one asked. He was a short, squat, dirty man, dressed in a tattered cotton shirt, ripped trousers and a hide vest with a conspicuous bullet hole in the back, just under the shoulder blades. A dark stain attested to the fact its former owner no longer required its services.

The man was a hider, a rough, tough, mean scavenger of all things saleable. His handle could have been "Bowie Knife," or "Tanner," or "Skin-Flint" and his ancestors were the buzzards and the rattlesnakes.

Claw Kiley had never seen him before, but he understood one thing perfectly as he approached. Whatever name this man went by, however loathsome his appearance, no matter his foul stench and dirtier language, he was the heart and soul of Hellhole. This hider, skinner, thief and brawler - he and the men like him - were the economic force around which the commerce of Hellhole flourished.

The year was 1868 and the town, neither incorporated nor regarded as any more than a dusty trading post for hiders, had a lot to prove. Without a railroad, and far off the beaten path of the Texas herds, Hellhole had only two claims to fame: its status as a gathering point for hiders and its unconsecrated graveyard.

There were no civic groups, no ladies charities, no newspaper, no Cattleman's Association. The bank had a reputation for being easy pickings, and more lawmen had died on Hellhole's streets than the town could count respectable women - or trees. There was an aura of violence, of hardship and broken dreams carved out of prairie dirt, tumbleweeds, baranka and bleaching skeletons.

The scattered population was unequally divided into three types. There were the respectable, "gold" folk: the banker, the few professional men, the distant moneyed ranchers, nearly all of whom looked down upon the less fortunates as being descended from the convicts Great Britain had shipped over in the years before the great War for Independence. Next followed the clerks and the laborers, the saloon girls and the lawmen, all of whom were judged by income rather than merit. Finally there were the transients: the drunks, the sharpers, the hiders.

Of all the myriad types residing, however temporarily, in and around Hellhole, the hiders and buffalo hunters were the most important. It was the sweat of their work, the skins and furs they shot, trapped and sometimes stole, which brought in the dollars. Like so many scratch-towns before her, without a viable economy, Hellhole was doomed.

Money was the true heartbeat, the pulse and soul of a town. It could rain cats and dogs and wash away half the buildings, but as long as the hides were safe, no one complained. Fire, pestilence, drought, starvation were all evils to be feared. They were natural forces to be fought and ultimately endured. But no one, including the marshal, could survive without the hides.

Hellhole was not a cow or tanning town, a manufacturing town, a shoe or clothing town. Its distinction lay in being the one great way-station between the frontier and civilization. Hides were no good if they rotted on the desert; equipment and cheap, imported Irish laborers slaving in Back East factories were worthless without leather and skins from which to make saddles, boots, vests and harness.

Violence, bloodshed, murder and mayhem could be endured, so long as the stages carried away the precious cargo to their destinations east coast destinations. The Second Great War for Independence had been fought and won. Northern factories were bursting to the seams with orders.

Before the War, it had been England which sought and bought the Southern cotton and the Western hides, but four years of civil war had seen a tremendous, unprecedented explosion in Yankee manufacturing. From guns to shoes, cotton gins to textiles, the northern states were reaping the benefits of post-war experience, the euphoria of winning and the influx of returning soldiers.

Queen Victoria loathed the idea of slavery and England had sided with the Union, but that staunch position had dragged her once proud nation to the brink of disaster. To reward her valiant sacrifice, she should have been granted the benefits which came from choosing the winning side. Her gain, however, was more intangible than substantial. England had gambled and won, but by winning the war, she had lost the battle.

While the soldiers in blue had been defending "one nation, under God, indivisible," their civilian Union brothers had been weaning themselves away from Europe. If it could be built, manufactured, invented or dreamed, the Federals were the ones to do it. Whereas England learned she could not survive without Southern raw materials, Yankeedom had discovered it could thrive without England.

Ship the cotton and the leather, construct the railroads, carve out the roads, create the western frontier towns, all to serve the new masters, the lords of manufacturing.

The hider standing with a gun pointed at Marshal Claw Kiley's midsection had never heard of Manhattan or Boston. He did not know the difference between a steamboat engine and a locomotive, but he understood how to slip the skin off a still-quivering buffalo. In the greatest and newest scheme of things, he was a prince smelling like a gutter rat.

"Who be you?" the hide-sticker demanded, eyes squinting in the brilliance of the sunset.

"Claw Kiley, United States marshal. Put down the gun. What's going on, here?"

One identification, one order, one question. Of the three, only the last held significance.

"This sonofabitch, good-fer-nuthin' bastard says he's closed his store an' won't open it till tomorree. How'm I gonna get what's cumin' to me tonight, iffn he don't open up now?"

"He came after me, Marshal!" the clerk whined, extending his arm to display a hole in the sleeve where a knife blade had severed the cloth.

"Where's your boss, Mr. Barbre?" Claw demanded. "Go and get him."

"He's gone home to eat."

"You heard what I said. Git."

"Who's going to watch the store if I run off?"

"I will."

The clerk, whose name Claw did not know, sniffed and scurried away. The two combatants and the Badge watched him go in silence. It was not until he was out of sight that the lawman broke the verbal fast.

"You'll make good to that boy; pay him the cost of getting that shirt mended."

"He was standin' in my way. Don't he know nuthin'?"

"Put the knife away."

The hider hesitated, clearly torn, then did as he was ordered. The weapon hung from a sheath which dangled between the hiders legs, giving it an evil, ominous appearance.

"Don't know you," the cutter remarked slowly, maintaining eye contact with the taller, younger man. "You new?"

"That's right."

"What you say yer name was?"

"Claw Kiley."

"Claw Kiley." There was a flavor, a taste to the words which the hider ran over his tongue, as though debating whether to split them out or swallow them.

"Where'd you cume frum?"

"Here are there."

Claw Kiley had danced a similar dance with Cougar Bradburn less than an hour ago. The tempo was different and the setting more comfortable, but the rules had been the same.

You tell me what I already know, so in the telling - or the not telling - I can decided whether or not to trust you. Whether you are worthy of my confidence.

In the case of the two skinners, they were judging whether or not Claw Kiley was worth the killing. Or the saving.

"How's cume you're a U-nited States law bastard?"

"I'm nobody's bastard."

The first hider took a step back, running the back of his left hand across his mouth. A man might fight for honor, to accept a challenge, or from boredom. He might run when the odds were against him, or if his luck were running the wrong way. But a man who would tolerate a slander, even an indirect one, against his mother, was worth, exactly, the powder to blow him to hell.

And hide skinners were notoriously cheap with their shot.

"No offense meant."

It was a backing down, a surrender without admitting guilt. How Claw answered it would determine the destiny of three men.

And the future of Hellhole.

"None taken."

The tension eased.

"Claw Kiley," the first man called. "Didn't I hear sumthin' aboot you in the Cimarron?"

"Never been there."

The hider scratched his face, then hitched up his trousers, incidentally resting his hand on his knife.

"Mebbe it were some other place, at that. Sumthin' aboot killin' the man what shot Marshal Jack Duvall, was it?"

"Might have been. People talk."

"I knew ol' Jack. He was a short fella - wid a streak of yeller in his hair. Ain't that right?"

Claw pretended to consider the question, then finally heaved a long exhalation.

"He stood about five-foot-six, was as bald as a buzzard's head and was the meanest son of a wolf I ever met."

"His wife's name were Ida, weren't it?"

"Ada."

"Right. Right ya are."

The man's hand drifted away from his knife and he turned to spit downwind. A long stream of watery brown fluid dribbled down his chin.

"Coming, Marshal! Coming!" called a man. All three turned to see an out-of-breath townsman hurrying toward them. He was waving his hand over his head in greeting, or perhaps just because he was unaccustomed to running and did not know what to do with his arms.

"If it ain't Mr. Barber," one of the hiders joked. "Know why we call him Mr. Barber, Marshal?"

To spoil the joke would have been a bigger mistake than not knowing Jack Duvall was a six-footer with brown hair, a scar over his left eyebrow and married to a woman named Ada. Of the description Claw had given, only the last mattered. In a land where women were as scarce as hen's teeth, a man's "gal" rested closer to him than anything but his gun.

"No. Why do you call him Mr. Barber when his name is Mr. Barbre?"

"'Cause the last time we was here, Phil and me give 'im a shave!"

Claw laughed until his sides hurt.

"That's a good one," he admitted. "But - doesn't that make you two boys Mr. Barber, and doesn't that make Mr. Barbre, Mr. Customer?"

There was a stunned silence, then a roar of shock shot, as true as an Injun's arrow, out of both hiders. Claw knew he had given the men a topic of conversation important enough to chew over for the next twelve months, or until their return to Hellhole.

"Don't that make us the Barber boys, now, Phil!"

"It do, or I'm pushin' up daisies," his partner agreed. "Ain't we Phil and Adam Barber!" And they would be, from this day forth. Whatever handles they had carried into Hellhole could now be said to be "pushing up daisies."

Which was a sight better than the alternatives.

"Howdy do, Mr. Customer!" Adam Barber greeted the shop keeper. "We got a crap load o' hides fer you, if you got a riverboat gambler's stake fer us."

"I do, I do," the newly christened Mr. Customer deliriously agreed. "Good to see you boys again. Sorry for the confusion. Just let me open my shop and you can bring all your hides inside."

"Yeah. Git 'em outta the rain," Phil laughed. "When, 'zactly done it rained here last, Claw?"

"Not since the Flood," the lawman remarked sagely. "Not in my time, for sure."

"Give us a hand, Claw?" Adam asked casually.

"Claw" looked down at his hands.

"You know, it's been a long time since I did any hard labor."

"Not since you been in that Federal prison, ain't that right? Say, Adam, didn't we see ol' Claw up there last time we was jist visitin' that cousin o' yern?"

"It weren't my cousin, it were yer brother. An' I know damn well we didn't see him there."

"It were some other giant, then?"

"Yeah. But he were goin' by the name o' Lincoln."

"Bet Mr. Lincoln wishes he had seen you boys up in Federal prison last year," Claw cracked.

The two hiders paused, mulling the statement over.

The War was over and the federal lawman was not holding grudges - not if the boys he had fought against were willing to keep the peace.

"I guess it weren't *Mr.* Lincoln at that," the taller of the two Barber boys decided. "But what was his name, then?"

"I guess it wasn't *Mr.* Davis, either, if I stand correct," Claw countered.

"I know who it were!" declared Phil with a happy chuckle. "It were Varina."

"And she was cussing up a storm," Claw agreed. "How 'bout you boys let me give you a hand? That way, we can get done faster and get over to the saloon."

"Let's do 'er! An' iffn you got a hand left when we're done, I'll shake it."

"Deal."

Being the one who had offered, Claw turned and grabbed a bundle of hides off the wagon. It was tied together with rope so worn from use and slick from blood it might have been sinew and not hemp.

Claw grunted under the weight, muttered a low curse under his breath, then hoisted the dead weight over his shoulder, slipping it easily to his back.

"Where to, Mr. Customer?"

The former Mr. Barber, also known as Barbre, prudently sidestepped his customers and pointed inside.

"All the way to the back, if you can make it," he politely requested.

"I'll make it twice around Hellhole, if that's what it takes for my friends to get top dollar from you."

Phil and Adam whooped an approval and grabbed bundles from the wagon.

"'Bout time Hellhole got a real law man," they remarked to one another as they followed Claw inside.

"Yessiree, he's gonna put Hellhole on the map."

It took the better part of an hour for the three men to unload the wagon. When they had finished and Mr. Customer was eagerly pouring over the merchandise, the two hiders made good their promise.

"Put 'er here, Claw."

Claw's hand met Phil's and shook it, then slipped easily over to Adam's.

"Glad to make your acquaintance."

"Yer a right fine fella, Marshal."

"Yeah. All my friends tell me so."

The three laughed again, then peered over at the shop keeper.

"We're the first in, ain't we?"

"The first," he agreed. "If I hurry, I can get these hides boxed and out by Thursday's stage."

"Top dollar fer bein' the first. Right?"

"Right."

It was Claw who answered.

"How much, then?"

"I have to count them, sort them out, check for blemishes...."

He had not finished the sentence before Phil had a knife at his throat.

"How much, then?"

Claw made no move to prohibit the hider from cutting Mr. Customer's throat, merely shaking his head as a warning.

"How 'bout giving my friends an advance on those mighty nice hides so we can drink to your health, Mr. Customer?"

The man so addressed jerked his eyes up and down so fast he might have been making a pass at any one of the three.

"Certainly. Certainly. An advance, so you boys can go over to the saloon and have a drink. Just let me get to my cash box."

The compromise was agreeable to all parties and the knife was sheathed. Mr. Customer slipped away to the counter, reached under it and retrieved a small hinged, wooden box. He removed two ten-dollar gold pieces.

"Will this do for now?" he pleaded. Phil and Adam waited for Claw to make the decision for them.

"Make it twenty-five and give them a receipt for the hides." Then, turning to the hiders, "You boys have your mark on those bundles?"

"Yes, sir. See here."

Adam indicated a knotted piece of latigo attached to each rope.

"That's our mark."

"Good," Claw approved. "Mr. Customer, count the bundles, give these boys their paper and we'll leave you to your work."

"It might take me all night...."

"They'll be here in the morning to collect their due."

"Fine. Fine."

The shop keeper counted the bundles then quickly wrote out a receipt. Both hiders made an "X" on the paper and declared themselves satisfied.

"Claw, how 'bout you and us going over and gettin drunk?"

"Sounds good. But how 'bout telling me - how many other hiders were behind you fellas?"

Phil and Adam poked each other in the sides and laughed at the foolery.

"Oh, we's the onlyest ones we ever did see, Marshal. Cain't say there's inny more followin' us."

"Yeah. But just supposin' there was - how many would you say? A dozen? Two dozen - make it twenty-four, twenty-five men, divided into, say ten partnerships?"

"Now why'd you wanna ask a question like that?"

"Pretty simple, I expect. You two represent the first hiders come in for trading. You're like the big cattle herds that drive through Texas. One herd arrives, the other herds can't be far behind. Of course," he added rakishly, "You boys are a lot prettier than cattle."

He set the hiders off on a new spasm of laughter, which continued while they walked him, arm in arm, into the street.

"Where to, ol' Claw? It's your town. You pick the place."

"Well, I don't want to appear to favor one drinking establishment over another," he mumbled, hiding a grin behind his hand. "But personally, I drink at the Lowdown."

"Why is that, friend Kiley?"

Claw had his answer ready. In point of fact, he had rehearsed it from his first day in Hellhole.

"It's closer to my office."

Amid whoops of joy and celebration, the two forerunners in the mad dash on Hellhole that opened hiding season, took their boon companion to the Lowdown.

Bursting through the swinging doors of the saloon, they quickly reacquainted themselves with the layout, then marched over to the bar. Not surprisingly, Steve was behind it and Miss Bradburn stood in front, her new place of ownership.

"Welcome, boys!" she greeted. "I'm Cougar Bradburn and I own the joint. First drinks are on the house. Make yourselves at home and don't worry about drinking the place dry. There's a new shipment due in first of the week."

Both men grinned from ear to ear, then feigned astonishment and turned to the badge.

"You allow womenfolk to own drinkin' parlors in yer town?" Phil asked.

"Allow?" Claw retorted, arching an eyebrow. "I reckon you could say that I allow Miss Bradburn to own a saloon. But then again," he added hastily, "She allows me to keep the law here. It's sort of an agreement we have."

The boys thumped him on the back and winked at Cougar, removing their hats in tribute to long-ago parents.

"Pleased to meet you, Miss Bradburn."

"And I'm pleased to meet you boys. Care to introduce your friends, Marshal Kiley?"

"This here is Phil Barber and this is Adam Barber. They're not brothers, exactly, but they are the first buffalo hiders of the season and that makes them princes around here."

"Then break out the champagne, Steve," Cougar ordered. "And just to show my appreciation of them calling the Lowdown home while they're in town, I'll only charge you fellas fifteen dollars a bottle."

"Kin we git two fer twenty-five?" Adam asked, slapping their advance on the bar.

Since the Lowdown routinely charged ten dollars a bottle, selling two for twenty-five dollars seemed a bargain all around.

"You sure can. And when that's gone, you can start a tab. I know you boys are good for it - seeing as how you're the princes of Hellhole."

Phil gave a Rebel cheer, tossed his hat in the air and threw his arms around Cougar. As he whirled her in the air, he whispered hoarsely, "Wasn't you one of the girls here last year when we was by this way?"

"I sure as hell was, but as you can see, I've grown up some."

The hider planted a kiss on her cheek, set her down and took up his glass of sparkling wine.

"To the best damn saloon keeper in Hellhole!"

"And to our new friend, Claw Kiley!" Adam added.

Two glasses later they were as drunk as skunks - an animal, incidentally, with which they shared much in common - and were standing on the bar, singing songs.

"I'm glad I ain't in Dixie, Hooray! Hooray!

In Dixie Land I made my home,

But in Hellhole I made my money,

Away, away out west in Hellhole,

Away, away, a fer piece away frum Dixie!"

"That works for me," Cougar acknowledged. "Full 'em up again, Steve. These boys have a lot of drinking to catch up on."

"Yes, ma'am," he agreed, opening the second bottle.

"And put it on their tab," she added in an undertone, as the lawman and the hiders walked unsteadily to a table.

"Yes, ma'am."

When Claw and the Barber boys were well into their next drink, the marshal leaned over and whispered drunkenly in Adam's ear.

"You know I gotta do my job, Mr. Barber. So tell me - how far back are the other hiders?"

"Two days, on my soul," Phil replied in the same confidential tone.

"Two hours, you say?" Claw asked, cupping a hand around his ear to imply the background noise had made it difficult to distinguish what Phil had actually said.

"Nah. Tomorrow afternoon," Adam corrected.

"And how many would you say were coming this way?"

"Sweet Jesus, Claw, fifty men an' a company of boys, wagons and mules."

"Good year for buffalo, was it?"

"A good year," Phil agreed. "But the competition's gettin' stiff." He laughed at his own joke. "Stiff? Get it, Marshal? Stiff, like hides been out in the sun too long."

Cougar, who managed to hear everything and was always in the right place at the right time, remarked, in passing, "I'll be puttin' on a dozen new girls by tomorrow, boys. But don't let that stop your fun tonight."

"Girls? Girls? Don't tell me, you got girls in this here town?"

"Ladies aplenty."

"I swear on my aching backside, Miss Cougar, we ain't seed a girl - ceptin' you, o' course - since the last time we was through this way."

"The closest we cume to a female was Phil's ol' bitch an' she ain't no good, although on cold winter nights, we fight to see which one she'd sleep on."

"She warmer than a blanket an' less trouble than a squaw."

"I don't doubt it."

"Miss Cougar, you too high an' mighty now, to sit on a man's lap?"

"That depends on the man."

The Barber boys hiccupped noisily and made room for her to share their combined "seat."

"It shore cain't be the marshal's lap you want to sit on," Phil observed.

"Why's that?"

"'Cause it's us what's got the money!"

"'An' the looks."

"Well, you're both a sight," she acknowledged, placing herself comfortably between them. "Wouldn't you say so, Claw?"

The marshal was not as sure as the lady.

"I've got my rounds to make," he said by way of excuse, standing up and towering over the small, intimate group.

"If you walk over to my place, Mary's kept dinner warm for you," Steve said, clearing away the empties and replacing them with full ones.

"Thanks. I'll do that later. See you by and by, Miss Cougar."

"We'll be open late."

It was a statement, not a promise.

"I'll look in then. To be sure things are quiet."

"If that's what you're lookin' fer, Claw, then don't bother," Adam promised. "We're the princes of Hellhole - the first cutters in - an' this town won't be the same till we leave."

That was the promise.

Claw nodded farewell and slipped away, pushing through the group of shop keepers, stablemen, clerks, gamblers, drunks and drifters, all of whom wished to be present at the opening of hider season. Hellhole was a hiders town and every one of their livelihoods depended, to a larger or lesser degree, on the influx of hiders and hides.

Relationships made in saloons created the possibilities for an exchange of money. Hiders bought supplies, holed up in the best hotel rooms, ate in the finest restaurants, drank champagne and paid well for entertainment.

Long before the cattle herds and the Texas drovers ever thought of turning their heads toward the dusty Kansas towns of Hellhole and Caldwell and the like, buffalo hunters, with their essential raw materials for the eastern manufacturers, were the lifeblood of survival.

They were, indeed, the princess of the fledgling western civilization.

To which the lawman and the saloon owner both paid homage, albeit in different ways and for different reasons.

And with varying degrees of enthusiasm.

CHAPTER 17

"They're like locus," Fiz groused, watching the influx of buffalo men from the window of his second story office. "Every year they come and every year I forget how repulsive they are. More like animals then men."

Claw looked at him in some astonishment.

"I've never heard you talk like that before."

"That's because you don't know me!" Fiz retorted in unaccustomed vehemence. He turned away, letting the curtain drop before the play had run its course. "No one knows me." Then, with his anger rising, he demanded, "What makes you think you know me?"

Claw shifted his weight from one foot to the next, then inched toward the door. But his friend was not through and no one, not even a United States marshal walked out on him before he was dismissed.

"It doesn't do your reputation any good, either, you know."

"What doesn't?"

"Consorting with the likes of those buffalo hunters. A man is judged by the company he keeps. I heard one of them call you 'Claw' this morning."

"So? You call me Claw."

"Am I in the same class as a buffalo hunter, now?"

Fiz grew increasingly agitated, crossing to the lawman and jutting his chin out in defiant challenge. It was not a physical confrontation the physician was seeking, but a moral one.

"I don't know what you mean."

"I'm asking you, if, in your mind, a doctor, a practitioner of the healing arts, is on the same level as a man who makes a living slaughtering animals without number, skinning them before they stop quivering, and bringing the hides into Hellhole to sell."

"Let's see if I can answer that," Claw replied slowly. "Two men are brought into your office. Both have been shot. One has a flesh wound. He's a well-to-do rancher and can afford to pay you well for your services.

"The other is a drunk, without a penny to his name. He was run down in the street by a wagon and has a broken leg. If he's not treated promptly, he'll bleed to death. Which one do you tend to first?"

"I'm not talking about me. I'm talking about you."

"But I can't answer your question until I know the answer to mine."

Flustered, annoyed and without consideration, Fiz spat out his reply.

"I'd take care of the drunk, of course. I don't see your point."

Claw nodded slowly, then took one step back before walking to the door.

"Wait a minute, damn you!" Fiz ordered in unaccustomed language. "You didn't answer my question!"

"I didn't have to. You answered it for me."

"Come back here!" But the marshal was gone. In utter fury, Fiz took a roll of bandage from the table and heaved it against the wall. It struck with a soft plop, fell to the floor and unrolled. "Now look what you've done!" Fiz hurtled at the spirit of the disappeared lawman. "I spent all morning rolling that!"

Outside, Claw hurried down the stairs, escaping into the street. Quiet was a thing of the past. The town hustled and bustled with activity. The morning stage had brought in seven men, all of whom were desirous of purchasing hides for shipment back east. They were men in a hurry; men for whom time was of the essence.

The stage had been bringing in buyers all week and many of the hides had already been bought. They would have to work fast - and spend some money - to obtain that which their Northern consignees wanted.

They knew as well as anyone that tomorrow and the day after more buyers would arrive. The Season was upon them. Their income for rest of the year, to say nothing of their reputations, depended upon striking fast and profitably.

The Hellhole House was full to the rafters and rooms to rent in boarding houses or with the locals went for two dollars a night. Finding an empty chair at any of the eating houses was almost impossible and there wasn't a bottle of French brandy anywhere in town.

"I say - you - the tall one," a buyer hailed Claw. "Direct me to the sheriff's office."

"The closest sheriff is in Caldwell."

"Caldwell Street? Where is that? Why isn't anything labeled around here?"

"I suppose because everyone who lives here knows that Caldwell is a town, not a street."

"Listen, boy, I was told in Hays there was law in Hellhole. Now, you tell me there isn't even a sheriff's office in town. Do *you* call that law?"

"That depends."

"Is there a deputy? Anyone at all in this town I can talk to?"

"You're talking to me."

"I mean, someone in authority. Not one of you gunslinger types. I know all about you."

"You do?"

"You and your kind flock to Hellhole when the pickings are good. Cut-purses, gamblers, bullies. How many men have you robbed today?"

"Come to think of it, I haven't robbed anyone today. Guess I better get busy. A man has to make a living, you know."

"That's what I'm trying to do. I need protection."

"Mind telling me from what?"

"From you."

Claw's eyes flew open in pure ol' astonishment.

"That might be a little hard to arrange."

"Yes, you all think that. Do you live here?"

"I do."

"Are you good with a gun?"

"I've heard people say that."

"Then I have a job for you. Do you understand money, don't you?"

"About as well as the next man."

The buyer lowered his voice.

"I have a great deal of money on my person. I need a body guard. I'm offering you five dollars a day to protect me."

"I thought you just said I was the one you needed protection against."

"I meant your type."

"Oh."

"Get me a room at the best hotel in town. I don't care who you have to bully. That's up to you. Then reserve me a table so I can get something to eat. After that, round up all the buffalo-eaters who have hides to sell, so I can make some quick purchases. Then stay close to me while I pay them."

"Why is that?"

"In case they decide to skin me alive."

"Your hide worth something to them, is it? I never knew a one who would bother skinning an animal like you."

"I know these men. They're rough, wild, uncivilized and heathen. Last year, my partner was shot in the arm by one of them."

"Did he deserve it?"

"What do you mean, did he deserve it?" The buyer stomped his foot in dire agitation.

"Did he provoke the confrontation?"

"How would I know? This town has the worst reputation for violence in the west."

"That a fact?"

"Yes, it is. I read it in the New York *Herald* before coming down here."

"Then maybe you should have stayed in New York."

"Are you going to work for me, or not?"

"I can't."

"Why not?"

"I already have a job."

"Doing what?"

"Taking a tally of all the dead bodies every night."

The buyer was clearly nonplused.

"Well... how long does that take you?"

"Depends on how many there are."

The man's voice quavered.

"How many are you expecting?"

"None."

Claw tipped his hat and sauntered away.

"Wait a minute! I said, I need protection."

"I'd say it was Hellhole which needed protection from you."

The conversation was mercifully interrupted by a loud shot. Claw trotted toward the sound, leaving the "back east" buyer standing unprotected and alone in the street.

Two buffalo hunters were exchanging fists as the marshal arrived. Without bothering to ask for explanations, Claw dove into the fracas, separating the two men and holding them at arm's length.

"No fighting," he warned.

"Claw, this yahoo tried to get into see a buyer befer me," one complained.

"I was in line first!"

"There are plenty of buyers around. What's so special about this one?"

"He's got girls in there."

"Yeah? Well, he's not trading them, is he?"

"But they're pretty, Marshal."

"You want to look at pretty girls, go to a saloon. You want to sell your hides, go to a buyer. There's one standing in the street back there. He's got so much money he can't move."

The two men hurried off. Before Claw could leave, however, he was accosted by the angry man inside the storefront.

"Why'd you go and chase my customers away?" he demanded.

Instead an answering, Claw pushed past him and entered the store. Three young ladies in scanty costumer were seated on a wooden slat suspended between two flour barrels. Seeing the new "customer," they jumped down and swarmed over him.

"I can make you feel good all night," one purred.

"And I can tell you some nice saucy stories."

"Want to look at my pictures?" the last inquired, waving a series of French postcards under his nose. "They'll make you feel like a man and show you things about what boys and girls do, you never dreamed possible. Straight from Paris."

The back room was filled with hides. The stench was nearly deadening. As he wrinkled his nose, one of the ladies sprinkled him with perfume.

"Like this?" she asked. "Just let Charles buy your hides and you can have a lot more than perfume."

Claw coughed and directed his attention to "Charles."

"What are you running here? A buying operation or a brothel?"

"I'm just supplying some entertainment, Marshal," Charles replied, eying the badge for the first time.

"Where'd these women come from?"

"I picked them up - I *hired* them - in St. Louis."

"Then that's where they're going. On the next stage."

"You can't order them out of town. If you sent all the working women away, there wouldn't be a damn female left in Hellhole."

Before the buyer could explain about "legitimate business practices, Claw landed a fist on the man's nose. As he staggered backward, falling into a stack of hides and tumbling with them to the floor, the lawman gave him his walking papers.

"Next stage. Be on it. With the ladies."

"I have a right to be here. I rented this place last year just so's I could conduct my business this year."

"Complain to Hays."

Claw kicked the buyer's leg out of his way and stomped off. He had not gone ten feet down the street when another fight broke out, this time in front of the Hay, Feed and Grain Shop.

Small fights, petty arguments and claims of "being robbed," from both buyers and sellers kept Claw busy until late in the evening. Tired, bone weary, hoarse and bruised from constant shouting and scuffling, he trudged down the street, eyes on the Lowdown. The two outside lanterns were still burning, giving him hope of a nightcap and a chance to speak to Cougar in private.

That hope was extinguished as Steve came out of the saloon, drawing the solid doors closed behind him. The lanterns were turned down then blown out as the marshal approached.

"Closing so soon?" he joked to make his lost opportunity less acute. Steve turned to him with surprise.

"Oh, hello, Marshal." He shook his head ruefully. "It's been a long night."

"And then some. No serious trouble, I hope?"

"No, sir. Leastways none Miss Cougar couldn't handle. She's a right smart operator. I didn't hear one hider give her lip all evening. And when it came to fighting, she had them outside before they knew what was happening to them."

Claw frowned and shook his leg in irritation.

"She ought to call for help; *you* ought to call, if she won't."

"Well, sir, I suggested it, but she wouldn't hear of it. She figured you had your hands full enough as it was."

"Yeah." But not full with what he wanted. His disappointment grew acute.

Seeing his expression, Steve hastened to reassure him.

"I'm sure she'll call you if anything gets out of hand. I don't imagine she wants the place shot up."

"I don't imagine."

But his problem was, Claw did imagine.

"You want me to open up so you can have a drink? You look like you could use one."

The offer was meant kindly.

"No. I'm tired. See you in the morning."

"I'll be there early. Stop by, if you want. Miss Cougar will be serving coffee and crackers until noon, when she opens the bar."

"I'll keep it in mind," Claw muttered, turning away. He did not want coffee and crackers. He did not want to wait until morning. He did not want to be alone.

Waiting until Steve was out of sight, Claw slipped into the alley beside the Lowdown and stared up at Cougar's window. It was dark. Telling himself he would not bother her if the window was lit, he took the lack of illumination to mean she was asleep. Ignoring his own rational, he scooped up a handful of dried dirt and pebbles, juggled them in his hand a moment, then tossed them up at the window.

While his effort fell short, the noise he desired seemed adequate. Ducking into the shadows, he waited, like a schoolboy behind the barn.

When Cougar did not wake and come to the window, he tried again, taking better aim. Several larger stones rattled against the pane. Again he hid.

Telling himself he was a moon-struck calf, he repeated the action a third time and was rewarded by the high-pitched squeal of tight wood being forced open. With his lover's heart pounding in his breast, Claw had almost completed a semi-circular wave of his hand when his blood turned cold.

"No, the wind ain't cume up," a man's voice complained. "Mebbe some night bird flew a'gin the glass."

"Well, leave it open and come back to bed."

It was *her* voice. Hot tears of shame burned in Claw's eyes. Cursing himself for being ten kinds of a fool, he turned away, walking into the barrel of a shotgun. Claw was so startled, he froze before the order came.

"Don't move, cowboy."

Humiliation came in many ways, shapes and times but never was it more acute than when inadvertently brought on by a friend.

"Joshua, it's me. Put the gun down."

"Marshal Kiley?" The cold steel was removed faster than a hound on the scent of a ring-tailed raccoon. "I'm sorry, sir. It's dark an' I heerd someone foolin' around out here. There's a heap o' money in the Lowdown, and -"

"That's all right. I told you to keep an eye out."

The lawman turned and walked stiffly away, ignoring Joshua' protestation he would be more careful next time.

He need not have bothered. "Next time" would be a long time coming.

It was close to 4 A.M. when Claw awoke, covered in a sticky, uncomfortable sweat. The night air was moist and heavy but that was not the cause of his sudden alertness. Pulling on his boots, Claw tiptoed to the window and stared out. The street, from what he could see, was quiet. No one was about. He silently withdrew the pistol from the gunbelt hung on the peg by the door and waited.

He stood ten minutes without moving, drawing air through his distended nostrils before he heard the sound again. The noise was a low, muffled, discordant clicking. It took him a moment to place it.

Toenails on wood.

It was only a dog, after all, wandering up and down the street, occasionally crossing and re-crossing some of the boards the merchants had placed to cover the larger holes on Main Street.

A dog. Nothing more ominous than a stray, scrounging for food.

Miss Cougar, his feral cat, hissed. It was a long, drawn-out warning, piling goose bumps on his clammy flesh. Claw turned his head cautiously, trying to make out the shape of the cat in the dimness.

Miss Cougar came out from behind the stove, back arched, fur around the neck ruffled and standing on end. Her tail whisked once, twice, then froze. Her eyes shone in the dark, giving her an otherworldly appearance

His instincts were right. Something was out there; an evil was afoot in Hellhole. What he heard had not been a dog, or if it had been, the dog was part of the conspiracy.

Making a small restraining motion toward the cat, Claw inched the door open and slipped outside. The smell of dirt was strong.

There were no street lamps and the moon had already set, making his journey across the street safe from prying eyes. He tiptoed to the Lowdown and placed at ear against the side of the building, listening. All was quiet. If someone was inside, he - or they - had stopped moving.

Joshua' words came back to haunt him.

They's a help o' money in the Lowdown.

Damn it. He should have demanded that money be placed in the bank. He hadn't wanted to intrude, to force his will on her. If she felt the money was protected in her safe, that was her business.

But it wasn't, he bitterly reminded himself. Protecting it was his business. That gave him the right to demand concessions. He had let his hurt pride get in the way of his duty.

If no one was stirring in the saloon, then the danger lay elsewhere. Claw slid around the side of the building and crept down the street, eyes wary, nerves taught. But his mind was not on the danger but rather in a bedroom two stories high. He was half a block away from the Lowdown before he verbally abused himself.

"Never again," Marshal Kiley swore through clenched teeth.

If he had not been talking to himself he would have heard the dog. It came up behind him, toenails clicking on the loose stones. It was not until the animal was midway into its leap that he sensed its presence.

Claw's sudden jerking movement to avoid the dog caused him to lose his balance as the canine landed, forepaws extended, teeth bared. He felt the cold nose, first, almost a nuzzle at his warm throat, before the frantic, iron-hard fangs sank into his flesh.

As his arms flailed, the gun fell from his hand, falling unheard in the struggle for survival. With no chance to draw a knife, Claw was forced to use his fingers, prying them against the hair and hide of the wild beast at his throat. Amid grunts of effort and growls of anger, the two combatants fought in time-honored desperation.

He wanted to scream from the pain of the sharp teeth slicing through the flesh of his hands and arms, to cry from the agony of the weight pressing down on him, but he made no sound.

His best chance had already been squandered. When attacked by a killer dog, a man had once window of opportunity: to seize the beast in mid-flight and hurtle it beyond him before the force of the velocity knocked him down and the frenzy of the snapping teeth tore into him. But Claw had not seen it coming, and now thrown to the ground, he could do little more than fend off the inevitable.

"Git him!" urged a voice that sounded miles over him. "Tear his throat out."

"It's the law dog," another observed, squatting down to have a closer look. "Claw Kiley."

"So much the better."

The last words he would ever hear.

It did not seem fair.

But no one had ever promised him fairness.

Claw awoke to the sound of his own ragged breathing. He knew he was alive because he was in pain. Suffering was for the living. He had heard that in a sermon, once, when religious fervor had swept through his regiment. The orator had been an Irish priest, dressed in a black frock coat and a top hat.

His specialty had been preparing men for death and he had caught his at Franklin. The man of God's head had been blown off by a Rebel cannon ball. Claw supposed he had not suffered long.

He had been identified by his dog tag.

Claw did not know where he was, nor could he place the location. He was inside a building, but which building and for what purpose, he could only guess.

A slight movement on his part drew attention to his plight. A man he did not recognize stuck his face into Claw's and peered, eyeball to eyeball, at him. From the way the man bent, Claw realized he must be lying on the floor.

"He's awake. If he starts yelling..."

"He won't yell. Will you, Marshal?"

"Who are you?" His tongue was thick and the words came out slurred.

"What's it matter?"

"I want a name to put on your headstone."

For his trouble, Claw received a vicious kick in the face. His nose began to bleed.

"I tolt you we shoulda let that damn dog kilt 'im."

"An' have everybody in Hellhole awake and sniffin' around befer we got any work did? No. We'll kill him, a'right, but we gotta make it look accidental like. That ol' vicious dog jist jumped 'im and tore his throat out. Mebbe its got the rabies. Come on. It's almost dawn."

Clearing his head by slow, steady intakes of air, Claw finally realized where he was. He was in Mr. Customer's store, somewhere in the back, amongst the towering stacks of hides. The two who had set the dog on him were out of sight behind the large bundles. At first he thought they were stealing them, but the idea did not make sense. Even if they managed to fill a wagon with hides, they could not hope to get far before being overtaken.

"Hurry up. Have you got all them markers off?"

"Jist got this last one."

Claw heard what he took to be a small piece of leather fall to the floor, then a muffled curse.

"Damn! Lost it."

"Find it. We cain't leave it here. If it's found, it'll back up thems other's claims."

What they were doing, Kiley realized, was changing the ownership marks on the bundles of hides, substituting their own for that of other hiders. When it came time to claim full price, the shopkeeper would have no alternative but to pay the men whose names were on the tags.

"Done!" came a triumphant cry. "This is all we dare fix here. You doctor that receipt whilst I git our friend ready for his journey."

Tied hand and foot, Claw was forced to endure the rough hands digging into his armpits and dragging him toward the back.

"He's a heavy sonofabitch," the thief complained. "He'p me."

With both men straining and grunting, they managed to carry Claw through the rear door and out into an alley. One whistled for the dog but he was stopped by his partner.

"Not here!"

"We cain't carry him no further. He's heavy!"

"Git the horse. We'll drag him a ways off and dump him behind the eatery. They's lots of dogs there. Hungry, too, and used to eating raw flesh off'n the bones."

A horse was brought around and a rope strung around Claw. He did not struggle. His only hope now lay in absolute cooperation. If they thought him placid, it might not occur to them he could yell for help.

The journey through the back alleys was slow and awkward. Without using his feet to push away the accumulation of trash, his body kept getting tangled in broken crates, newspapers, tin cans and piles of refuse. Bits of broken glass cut his arms and legs, while tangles of loose cord snared and temporarily restrained him in his forward progress.

"We're never gonna git there at this rate! Cain't we leave him here? We done gone fur enuf."

"Yeah. I'll rub some fat on him an' you go an' find that damn dog. Find a pack of 'em an' fetch 'em here. Tell 'em theys dinner awaiting."

He chuckled cruelly.

With his eyes closed, Claw could not see what the men were planning on doing, but he had heard enough. It was not a bad idea. With hundreds of homeless dogs wandering around, a man might be attacked and fall prey to their hungry appetites. Especially a lawman, whose job it was to check the back alleys and deserted lots. If ganged upon by a dozen vicious animals he might shoot one, perhaps two, but a man alone would have no ability to defend himself from a pack.

If the dogs bit and gnawed on his body, no one, not even a suspicious doctor, would realize he had been beaten beforehand. Once he was dead, the ropes could be removed, with no one the wiser.

Because he was such a big man, and because first daylight was not far off, the two were careless. They had forgotten to gag him. If he remained quiet until they backed off, he would have a chance.

It wasn't much but it was better than nothing.

It almost worked.

The hider who remained behind approached Claw with a stinking piece of lard in his hand. Stooping over to rub it on his throat, he tripped over Claw in the gloom and fell broadly over the prisoner's body. The sudden impact of weight was so startling, Claw forgot his need for absolute stillness and swore angrily.

Pulling himself up quickly, the hider shook with sudden revelation.

"You bastard!"

Before Claw could make a retort, a filthy rag was stuffed in his mouth and bound in place with a cord.

"You a'most tricked us, lawdog. You'd a got away, we'd be in a stew."

A jail cell was more like it, but the point was mute.

Claw could do no more than struggle helplessly as the rancid fat was smeared over his face and neck. Nearly gagging from the smell, he was compelled to breathe through his mouth, or vomit into the gag, aspirating himself.

The task was nearly completed when the second hider reappeared, whistling urgently.

"Here, boy, here boy. Come to papa. Here's a nice piece o' meat fer you."

The dog growled eagerly, rushing the man in its eagerness to eat. A chunk of rotten meat was dropped over Claw's body and the two hiders jumped back, wishing to be safely away before the frenzy began.

The dog was feral but it was not a killer. Raised as a half-wild pet, it had spent most of its life in the company of humans. Tearing away at the flesh of a man, even in a moment of starvation, was against its nature.

"Where's that other dog? The big black one? The one what a'most tore his throat out befer?"

"I didn't see it."

"Go on," the skinner wheedled plaintively. "It's a'right, boy. Jist dig in and he'p yerse'f."

The dog wagged its tail at the unaccustomed kindness of the words, then turned to sniff Claw experimentally. A tongue came out and licked the lard from his face.

"Good dog, good dog," Claw muttered. But his words were muffled by the gag and the harshness of the translated sentiment angered the animal. It drew back its lips and glared with a defiant state at the man smelling like food.

"Go to it!" the hiders encouraged.

They might not have succeeded in wearing away the layers of restraint bred into the canine but as a pack of dogs came scrambling into the alley, the first animal, suddenly threatened with the loss of precious food, took a quick nip out of Claw's shoulder.

In a moment a huge dog fight was underway. A dozen lean, sinewy bodies clawed, bit and snarled over and around their prey, fighting for a bite of food while fending off any who dared steal what they had claimed.

When the hiders saw their plan must succeed, they backed their horse out of the alley and hurried off. When the excitement was nearly over, they would "wake" from peaceful slumber in a nearby flop house and return to watch.

Claw could not hope the sound of a dog fight would attract attention. There were too many wild dogs and too many fights for anyone to bother about. Unsanctioned, man-induced dog fights and subsequent betting were as common as flies, and of little more interest. If he were to save his hide, he would have to fend for himself.

It did not help that being torn to shreds by sharp, vicious teeth caused an uncommon fear in a man's breast. As a means of death, it ranked slightly above rattlesnake bites, poison water or a ruptured bowel and made expiration from gunshot almost desirable.

With a frightened roar of indignation, Claw lashed out with his bound feet, striking one animal in the ribs and hurtling it twenty feet in the air. As it landed with a hiss of exhalation, it was immediately set on by other, less daring animals. In the world of survival, one did not have to be the bravest or the strongest to eat. In Darwin's On the Origin of Species, luck, too, had its part to play.

With the odds against him and no logical, fair-play scenario presenting itself, Claw's instincts were served by utter despair. With a mighty heave, he rolled onto his stomach, crushing two dogs beneath him as he altered position. Perversely, the feel of their terror served to calm his nerves and with renewed dedication, the lawman jerked and twisted.

It required sublime effort, but as he turned again, Claw used the momentum to move forward, awkwardly getting to his knees. Height signified power and the dogs, startled by the new development, slunk back, ears pressed close to their heads in uneasy tension. They began a slow circling of their prey, tails wagging, half from confusion, half from a craving for praise. This was a man-beast, after all, not a calf or a cat or an alley rat. In their limited consciousness, there were remembrances of times past: of warm campfires, roasting meat, a caress, a soft word.

Claw could not hope to rely on those fleeting, blunted images. He, too, remembered other days, other times of comfort and dependence. Age and experience were the same for canine and man. Both understood that times change; that a gentle pat could turn to a deadly blow without the slightest provocation.

It was too late for kindness. Fear was his greatest weapon. Fear and the threat of dire punishment. As the ever-closing circle drew the dogs into striking distance, Claw growled a vicious noise deep within his throat then used their momentary distraction to raise himself to his feet.

If he were formidable at half his height, he was twice that on his feet. More godlike now, the bleeding, sweat-stained man towered above his attackers, still smelling of raw meat yet emanating a danger as old as fire.

Claw knew his life was reduced to a showdown. It would be one dog, either the biggest or the most abused, which would determine his fate. It was to be, then, leader against leader, marshal versus top dog. He would stare that animal down and live, or he would be torn down and die.

Scanning the dark alley, Claw squinted to improve his eyesight, finally identifying which dog it would be. Not by size or color or breed; he determined the head of the pack by the cold, calculating eyes, the tilt of the head, the partially extended tongue. This was the canine which would make the decision for the others; the one which would determine the chances of success, weighing it against the hunger in its belly.

Aggression was the key. Claw jerked to his left, hissing through the gag, then hopped forward. The dogs growled and withdrew. All but the spit-yellow cur with the demented, betrayed eyes. This one inched closer, fur at the ruff standing on end, tongue lolling in anticipation.

Breathing through his nose like a fire-breathing dragon, Claw growled from deep within his throat, then jumped again. The dog retreated a step, no further, then tensed its haunches, calculating, appraising, hating.

If the dog launched itself at him, Claw would be unable to protect his face and neck. That much knowledge they seemed to share. The weight of the dog's forward momentum would carry them both back, off balance, onto the hard earth. Once down, the man-prey would be no more dangerous than a grizzly devoid of claws and teeth.

Once down, the contest would be one-sided.

Claw had to get his back to a wall. Only then, like the wounded bear, could he hope to defend himself. Without moving his head and thus inadvertently giving the dog a signal to attack, he shifted his eyes, scanning his surroundings with feline serenity. The alley he found himself in was twenty feet wide, perhaps fifteen feet to one side of him, five to the other. If he must fall, he would twist to the right, possibly striking the wall of a building with his head and shoulders. If nothing else, that might hold him up long enough to catch his balance.

Or do no more than break his neck.

Claw Kiley did not want to die. Dying was a fearful thing. To survive was in his makeup as deeply rooted as it was in the dogs. He would fight until there was no breath left, no strength to carry on. It was the way of all wild things, and as he stood facing his adversary, Claw Kiley was as wild and untamed as they.

He did not think of the comforts he would lose, the friendships he would miss. He thought now only of kill or be killed.

He growled again, then hopped once, twice before the leader of the pack made up its mind. Like the man, the dog-beast interpreted the wall as a place of safety. As much as Claw strove to obtain that respite, the dog yearned to deprive him of it.

With a rush of ancient fury, the dog tightened its muscles. A quivering of anticipation shot through its tough hide, rippling the fur which once might have nestled a child's head upon its warm underbelly. Once, but no more. Starvation was a good teacher, serving as an eraser to past lessons.

While the dog was in midair, Claw turned, absorbing the blow with his shoulder. The force staggered him and he toppled, hard, against the building. Boards creaked, one giving way against the combined weight of two struggling animals. They crashed through the half rotten structure, suspended for a moment between standing and lying by the remaining portion of shattered wall.

Caught, then, trapped by the dog and pinned between the boards, Claw felt an utter sense of terror. Death was upon him with all its stark unknown, searing pain, bitter recriminations.

To die like a dog.

The words shot through his being with the nervous energy of a galvanic battery. To die like a dog.

"No!"

Tightening his stomach muscles, Claw pulled back, managed to come to a standing position, then caught the cur's ear between his partially bared teeth and ripped it away. As the animal snarled, temporarily caught in its own life and death struggle, the marshal spun with it, holding the dog in his teeth for one second longer before pushing it against an out-jetting of splintered wood. With incalculable urgency, Claw pushed the dog's tender belly into and then through the wood. Blood from a severed artery shot into the air like a rocket.

The dog howled, cried and twisted, further imbedding itself on the wooden pike. As life ebbed away it barked, whimpered and finally succumbed to blood loss. The mad throbbing of its heart, empty of life-sustaining fluid, stopped beating and the spirit fled, leaving its killer, still a man for all the torture and the fright, to shed a sudden tear for it.

Where Mankind had betrayed, death had redeemed.

The other dogs, which had crept closer, now slunk back, eyes wary, tails down. As Claw tottered, then growled, they retreated further, eyes no longer on him but on the limp meat suspended by the broken board.

Inching away, Claw watched as the remaining dogs crowded in, tearing at the flesh, ripping the hide of the bravest and the best of them. It was not a fitting ending but it was a finale.

No loving creator had ever said life was fair.

Or just. Or painless.

CHAPTER 18

Claw Kiley thanked God for small mercies, for those were all he had. They were better than none.

With a muffled groan, he half hopped, half baby-stepped around the side of the building, arms and legs still tied. He could not hope to reach his own office traveling in such a fashion, but did not wish to be seen hurt and in an undignified position. His dilemma was solved, as a pair of strong hands grasped him, lifted him off his feet and dragged him back into the alley.

"You're bleeding some, pardner," the hider observed with genuine concern in his voice.

"Yeah," Claw admitted as the gag was removed. "Obliged."

"Who was it done this to you, Claw?"

The hider sliced through the bonds with a movement so fluid and seamless he might have been spreading warm butter over bread. When he saw the circulation was returning to Claw's swollen and purple hands, he grinned lopsidedly at the marshal.

"One good turn deserves another. That's frum the Good Book, yuh know."

Before Claw was forced to make an obvious point of ignoring the question of who had hurt him, or of acknowledging his pain by holding a hand over his wounds, a loud shout of alarm caught his attention.

"That sounds like -" the hider remarked, but his recently released companion was ahead of him and gone. The man shook his head in wonderment, then followed.

The one-sided argument between a hider and Mr. Customer was unceremoniously conducted with screams of anger, wild hand gesturing and threats. As the marshal approached, the scruffy plainsman flashed a knife under the buyer's chin.

"I got this here paper. You cain't deny it. It says I checked in fourteen bundles, 'an now yer sayin' my mark's onlyest on ten."

"The original count must have been wrong," the flustered businessman explained.

"Stand back!" Claw called as he hobbled toward the store. Staring the hider down, he demanded, "What's your name?"

Placed on the defensive with the unexpected question, the man babbled, "Keystone."

"All right, Mr. Keystone. Put the knife away. As the man debated with himself, Claw made a sweeping motion with his hand which not only established his authority, it covered the fact he was not holding a gun. The hider pouted then reluctantly sheathed his knife.

"Marshal, he's tryin' to cheat me."

Had the situation not attracted as many men as it had, Claw would not have taken the time to explain.

"No, he's not. There's been a fraud committed here." Then, to Mr. Customer he demanded, "Have two hiders been in here within the last half hour - men with receipts for thirty, forty bundles?"

"I just paid off two fellas. They called me out from my bed; said they had to leave an' couldn't wait until regular business hours to get paid There wasn't anything wrong, was there? They had their receipts and their markers matched the count."

"Where'd they go?"

"I didn't notice."

Seeing Joshua running toward the store, Claw shouted an order.

"Over here." As the deputy joined him, pistol at the ready, the marshal directed him toward the door of the shop.

"Don't let anybody in or out. No more transactions until I can find -"

"Sir," Joshua interrupted with concern. "Yer all cut up. What happened?"

"Tell you later."

"Tell me now."

"Do as I say."

The thieves who had switched the name markers had only one horse with them. That meant they would have to go to the livery to get the second before they could leave. Claw ran at a gallop, or the closest to running he could approximate, toward the stable. Behind him he heard Joshua' reassuring voice and felt a flood of relief.

He had come to Hellhole alone and was solitary no more.

"All right, you yahoos, stand back. You heard the marshal. No more wheelin' an' dealin' jist now. You all go on down to the Lowdown an' git some free victuals while we git this mess sorted out!"

Oblivious to the stares of curiosity he received from the early-risers who had come out to see what the commotion was about, Claw reached Bark Barker's just as the doors of the stable were being opened.

"Thanks fer yer business," the proprietor was saying as he emerged from the dimness.

"Think nuthin' of it. We'll see you next year fer sure."

The familiar sound of his would-be murderer sent Claw's blood cold. If he lived to be fifty, he would never forget either the voice or the face which went with it.

"Hold it right there!" he called as the two, mounted on fresh horses, come into his view. "You're under arrest!"

"Damn!" cursed the first man, reaching for his gun. "I tolt you we shoulda shot that law dog."

Claw was faster than he, his hand already at his holster before the hider's arm had dropped.

"Drop the guns and get off the horses before I plug both of you in your tracks. I mean it," he added with deadly certainty. "Give me an excuse."

The first man had already dropped his pistol before his partner drew alongside him, on the outside.

"Fool," he hissed through rotten teeth. "He ain't got no gun."

Claw had remembered, too late, his own pistol had been taken from him. The bluff had worked once, but not twice.

A shot rang out, striking the nearest hider. Caught unaware, his lifeless hands flew up, then as dead as a puppet whose strings had been severed, he tumbled forward, striking the ground at Claw's feet. The other aimed his pistol at Kiley's chest but before he had a chance to fire, a second round struck him in the head, taking off the top of his skull. Propelled backward amid an explosion of blood and brains, his body was momentarily pinned against the wall of the livery in fair imitation of the dog Claw had killed. But unlike the cur, no tears were shed for his untimely death.

Spinning around, Claw saw Joshua come up behind him, pistol extended, eyes blazing.

"Marshal Kiley, what in tarnation do you think yer doin?" he demanded. The question was not meant to be answered, so much as he was expressing his own fear and admiration. "You ain't got no gun."

"I don't need one," Claw grumbled, hoping his own fear was not as expressive. "Not when you can shoot like two men."

"I onlyest squeezed off one," Joshua protested. Surprised, the lawman turned and looked for the second gunman. No one was in sight.

"Then who shot the other?"

"It weren't me," Joshua protested, seeing Claw's skepticism. Holding out his gun, he slipped the chamber open, revealing five bullets.

"Then - who?"

No one stepped forward to claim the honor.

"Never mind," Claw shrugged.

Pushing the terrified horses out of the way, he approached the two hiders, warily eying them in case either were reading themselves for a second attack. A quick glance proved his concern to be unfounded. Both were dead. Joshua pointed to the front man.

"It were him I was shootin' at. Hit him right on," he admitted. "But this other'in. He didn't shoot hisself." Claw kicked the body, rolling it over on his face. A bullet hole had been drilled through his eye socket. "That's pretty fancy shootin'," Joshua acknowledged with a whistle of appreciation.

"Yeah, well, he's dead. Let's get them over to the undertaker's."

"Looks like you got yerse'f a guardian angel, sir."

Claw paused, then shot a glance heavenward.

"One good turn deserves another."

Joshua did not inquire further. Who was he, after all, to question the marshal's relationship with God? Or with another order of the lower species, for that matter.

That evening, after Claw's wounds had been treated and the ownership of the hides rightfully established, the Lowdown was buzzing with excitement. Adam Barber sat perched on the bar, arms spread for dramatic effect. Every eye of the one hundred men stuffed into the drinking parlor was on him.

"There he was, boys, standing in front of them desert rattlers, starin' 'em down. 'Don't move,' he says, 'Or I'll drill you full o' lead.' But here's the kicker," Adam drew out in melodramatic fashion. He ain't wearin' no gun. He's been set upon by them rats an' torn up by wild dogs an' didn't have no weapon. He knew it, too, but did that stop him?"

The speaker paused. Several listeners in the front urged him on. They had heard the story two dozen times before the sun had set, but it was a tale which only grew better in the retelling.

"No, sir. Nuthin' was gonna stop Marshal Claw Kiley. He's as brave a man as ever wore the star. He jist stands there, calm as a cow chewin' 'er cud, eyes flashing fire an' brimstone.

"'Git off'n them horses or yer dead men,' Marshal Kiley warns 'em. So the first drops his gun, real scared like, an' the second gets to twitchin' like he's gonna face the marshal. And boom! Claw Kiley draws his gun - courst, he ain't got one - an' the feller jist falls dead away. How did he do it, you ask?"

A man from the back called, "How did he do it?"

"Yeah! How did he shoot that hombre without a pistol?"

Phil Barber chuckled. He had come to the good part.

"Why, he shot 'em like this!" Holding up his hand, fingers fashioned like a pistol, he went "Boom!" and then pretended to blow away the gun smoke. "That's how he done it!"

"Why, that's magic!" another called with dazzled respect.

"More like *black magic,*" Fiz groused, rubbing his hand across his mustache and shaking his head.

"It wasn't like that," Claw softly protested. Fiz exchanged a glance at Cougar before replying.

"Of course it was. It was *exactly* like that. Why, half the town saw it. Each and every one of them can testify to it. Of course," he added, staring down and contemplating the pile of sawdust at his feet, "Tomorrow it will be another story and the day after that, another. And they'll all be exactly true." He looked back up. "You know why that is?" he asked Claw.

"No. But I have a feeling you're going to tell me."

"The reason all those wild, imaginative, totally implausible stories can all be true is because you're a legend. That's right. A legend. You're larger than life."

"I'll say," Cougar agreed.

"I don't want to be a legend."

"It doesn't matter what you want or what you don't want. I don't recall anyone asking you if you wanted to be a legend. Do you?"

"No."

"And they won't, either. Especially after this. One tall tale will heap on top another until before you know it, some writer from Boston will be down here wantin' to write your life's story."

"I don't want anyone to write my life's story."

But Fiz was on a roll and there was no stopping him.

"Don't worry. He won't ask your permission."

"I won't talk to him."

"When has that ever stopped a writer? Especially a Back East reporter? Whatever you don't say, he'll fill in for you. By the time he's done, you'll be the son of a grizzly and rattlesnake, you'll shoot faster than greased lightning, have steely blue eyes which pierce through a man's soul, and are kept so busy shooting outlaws, having fast-draws on Main Street and drinkin' at the Lowdown, you won't recognize yourself."

"I don't know about that," the marshal protested with a smile. "I recognize myself from that description.

"Say, I've got an idea," Cougar pursued. "Since you've already given the matter considerable thought, why don't *you* write the story and send it Back East?"

Fiz was incredulous.

"Me?"

"Yeah," Claw seconded. That way, I'll know who to go gunnin' for when Matthew Brady comes to take my likeness."

"He's got a point, Fiz," Joshua agreed.

"Oh, shut up. Who asked you?"

"Courst, sir, they's a heap to think aboot befer having one o' them picture-takin' fella set you down fer posterity."

"Posterity?" Fiz exploded. Joshua ignored him.

"I knew a man onest who had his picture taken. One o' them daguerreotypes. Courst, you know, Marshal, aboot the Injun superstition that gettin' yer picture took robs a man o' his soul?" Claw nodded and he rambled on. "Well, this fella I knowd didn't believe in inny such nonsense. So, he goes an' plunks down good money to git hisself all set out in pictures."

"Did you ever know anyone who had bad money?" Fiz demanded. No one bothered to answer.

"They cume out pretty nice, too. But then this pe-culiar thing started happenin'. He got to twitchin' all over, like he had the scabies an' then his own dog wouldn't go near him -"

"Doesn't sound all bad," Claw mumbled, gingerly touching the bandage at his throat.

"Next thing you know, the fella's voice starts changin' an' he gits all pale like, so's he resembles a ghost."

"A ghost without a soul," Fiz muttered.

"I'm getting out of here," Claw said. His departure went unnoticed.

"Well, this feller -"

"I know," Fiz interrupted. "He sprouted angel's wings and 'jist' flew away."

"Now, why would you say a thing like that?" Joshua protested. "I ain't talkin aboot an angel; I'm talkin' aboot a man-ghost."

"Man-ghost? What in blue blazes is a man-ghost?" Fiz exploded.

"Why, a man what's half dead an' half alive."

"That sounds like an excuse not to pay his doctor's bill for the 'half alive' part. Now, be quiet. I want to hear how Claw Kiley shot a man to death in cold blood without a gun."

"It weren't in cold blood -"

The excitement over the marshal's prowess did not die down all season and might have continued until next season had not something more unusual occurred to take its place.

"Transport coming in, Miss Cougar," Steve sang out from just outside the double doors. "The wagon's toting a big crate."

Cougar joined him and looked out.

"Yes," she agreed. "That's a big crate, all right. Why don't you stop him right there and ask if the delivery is for the Lowdown?"

"I'll do 'er," he agreed, slipping away.

The owner of the saloon and coincidentally the purchaser of the delivery "big enough to be a buryin' box" watched as the wagon was halted. When the driver nodded, she gestured with her hand.

"Have him bring it around back, Steve." Seeing Joshua emerge from the Marshal's Office, Cougar summoned him over. "See if you can help unload that crate, will you, Joshua?"

With eyes as wide as saucers, he tipped his hat and hurried to be of service and so be the first to have news of what the box contained.

Gossip, as he knew from experience, made a man healthy, wealthy and wise.

And also made him the recipient of invites to "cume on in an' set a spell an' drink some lemonade," while he reported the news.

"Shore is heavy," the deputy observed as he hoisted one end of the crate down off the wagon. "What is it?"

"I don't know," the driver confessed. "Guess if it's for the Lowdown, it must be some new-fangled gamblin' machine. Or mebbe a pianee."

Joshua thought the man must be right.

It took them, Steve and three more men to carry the Very Heavy Crate through the back door of the drinking establishment.

"Place it in that room there," Cougar directed.

"I'll get a crowbar, Miss Cougar," Steve volunteered. "So we can pry the top off."

"Good idea."

He returned in under five minutes, which, to the waiting group, seemed an age.

"Hurry, Steve," the driver encouraged. On Cougar's look he added defensively, "I got to have it signed for. I'm to witness nuthin' is broke."

"Of course," Cougar agreed.

As the top came off and the blanket of padding removed, the sighs of disappointment and confusion were loud and unmistakable.

"It ain't no gamblin' wheel, at all," the driver exclaimed. "It's nuthin' but a bath tub!"

"A bath tub? Who's want a bath tub in Hellhole?"

Even Joshua was nonplused. Removing his hat and wiping his brow in the classic, "I need a drink" attitude, he stared at the gleaming white porcelain-over-metal object.

"Might do fer a waterin' trough out front," he acknowledged reluctantly. "But it's mighty fancy. Is that what you figure to do wid it, Miss Cougar?"

"No. I figure to take a bath in it."

"What fer?"

"It's a little difficult to explain," she admitted.

"I reckon its aboot big enuf to float a birch bark canoe in."

"Something like that," she admitted with a twinkle in her eyes.

The marshal was not seen near the Lowdown Saloon for three nights and two days. It was said he had "marshaling business" to attend to.

On the morning of the third day Claw Kiley made his appearance at the Lowdown. He bore a striking resemblance to a man-ghost.

"I heard about your new bath tub," he admitted as Miss Bradburn joined him.

"Did you, now?"

He nodded solemnly.

"Heard it was about as big as a pine burying box."

"Oh, don't worry," she scoffed. "If a coffin was all I wanted, I would have ordered one from the undertaker. This came all the way from Saint Louie."

"That a fact?" He spoke as though the significance were lost on him.

"That's a fact."

"Heard you've been charging admission for a fella to take a look at it."

She laughed. The sound was light and amused.

"You know how rumors start. Never knew a man who wasn't a gossip at heart."

Claw was not sure whether or not to agree, so said nothing. It was the habit of a lifetime, which would only grow into an annoying character trait.

"Want to see it?"

"I don't have a dime on me," he flatly confessed.

"It'll only cost you a nickel."

"I'm broke."

"I'll put it on your tab."

Before he could protest he did not keep a tab, Cougar slipped her arm through his and dragged him off to the Infamous Back Room.

Seeing the bath tub, stripped of its packing crate, in all its wide wonder, Claw gasped.

"It's big," he admitted.

"Very big," Cougar agreed. "I had it special ordered."

"What for?" Claw's eyes snaked over toward the very open and extremely conspicuous window. "I'd close that and board it up, if I were you."

"Why is that?"

He thought Miss Bradburn and Doctor Ward occasionally sounded a lot alike and decided it was not a good thing.

"That open window gives men a pretty good peep show. Without paying his dime," he added morosely.

Cougar appreciated his concern for her livelihood.

"I guess I could nail a sheet over it," she conceded. He glanced at her and she smiled. It was self-evident. "A curtain would look pretty peculiar on the window of a saloon."

"Oh." It was as much of an agreement as he could muster.

"I expect you'll want to come over one evening and try it out."

"Why would I want to do that?"

"For the novelty."

He noted, but failed to comment upon, her drollness.

"I better get back to work."

"Me, too," she agreed casually. "Let me know when you're coming back. I'll start the water heating. The brochure said it takes one hundred buckets to fill."

Claw shivered.

"Someone walked over my grave," he explained.

"In that case, we can use the crate it came in as a burying box. Would that make you feel better?"

He shivered again.

"Maybe I'm catching cold."

"In that case, a good soak in a hot tub will do you wonders."

"In the army," he laughed nervously, "they dosed a soldier with blue mass when he came down with a cold."

"Blue mass," she informed him gaily, "is for constipation."

"Oh. Yeah. Well... it's commonly thought of as a cure-all."

"I was never a soldier."

"I forgot."

"I'll see you later."

"Don't wait up for me."

"I have no intention of it."

Claw swallowed and cursed St. Louis to Hades.

"Marshal, I ain't seed you over ta the Lowdown lately," Joshua observed. He had been whittling a piece of tree branch down into the size of a toothpick. Claw looked up from the report he was not writing and frowned.

"Aren't you ever going to finish that?" he complained. Joshua stared benignly at him.

"By and by."

"What are you making?"

"A peg."

"A peg? A peg for what? To hold a doll hat?"

"In case I ever need one."

Had there been sulphur on the tip of the peg, Claw's glare would have ignited it.

"I'm not going to the Lowdown," he announced out of the blue. Joshua appeared not to hear. He had gone back to his carving job. "I said, I am not going to the Lowdown," Claw repeated.

Joshua had apparently gone deaf.

Claw pushed back in his chair, stretched, yawned, then crossed by the busy deputy. Joshua had apparently gone blind, as well, for he did not look up.

"I'm going to make rounds."

He did not offer to go with him. He did not even acknowledge the marshal's departure.

Claw left, slamming the door behind him.

It was early, not past seven o'clock. Too early to make rounds. The sun had not even set. Claw looked up into it, wondering if it were true that a man who stared at the sun too long went blind.

He decided he would go and have a cup of coffee with Fiz and maybe a game of checkers. With long, sure strides Claw crossed the street, keeping his eyes fixed on a point up the street. He did not even glance over at the Lowdown. He definitely did not see Miss Bradburn at the doors watching him.

If asked, he would swear he had not seen her.

Short of being required to place his hand on the Bible before doing so.

Taking the stairs to Fiz's two at a time, he jerked open the door and stuck his head in. Fiz was not in the outer room but he could hear him fussing in the back.

"Hullo!" Claw called cheerfully.

"Who's there?" came the surly demand.

His feelings hurt, Claw retreated. He knew Fiz recognized his voice. It was a conspiracy. He thumped down the stairs, three at a time.

Bark was standing outside in the corral when Claw came up behind him. He was leading a colt around by a rope.

"What you got there?" the lawman inquired. Bark shrugged.

"A horse."

"I can see it's a horse. Just buy it?"

"Took it in trade."

"What you going to do with it?"

"Want to buy it?"

"No."

That ended the conversation. Claw drifted away.

The doors on the bank were locked, the hiders had either gone their separate ways or had gathered at the drinking holes to water themselves and no one likely challenged him to a duel on Main Street. In desperation, Claw entered Ma Smit's boarding house.

"Hello, Marshal!" Ma called. Her face lit with unexpected glory. "Sit down. Did you have your supper? Can I get you anything?"

His intent had been to drink a cup of coffee and spend an hour reading the newspaper, but the smile on Ma's face disconcerted him.

"Looking for a fella," he lied. "About five-foot-seven, dark hair, brown eyes. Anyone like that been in here?"

"Goodness, Marshal, that description fits most of the men in Hellhole."

"Yeah, well, the wanted poster wasn't very specific."

"What's his name?"

For the life of him, Claw could not come up with a name. Any name. Then he laughed.

"Bradburn."

"Bradburn?" Ma sounded shocked. Her eyes narrowed. "Nobody by that name's come in here."

Claw left quickly. He did not bother to thank her for the information.

Despite the hour, he made his rounds, taking his time, pausing occasionally to speak when spoken to. No one in Hellhole seemed in the mood for conversation. Just a "hello," or a "good evening, Marshal," then hurried on their way.

Everyone, he supposed, had someplace to go. Everyone but him.

By eight o'clock he had walked the perimeter of the town twice, stepped in eleven piles of dog feces, twisted his ankle in a hole in the street and worked up a powerful sweat, which had nothing whatsoever to do with his exercise.

He imagined he would turn in early. It wasn't just any evening a man could get to bed by eight-thirty.

Joshua was exactly where he left him. The peg had been reduced to a splinter. The pile of shavings had been neatly swept over by the stove.

"I'm going to bed," Claw declared. Joshua seemed to think that was a good idea. "I've made rounds." Joshua approved. "Good night." No answer. "See you in the morning."

"What morning would that be?"

"Tomorrow morning. What do you think I meant?"

"You bein' so tired an' all, I thought you might sleep fer two or three days."

"I'm not that tired. I just want to go to bed."

Joshua coughed. Claw supposed he had gotten a fleck of sawdust in his throat.

"I won' be needing you anymore this evening," he continued, temper rising.

"I reckon I'll jist mosey over to the Lowdown, then."

"You do that."

Joshua remained nailed to the chair.

Claw sat on his bed. The mattress felt as hard as a rock. Someone had switched it. He stood, ambled over to the water bucket.

"I'll just fill this for the morning."

He bent over to grab the handle, saw it had already been filled and jerked back, as though he had seen a water snake inside. He glowered at the deputy.

"I thought you were going out."

"Oh, I am."

"When?"

"By and by."

"If you wait any longer, there'll be snow outside."

Joshua turned wise, sad eyes on his friend.

"It ain't so bad," he slowly observed.

"What ain't?"

"Takin' a bath."

"What's any of this got to do with taking a bath?"

"Miss Cougar took a bath this afternoon."

"How-do-you-know?"

"She told me."

"Oh. Yeah. Well, ladies to that sort of thing."

"Ain't that a right funny thing," Joshua began, swinging one leg over the other and settling into the chair. "I remember the first time I ever did see a bath tub. You know where that was?"

"No."

"In the back of a covered wagon. This here family were goin' 'west,' they called it, an' they had all their belongin's in this wagon. Marshal, you never did see a wagon so overloaded in yer life."

"Really?" came the less than enthusiastic acknowledgement.

"Them poor horses was aboot done in. They couldn'a gone another step, I swear."

Claw knew the feeling.

"They called me over an' asked me what I thought was wrong with 'em. The horses, I mean. I tolt them the wagon was too full. Guess they had been told that befer, cause the womenfolk got all teary-eyed an' started making noise.

"I offered to hep them empty the wagon. Took out all sorts o' things. Like books an' this gi-gantic lookin' glass. And then I seed this tub in there. 'What's this?' I asked. 'It's a tub,' the feller tolt me. 'What do you use it fer?' 'Taking a bath.' "Ain't that what the creek is fer?' I asked."

"Never mind. I don't want to hear any more."

"'So the fella said, 'No, the creek is fer waterin' the horses. The tub is to set in.' So I says, 'Now ain't that a pe-culiar thing. Why would a feller want to set in a tub?' An' he says, 'To git clean.' So I says...'"

Claw did not hear the rest of what Joshua said.

It was one of those stories which never ended. He had a suspicion if he stayed to listen, he would need that burying box, after all.

Would, in fact, volunteer to crawl into it.

"I'm going to the Lowdown."

Joshua continued the story for the elucidation of Miss Cougar, the cat.

CHAPTER 19

"Hello, Giant," Miss Cougar, the proprietress, greeted the marshal. "Haven't seen you in here for a while."

"Wonder why that is?" he muttered.

"I thought you were broke. And didn't want to run up a tab."

"Steve, pour me a beer."

"Sure thing."

Steve drew Claw a beer and accepted the nickel placed on the bar. Claw sipped it gingerly.

"It's warm," he complained.

"It is getting pretty hot," Cougar agreed. "But it's that time of year."

"The beer."

"I expect we could use some rain."

Claw put the glass down and turned to face his tormentor.

"Will you kindly tell me what's so important about my taking a bath?"

She appeared surprised at the question.

"I don't know what you're taking about."

"I'm no dirtier than anyone else in here."

"I took a bath this afternoon."

"I didn't mean you."

"Who did you mean?"

"Them." Claw indicated the assortment of townsmen, card players, hiders and drifters.

"I don't suppose you are."

"I don't see you asking any of them to take a bath."

"My tub is not open to the public. If they want a bath, they'll have to go to the tonsorial."

"You know, if a man takes too many baths, his skin flakes off."

"How-would-you-know?"

"I heard it said."

"What else did you heard said?"

"You had a fella in your room the night I got hurt."

"Who said it?"

"No one."

"Then how do you know?"

"I... heard him open the window."

Cougar considered for a long moment before speaking.

"I wondered," she said, more to herself than to him. When she looked up, her eyes were a steely blue, of the kind legends were made. Gone was the hurt, the confusion, the betrayal... if those emotions had been there in the first place. "What did you do? Throw pebbles at the window?"

Claw blushed to the roots of his hair.

"I... thought you were alone."

"Why?"

"Because I wanted you to be."

His reply, so simply and honestly stated, melted steel.

"That's it," she declared with vim.

"What's *it?*"

"You maybe are going to be senator one day and you maybe are going to marry a governor's daughter one day, but tonight you're mine."

He did not know whether to say, "Be what?", "Marry who?", or "Only tonight?" so said nothing.

In the long run, it was just as well.

Grabbing him by the arm, Cougar dragged him toward the back. As he realized her intent, his knees bent at the joint and a low moan of 'Whoa is me,' escaped his lips.

But he did not "whoa," nor did he protest too strenuously, as Cougar shoved him into the back room and slammed the door. He noted, in passing, a sheet had been nailed over the window. As far as consolations went, it was right up there with Saturday nights and warm beer.

"Strip!" Cougar ordered. Then, over his protest of "Strip?" she shouted, "Joshua, start the bucket brigade."

From out of nowhere, Joshua Jackson appeared, a bucket of steaming water in his hands. His face was flushed, no doubt from standing over a hot fire.

The kind which simmers in Hades.

"Right here, Miss Cougar."

"Dump it in the tub." "It" referring either the water or the marshal, his choice.

"Right you are."

Joshua opted for the water. It made a distant, hollow splashing noise as it landed against the sides of the huge tub.

"I'll have twenty more buckets in there befer you can pull an ace o' spades frum a deck of cards.'" he informed the marshal smugly.

"I didn't know you were a gambler," issued from blue lips.

"So you might as well get undressed an' hop in. No worry aboot freezin'. Not on a night like this."

"Freezing" reminded Claw of the expression, "Not until hell freezes over." Wisely, he refrained from speaking his thought out loud. "Maturity," Miss Cougar would say, "was a wonderful thing to behold."

"Here," she said, tossing him an irregularly shaped mass of white material, resembling a bleached rock.

"What's this?"

"Castile soap. I carved out a chunk from the fifty pound block I bought. You rub it over your body."

"Would you care to demonstrate?"

"Maturity," Miss Bradburn would say, "was a highly unattainable goal for most men."

Joshua hightailed it out of the room. In his haste, he forgot to close the door tightly.

There was not enough water in the tub - yet - to drown the tall man over his remark concerning what he wished her to demonstrate. So Cougar opted for the next best solution.

She laughed.

"Maybe."

Claw crumpled to a heap on the floor.

She left him there and he seemed perfectly content to simulate a floor board. In half an hour, the hot water reached the mid-way point.

"Time to get in," Cougar announced. Claw grinned drunkenly, although he had not had a drop of alcohol in recorded memory, the warm beer notwithstanding.

"I will, if you will."

"You will, or I'll kill you."

Claw thought he would.

Pulling himself up by holding onto the edge of the tub, he stared bleakly into the depths.

"Bath tub," he muttered to himself, properly identifying the object. "Water." He was two for two. "Soap." Correct, again. Two more and he would have a flush.

"Strip."

Proving she was the better poker player.

Claw removed his vest, than began unbuttoning his shirt. There were not as many buttons as he remembered. He was done in a flash. The shirt came off his shoulders and slid slowly to the floor.

Cougar perched on the top of an upturned barrel to watch.

Claw sat on the edge of a rickety chair and removed his boots. It was a peculiarity of Fate that they pulled off easily, without the least prodding. On most hot nights he was compelled to give the toe a stiff cuff with the side of a stiffened hand to loosen it.

He placed the boots side by side, parade-fashion.

The socks were even easier to remove. Set on the floor, they stood at attention, perfectly retaining the form of his feet.

The trouser buttons proved a problem. The button holes had grown three sizes too small. The harder he worked at them, the more they refused to budge.

"Shall I give you a hand?" Cougar inquired.

After that, the buttons slipped through the holes as though they had never been fastened.

The drawer strings were the last obstacle between dressed and undressed. Claw gulped audibly.

"Just pretend I'm a squaw and the tub is the creek," Cougar suggested. Claw swayed like a sapling in a tornado.

"That-won't-help," he confessed.

Amazingly, it was not meant to. He had misunderstood.

"Filled up as fer as she'll go, Marshal!" Joshua cheerily sang out. "Oncest you sat awhile an' the water gits cold, I'll take some out an' put some more hot in."

"How long am I supposed to 'set' in this thing?" Claw demanded sharply.

"Till Miss Cougar lets you out," he guessed.

"That sounds like a life sentence," the marshal observed without humor.

"Then be glad I'm not the Hanging Judge," Cougar supplied.

He thought "glad" was an odd choice of words. Not one he, personally, would have chosen.

"You can go now, Joshua," Cougar directed. "And thank you for the trouble."

"Weren't no trouble a'tall," he confessed. With a wink at the lady, the deputy slipped away. The door, as doors will, failed to click shut behind him.

"Well, Giant? Are you going to take the plunge?"

"Do I have a choice?"

"Between soaking and hanging?"

His drawers dropped to the floor in good approximation of a dead body being cut down from a tree.

Stepping out of them, the very conspicuously naked marshal gulped, eyes wide from fright. He reminded Cougar of a sugar decoration she had seen once on top of a wedding cake.

"You're not going to melt," she advised.

He laughed like a nervous groom.

With careful steps, Claw inched toward the tub, strategically placing himself between the dreaded object and the woman. She might have done him the service of looking down to inspect a fingernail or adjust the hem of her dress but she did not. Apparently, she was perfectly groomed.

Lifting one long leg, Claw raised it over the edge of the bath. Finding this an undignified position, he summoned his courage and vaulted over the side. As luck would have it, his foot landed on the soap and he slipped, his torso and other leg following him into the water with a splash of leviathan proportions.

When his head reappeared several minutes later, he was red from stem to stern.

"I'm being parboiled!" he sputtered.

"If only you were a lobster," Cougar rued hungrily.

He decided it best not to ask what a "lobster" was, for fear she would elucidate him.

Cougar began a slow trek around her property.

"Not bad," she decided after completing a tour of the circumference. "You fit perfectly. I knew you would."

"How much did this *thing* cost you?"

"Not nearly as much as it would have cost you to refuse trying it out."

"I don't doubt it." She nodded. "What do I do now?"

"Soak. Rub soap over your body. Relax."

"Relax?"

"You'd be surprised to learn most people consider taking a bath a luxury. Here." She tossed him a wash cloth. "Use this."

Claw suspended the cloth over his face.

"To clean yourself with."

"Oh," he said, or something close to it.

"I know you've bathed before, Claw," Cougar continued, a merry gleam in her eyes.

"Not like this."

"Not like what?"

"Not in front of a woman."

"If you'd rather bathe in front of Joshua, I can call him back. I doubt he's gone to bed for the night."

"No!"

"Suit yourself."

He thought if he could "suit" himself, he would.

"Don't forget to wash your hair."

"Yes, ma'am."

She settled herself more comfortable on the barrel. Her feet dangled an inch from the floor. Claw remembered she had lovely legs and forgot about being distressed. He retrieved the soap and began scrubbing. In a moment he was covered with bubbly white foam.

After he had removed his outer covering of sand, sweat and hide, he rubbed the soap on his head, spitting occasionally as his mouth took in more than its share of bubbles. When he had scrubbed the prairie from his hair, Cougar took an empty whisky bottle, filled it with water and poured it over his head, washing away the foam. He signed in hedonistic delight.

"This isn't bad," he confessed.

"Imagine that."

But his imagination was on other things and he did not hear her.

After working on his long legs, which he did not fail to display to best advantage by resting them over the rim of the tub, the marshal frowned.

"That's a long distance from here to my feet," he demonstrated, holding up his hand and wiggling his toes. Cougar arched an eyebrow. "How am I going to get to my toes?"

Cougar was all softness, barely concealing her eagerness.

"Are you asking for help?" she purred. He nodded eagerly, then sank deeper into hot water. "You might consider washing my back, too."

"Oh, I wouldn't want to forget your back, darling."

For the life of him, Claw Kiley could not remember why he had put up such a fuss about the phenomenon of bathing in the first place. He would never do so again, he promised, discretely balling a head of bubbles over his groin area.

"This can be most relaxing," he confessed. She smiled sweetly at him, the tip of her tongue playing with the underside of her front teeth, then snaking with alluring delight over the points of her canines.

"I'm glad you think so."

"There's something else I was thinking," he confessed, the heat from the water obviously rising to his face. "This tub is big enough for two!"

"You don't say!"

The thought, apparently, had never occurred to her. It was a good thing he had come along in her life, Claw decided. And then spoke his thought aloud.

"It's a good thing I came along when I did."

"You can say that, again, mister."

Unfortunately for Claw, he did not realize the playing field was just slightly uneven.

"Some things men do better than women."

"I was just thinking that very same thing," she unexpectedly agreed. He grinned broadly.

His grin, as all things must, died an untimely death.

"What are you doing?" he asked. His bravado mysteriously joined Davey Jones in his locker, deep below the water line.

"Merely going along with your assertion that men do some things better than women," Cougar said with a smile, beckoning to someone outside his line of vision. "Would you come in here, please?"

"It would be my very great pleasure," a deep, masculine-sounding voice responded with sincere politeness.

Frankie MacPhearson stepped into the room, wearing the grin Claw had abandoned. Strange to say, Frankie had abandoned his black lawyer's suit coat, and his shirt was rolled up to his bony elbows. His hands, Claw thought, looked pruny.

"Frankie has been washing the spittoons," Cougar informed the bather. Claw quickly swallowed a mouthful of soapy gall. "And has done a very good job of it, I do say."

Frankie's smile widened as he made a slight bow.

"I was always taught - and it has always been my belief - that if you set out to do a task, you should perform it to the utmost of your ability."

"I pay Frankie fifty cents a day to help around the place," Cougar continued, oblivious to the thin stream of bubbles which had replaced the form of Claw Kiley on and over the surface of the water. "He cleans the spittoons, sweeps the sawdust out and replaces it with fresh, helps wash the glassware and cleans up out back where the customers occasionally fail to successfully navigate their way to the outhouse."

The stream of bubbles petered down into an isolated one or two, bobbing desultorily on the surface.

"The marshal, Mr. MacPhearson, has asked for someone to wash his feet and rub his back. If you do could him this SMALL service, I would be most grateful."

"The pleasure is mine."

Frankie looked expectantly for the lawman. He was nowhere in sight.

"Just help yourself to any body parts you find," Cougar instructed her employee. "Claw has had very little experience in this type of bathing and - he assures me - would be most grateful for any services you can provide."

"Jist like washin' a horse," Joshua piped in from the doorway.

"Very similar," Cougar agreed.

She tossed Frankie a washcloth. The gentle man dipped it discreetly in the water, then rubbed soap onto the cotton before attacking the problem of the marshal's dirty feet.

"Iffn you take one hoof an' I do the other, we'll git done in half the time," Joshua volunteered, which forever endeared him to the lady, if not the lawman.

"Good idea," Cougar agreed, tossing him a second wash cloth.

Less genteel than the spittoon-washer, Joshua grabbed a foot from its watery grave and ran the cloth between the toes, employing enough vigor to initiate spontaneous combustion.

Claw shot up and hissed like a snake.

His words, if not the sentiment, were as unintelligible as though he had been a serpent and not a man.

Not understanding the warning, Joshua continued his job.

"What-are-you-doing?" Claw demanded, holding his hands over his chest in a totally ineffectual attempt to preserve modesty.

Miss Bradburn suffered from a slight spasm of the funny bone and was compelled to retire a step and recover, out of splash range.

"Don't worry, Marshal," Joshua happily reassured him. "Where I cume frum, grandmas a'ways say, you 'got enuf dirt between yer toes to grow potatoes.' But I'll git it out."

"You made that up!" he wrongfully accused. The unfounded accusation went against him as an officer of the law. Fortunately, he was among friends and the transgression was overlooked.

"'Courst, grandmas general directed that observation to a boy's ears," Joshua prattled on, refusing to believe a United States marshal could mean a slight against grandmothers. "Why, Marshal, she'd cume after us wid a rag the size o' a field of four-leaf clovers an' shove it down our ear holes like she was furrowin' us fer spring plantin'. I'll be more gentle than that, though seein' as how yer a growd man an' we were jist boys..."

"Cougar!" the marshal roared in a lion's voice and a supplicant's pleading. "Help me! Please!"

She was, as might be expected, all sympathy.

"You want me to call Steve in, too?"

Had his face not been wet, a casual bystander might have thought the tracks down his cheeks were tears.

"Please?"

To get out of the tub and beg would have been unseemly. Also, it would have gotten sawdust and dust bunnies all over his spanking-clean body.

It was not a question of repenting, but rather one of penitence.

"Please, please, please? Pretty please?"

The lady's heart finally melted in good approximation of a cube of sugar submerged in a cup of hot coffee.

"All right, boys," she announced with an authority in which they could not fail to respond. "I'll take it from here. Thank you. Tell Steve to reward you both with a bottle of bourbon, and I'll pay you for your night's work in the morning. *Afternoon,*" she amended rakishly.

The two "boys" happily disappeared, leaving the lady alone to savor her victory.

The next step would be as tricky as walking over a floor strewn with soap chips.

Claw was out of the tub in the bursting of a bubble, the nakedness of his feet making little noises as he puddled around the room after her.

"You're dirty, Miss Bradburn," he informed her. "You need a bath."

He caught her with less trouble than he had anticipated. With an eager, boyish excitement, Claw slipped his hand between the cloth of her dress and her bare back, popping the buttons as a unit, rather than taking them, one-by-one. A low moan of delight escaped his breast as he saw naked flesh emerge from the confines of civilization.

"There, isn't this better?" he gulped as the dress slipped over her shoulders. Amazingly, the lady was not wearing anything at all beneath her outer covering. One step and she was out of the dress completely.

"Much better," she agreed. "So - what took you so long to get the right idea?"

With a laugh of innocent joy, Claw scooped his lady up in his arms and very gently deposited her in the tub, taking care not to overdraw his account. As she moved to the side, he leapt in after her, water spilling over the edges.

The event went unmarked. The two bathers were too busy depositing kisses on one another's lips.

After enough interest had accumulated for each to count him and herself wealthy, their arms intertwined and they attached themselves together, as close as twin soap bubbles.

"Will you be my gal?" he whispered into her lips as they broke the boundaries separating them, merging into one larger, stronger unit.

"I will be your gal," she agreed, lying back against the side of the tub and drawing his face down to hers, fully aware that soap bubbles burst, and "gals" were not "wives."

But equally aware that soap bubbles washed away dirt. And that being a "gal" was leagues ahead of being just a "girl."

Never before in her life had she dreamed of sharing a bath, making love under water, or of accepting a proposal - any proposal - from a man who wore a badge.

Life, she mused, was for the living. At the moment, Cougar Bradburn was more alive than she had ever been in her life.

It was a baptism of sorts. A transformation. A metamorphosis.

An awakening of faith.

A hope for the future - and for the flesh-and-blood legend she had fallen in love with.

And who, miraculously, had fallen in love with her.

It was worth every penny of the one-hundred-and-fifty dollars she had paid for the bath tub.

"Stage only stops long enough to change the horses," the driver called to his passengers. "Those who're gittin' out, git out. Those who want a bite to eat better hurry. We're behind schedule as it is."

There were four people in the stage, three men and one woman. After fifty miles of rough, pitted roads, whipping winds and grinding sand, there were nearly indistinguishable from one another.

Two of the men pulled their hats down over their eyes and made no move to stretch their legs. One man, a peddler, pried open the door and nearly fell flat on his face as his feet, gone to sleep hours ago, failed to hold his weight. Several of the townsmen, loafers who had nothing better to do than see who came in and left on the stage, snickered.

The tradesman pulled himself together and accepted his carpet bag from the driver.

"Obliged," he said. His throat was parched and the words came out harsh. "Can you direct me to the nearest hotel? Not the best," he hastened to add. "Just a place where a man can get a good night's sleep and a decent meal."

"Try Topeka," one of the loafers suggested. The peddler smiled. It was an occupational hazard.

"Hello," he tried, wanting to make a good impression.

His overture was ignored and he departed, hoping to find more congenial men from whom to ask directions.

The woman, shawl wrapped around her shoulders, got out the other door. She had never been in Hellhole before, yet started walking with a purpose.

"Jist a minute, ma'am," the driver called. She paused but did not turn back to him. "Yer bag," he reminded her.

"Leave it where it is."

"I'm leavin' as soon as I git the team changed," he reminded her.

"I shall return before then."

After watching seventeen team-changes in the last week, she had timed the operation to the minute.

"This is Hellhole," he tried. "Wasn't you gittin' off in Hellhole?"

This time, her pause was longer coming.

"No," she said finally. "You are mistaken. I am going to the end of the line." And then added bitterly, "I am going back east."

The stage driver readjusted the hat on the back of his head and spit over the side.

"I must have been mistaken."

"Yes," she said. "That happens."

The hour was late and most men who would otherwise have drifted the streets were either in bed or drunk in one of the saloons. It was, she thought to herself, the witching hour; the time when a lawman started his rounds. The hour when his wife - if he were unfortunate enough to be married - started worrying.

"Rounds" had such an innocuous ring to it, she thought as she walked. One word, simple enough. "Rounds." Who would ever associate it with bone-jarring, soul-eating fear?

The sun was round. A child's play-toy was round. The hoop of a wagon wheel, the bowl of a pipe. These things were round.

Coins were round. Gold coins, silver coins. The type which filled bank vaults and lined gamblers pockets. The kind which a saloon girl slipped down her dress, between her warm breasts.

Excuses went 'round and 'round.

Wedding rings were round.

Wound tightly around a woman's heart.

She paused for a moment to stare at the ring finger of her left hand. In the deepening gloom of an overcast night, she could just make out the glint of tarnished metal. She had forgotten until now, her ring was not round. It had gotten dented somehow, along the trail stoking a dying fire or from lifting a box off a wagon.

Perhaps she had struck her hand against a wall by accident or anger, or fright, while she waited for him to finish his rounds.

A noise caught her attention and she turned, staring with sharp, piercing eyes toward the source. It was laughter she heard. Coming from the saloon, or more accurately, from a room in the back of the drinking parlor. The conversation was muffled but she made out two voices: that of a man and a woman. Her left fist clenched tight. It took more willpower than she thought she possessed, to unlock it.

Though time pressed, she paused to listen. The stage would wait for her.

"Cougar!" she heard him say. There was tenderness, naughtiness, boyishness in the voice. She did not have to see the speaker to envision his face. He was a young man, a brave man. He was good with a gun. The best there ever was, she had heard it said.

That was a lie. No one was "the best who ever was."

She wondered if the woman named "Cougar" knew what she knew. She wondered if she ought to tell her what she wished to God someone had told her, way back when.

But love was blind. As blind as a man dead drunk or a dead man.

Ada Duvall had heard a preacher say once, that love opened a man's eyes. Opened them round to the wonders of God's world.

God, she thought, pulling the shawl more tightly around her shoulders, could have His world back.

She had no more regard for preachers than she did for lawmen.

Bullet holes were round, too. She ought to know. She had seen more of them than she had ever seen of coins.

She continued her journey.

There was a small lamp burning inside the Marshal's Office. She knew there would be. She knew the door would be unlocked and the two-room bastion of justice would be empty.

Right again.

She was always right. She was on the side of right.

Neither of those virtues had saved her husband.

Ada paused inside the door and looked around. She was not curious. That virtue had died in her breast years ago. Along with all their unborn children.

It was exactly as she had imagined it. With a little time, she might have closed her eyes and heard his footfalls on the hard-packed earth, heard him whistling a tune, or pause to lift his nose to the air, like a dog, sniffing out trouble. There was always trouble.

Like excuses, trouble went round and round.

The widow of Marshal Jack Duvall went to the desk. His desk. Not Jack's desk. Jack had never made it to Hellhole. He had died on the street of some worthless, easily forgotten town, long before ever hearing the news about Claw Kiley's new position.

Federal marshal. Jack would have wept.

His widow wept for him.

Ada took a letter out of her hand bag. It was warm to the touch, like blood. Just like blood, it would cool.

She placed it on the desk, address facing him when he sat. It was his letter to her. She had written a note on the outside, in ink. She had not bothered to disguise her handwriting. He would not recognize it.

Her final task complete, Mrs. Jack Duvall paused to turn down the lamp. It was the habit of a lifetime. No sense wasting fuel. It came dear. When the government was late with his salary, he would have to buy more out of his savings. The accumulated worth of which would just cover a quart of oil.

She hurried, now, for the stage was waiting. She did not wish to be left behind. Stages, like death, could be put off only so long.

She had told the driver she was going "back east." Lies, like excuses and trouble, went round and round.

Like "round," and "rounds," the note Ada Duvall had written on Claw Kiley's letter to her, consisted of one word.

"Undeliverable."

In a world of lies, excuses and trouble, a simple truth covered a multitude of sins.

The widow-woman in the shawl closed the door behind her and hurried away. In the returning quiet of the night, a small feral cat leapt off the marshal's unmade bunk and prowled around the office, her nose sniffing the subtle wind currents.

It was evening.

Time to make rounds.

The End

GSFE

ALSO BY: S.L.KOTAR AND J.E.GESSLER

A character based historical 1950's courtroom based murder mystery entitled "**The Hugh Kerr Mystery Series**"..

- Book I   **The Conundrum of the Decapitated Detective**
- Book II   **The Conundrum of the Absconded Attorney**
- **Book III   The Conundrum of the Sins of the Fathers**
- **Book IV   The Conundrum of The Two-Sided Lawyer**
- **Book V   The Conundrum of the Clueless Counselor**
- **Book VI   The Conundrum of the Loveless Marriage**
- **Book VII   The Conundrum of the Executed Defendant**
- **Book VIII   The Conundrum of the Jettisoned Jury**
- **Book IX   The Conundrum of the Perjured Pigeon**
- **Book X   The Conundrum of the Haunting Halloween**
  - **Party**
- **Book XI   The Conundrum of the Tuneless Tunesmith**
- **Book XII   The Conundrum of the Meddling Motorcar**
- **Book XIII   The Conundrum of the Blundering Bear**
- **Book XIV   The Conundrum of Shooting Fish in a Barrel**
  -
  - **To Be Continued!**

Next a series is "New Beginnings" a 1950's medical drama.

- Book I   **The Believer**
- Book II   **The Heretic**
- Book III   **Arrow Song**
- Book IV   **Peas In A Pod**
-
  - **To Be Continued!**

"**the ReproBate saga**" is a character-based series in the 1860 American Civil War

- **Book I**   **Beneath the Rose**
- Book II   **skull and cRossBones**
- Book III   **Redefining Bastions**
- Book IV   **thicker than Blood**
- Book V   **prioR Battles**
- Book VI   **Requited Blasphemy**
- Book VII   **The waR Between**
- Book VIII   **To Richmond or Bust**
- Book IX   **carrying Battlescars**
  - **To be Continued**

"**the Hellhole saga**" is a character-based series from the American West

- Book I   **First Draw**
- Book II   **Audition for a Legend**
- Book III   **Strange Bedfellows**

"**The Kansas Pirate Series**" is another character-based series from the American West

- Book I   **Pirate Treasure**
- Book II   **Strawberry Fields**
- Book III   **The Drinking Gourd**

Stand-alone novels include:

- **Catman** *He was every man; he was no man*
-
- **ONE** Science Fiction space travel

- **Shepherd of the Kingdom** a modern-day horror classic

Non-Fiction

"**The Kepi Magazine**," A publication specialized in the Civil War and 19th century life.:

- **The Kepi Volume I and II**
- **The Kepi Volumes III and IV**

www.ingramcontent.com/pod-product-compliance
Lightning Source LLC
Chambersburg PA
CBHW020415150626
46554CB00014B/1407